"Epic in its scope, poignant in its prose, and profound in its themes, *The Last Dragon of the East* is an exciting adventure and a wrenching love story rolled into one."

—**Thea Guanzon, *New York Times* and *USA Today* bestselling author of *The Hurricane Wars***

"Rich with Chinese mythology, *The Last Dragon of the East* spins a heart-wrenching tale of love that transcends lifetimes."

—**Xiran Jay Zhao, *New York Times* bestselling author of *Iron Widow***

"This sweeping romantic fantasy has it all: epic journeys, characters to root for, and a romance that spans the ages. Packed full of mythology and gorgeously lush prose, the banter between the ever-upbeat Sai and the surly, secretive Jyn is top-notch. The twists kept me turning pages until I reached the incredibly satisfying, heartwarming conclusion."

—**Keshe Chow, author of *The Girl with No Reflection***

"*The Last Dragon of the East* is an enchanting tale of destiny and devotion. Led by captivating characters and rich with tender romance, this book asks us how far we would go for those we love."

—**Kylie Lee Baker, internationally bestselling author of *The Scarlet Alchemist***

"Katrina Kwan weaves Chinese myths of dragon gods and threads of fate into a delightfully heart-wrenching romantic fantasy. I adored Jyn and Sai's grumpy sunshine dynamic (one of my all-time favorite tropes!) and their push-pull dynamic. Lu

—A. Y. Chao, au

T0182751

The
Last
Dragon
of the
East

Katrina Kwan

SAGA PRESS

LONDON SYDNEY **NEW YORK** TORONTO NEW DELHI

AN IMPRINT OF SIMON & SCHUSTER, LLC

1230 AVENUE OF THE AMERICAS, NEW YORK, NEW YORK 10020

First Saga Press trade paperback edition October 2024

SAGA PRESS and colophon are trademarks of Simon & Schuster, LLC

Simon & Schuster: Celebrating 100 Years of Publishing in 2024

For information about special discounts for bulk purchases, please contact Simon & Schuster Special Sales at 1-866-506-1949 or business@simonandschuster.com.

The Simon & Schuster Speakers Bureau can bring authors to your live event. For more information or to book an event, contact the Simon & Schuster Speakers Bureau at 1-866-248-3049 or visit our website at www.simonspeakers.com.

Interior design by Lewelin Polanco

Manufactured in the United States of America

1 3 5 7 9 10 8 6 4 2

Library of Congress Cataloging-in-Publication Data

Names: Kwan, Katrina, author.
Title: The last dragon of the east / Katrina Kwan.
Description: First Saga Press trade paperback edition. | London ; New York: Saga Press, 2024.
Identifiers: LCCN 2024011199 | ISBN 9781668051238 (paperback) | ISBN 9781668051245 (ebook)
Subjects: LCGFT: Fantasy fiction. | Novels.
Classification: LCC PR9199.4.K89 L37 2024 | DDC 813/.6--dc23/eng/20240517
LC record available at https://lccn.loc.gov/2024011199

ISBN 978-1-6680-5123-8
ISBN 978-1-6680-5124-5 (ebook)

For my father, the other storyteller
of the Kwan family

Author's Note

The Last Dragon of the East is a fantasy intended for adult readers.

While it is a hopeful tale of love and devotion, the journey on which our characters will embark is one steeped in war, violence, and death. Readers who may be sensitive to more mature themes of self-harm, suicidal thought, and torture are encouraged to take heed.

Now, set forth and find your Fated One.

Part I

The
Thread-
Seeker

1

"*Gēge! Please tell me what you see!*"

The young woman peers up at me, her dark eyes wide and expectant as I carefully count the bronze coins she has paid. The money is all there and accounted for, but there's no harm in double-checking my math. Being shorted out of a week's worth of food once has taught me the value of diligence for the remainder of my lifetime.

Once satisfied with my tally, I tie the small purse of coins to the inside of my outer robe. "Very well, *mèimei*," I say with an easy smile. "Raise your right hand, just so."

She follows my instructions eagerly as she draws in a deep, excited breath. Her hands are those of a laborer: calloused palms and thick knuckles. She likely spends her days toiling in the neighboring rice fields. Her hands and nails are clean, however, scrubbed pink and practically raw to be rid of any dirt and grime.

She has a simple appearance. Her dull brown dress is cut from cheap, rough fabric. Her long black hair is pulled back into a simple braid that runs the length of her spine, cinched off with a short black ribbon. I can detect the faintest trace of floral perfume upon her hair, though the fragrance isn't very strong. It's clear that she has

put a lot of effort into looking her best despite her circumstances—
and likely spent well beyond her means for such a privilege—but I
blame her not.

I, too, would want to look my absolute best, were I meeting
my Fated One today.

I can see her red thread as clear as the blue skies above. The
shimmering magic loops around her little finger and then trails off
toward the center of the city. There's a good amount of tension, no
slack to be found, which informs me that the person on the other
end must be close.

"Are you ready?" I ask her.

She nods quickly, her excitement palpable.

With my hand tucked just below her wrist, we start off on our
merry way.

Her thread cuts straight through the marketplace by the har-
bor. The narrow streets of Jiaoshan are congested pipes, clogged
with merchants and customers alike. Vendors eagerly peddle their
wares while workmen treat themselves to well-deserved meals
made up of spiced meats, steamed buns, and dumpling soups.

The air is chilly—winter's first frost covering the rooftops—
though the cold does little to dissuade people from going about
their business. There are vibrant dyes freshly imported from the
western kingdoms, exotic spices from overseas, and beautiful be-
jeweled hairpins and rare silks from the trade routes farther up
north.

There is nothing from the South. Trade with our Southern
brethren has dried up since the emperor's declaration of war
nearly a year ago.

The city of Jiaoshan—so I have been told—was once nothing
more than a few straw huts built around the circumference of a
large lake. The more people who gathered to call it home, the more
they took from the water. Decades went by, the lake shrinking a

few inches every year as the population grew. People raised their homes closer to the water's edge, chasing after it, until the lake dried up and all that was left was the sprawling city built upon its muddy basin.

It's just as well. I loathe swimming.

The hustle and bustle of the marketplace fills my ears, but as we venture through, the whispers and curious stares follow without fail. Even the scantily clad courtesans of the local pleasure house lean out from their windows to cast their judgment.

"Isn't that him?" a woman comments, staring at me with barely veiled contempt. "The Thread-Seeker?"

"Who?"

"He looks a mere drifter."

"Why's he still here? Shouldn't he be with the other conscripts?"

"Probably weaseled his way out of it."

"Coward."

"Is he swindling that poor girl?"

"No, no—it's him, I'm sure of it. Sai was the one who helped my cousin find his husband not two moons ago!"

I ignore the comments and focus on the task—literally—at hand.

Because while it's true that I can see my client's thread, I can also see the ones belonging to everyone else. Vibrant red lines leading left, right, and center. They crisscross and tangle, weaving near and far. Some lie slack upon the ground, while others wrap over houses or get stuck in trees. Others are taut like clotheslines, or the snapped reins of a mule-drawn wagon. The threads of fate constantly shift throughout the day and night, much like a tangled pit of vipers, moving wherever the two souls on either end see fit.

Most days, I'm able to ignore it all. It's an ever-present, confusing web of magic that I have learned to see past over the years; same as one would with a large, faceless crowd. The threads are intangible, easily passed through, so I'm never at risk of tripping over them. Having a gentle hold on her hand helps me focus; it is much like the hand of a compass, pointing me in the right direction.

The girl's thread begins to vibrate, an overwhelming warmth radiating off the thin strand. She gulps, breaking into a light sweat despite the cold winter morn.

I continue to guide her through the market, climbing the base of the hill leading toward the Pearl District. The old wooden shanties that line the streets of the market slowly melt into bigger, grander homes, complete with tall cream walls, pointed roofs, and magnificent water gardens that have started to freeze over with the turn of the season.

We receive more stares from those around us, but they're not so much curious as they are disgruntled by our presence. Aristocratic women whisper behind their custom-made silk fans, pinching their painted faces at us as we carry on.

"Are you sure we're in the right place, *gēge*?" the woman asks me when we approach an estate with a massive circular moon gate, its red wooden doors firmly shut. The design of a fearsome dragon has been etched around the circumference, gilded in gold leaf; its snarling teeth and sharp claws on display to scare off bad luck and spirits with cruel intentions.

I glance down at her hand again. Her red thread is taut and vibrating from the tension of her and her Fated One's proximity. It begins to glow, a bright and rich crimson hue, sparkling like distant starlight. I'm the only one who can see the magic at work. The girl stares at me, none the wiser.

I nod encouragingly. "This is it, *mèimei*. Your Fated One is just beyond those walls."

She takes a step back, shaking her head in abject horror. "That's the councilman's house! There has to be some kind of mistake."

"Your red thread of fate is never wrong," I tell her. "You are destined to be with whoever is on the other side of that gate."

"But *look* at me. I don't belong here." Her bottom lip trembles, her thin brows knitting together into a steep frown. She tugs at the end of her braid, fraying her ribbon between her fingers. "What if they take one look at me and laugh? They'll know the second they lay eyes on me that I have no dowry to give. This was a mistake. I never should have come. This whole thing's been such a foolish endeavor."

I place my hands on her shoulders and hold her gaze, calm and steady. "I know you're afraid, but believe me when I say your Fated One will love you with all their heart. It matters not what you look like, nor how wealthy you are. True love will never fail you, but you must be brave enough to accept it in the first place."

I give her the lightest of nudges toward the gate, taking a step back to watch it all unfold with the gathering crowd.

She reaches shakily for the iron door knocker and bangs it against the wood—once, twice. The silence that follows is thick and heavy. Not even the wind whistles past, afraid of shattering the suspense sizzling in the air.

At long last, the door creaks open on its hinges. A man steps out, dressed in deep purple robes and a heavy golden chain bearing the seal of the city council. He blinks down at the young woman, his brief confusion almost immediately washed away by curiosity. There's warmth in his eyes, a kind smile tugging at the corners of his lips.

Between them, their thread sings. It glows with the brilliance of nine suns, their connection pure and true. Nobody else can see this blinding display, but they don't have to. The way they look at each other in wonderment and awe is more than enough to understand what's going on here.

It's a beautiful miracle, unmatched in all things worldly or otherwise. Happiness is a contagious affliction, but I do my best not to look down at the thread wrapped around my own finger. I'm never pleased at what I see, and there's no need to ruin my good mood.

I slip away into the crowd. My job here is done.

As exhausted as I may be after my morning spent matchmaking, there's still much to be done around the teahouse.

By *sì shí*, the hour of the snake, I've wiped down all the tables and given the kneeling pillows a good fluff, ready to welcome the day's first thirsty customers.

By noon, the hour of the horse, I've fixed the broken window shutters facing the street to better let in light, hoping the welcoming ambience will draw patrons into my family's humble business. No one has stepped in yet, but I haven't given up yet.

By *shēn shí*, the hour of the monkey, the sun is beginning to hang low in the sky. My optimism wavers, but I must take into account the dinner rush. The local farmers and fishermen will be passing through soon, done with their day's work. Surely I can convince a few stragglers to come in for a lovely pot of tea and a plate of sweet almond cookies.

I spend the remainder of my afternoon flipping through the teahouse's ledger, quietly lamenting the low figures. The coin I earned today should cover the teahouse's losses, but that leaves little room in the budget for food. Perhaps if I have a little less to eat and fill up on water, I can ensure that A-Ma gets enough to fill her stomach. I'm still young and strong. A missed meal here and there won't hurt me.

Just as I finish balancing the books, I hear my mother break into a coughing fit. The stairs creak beneath her weight as she descends, one step at a time, clinging to the rickety railing for stability. She's been asleep all day, as per her doctor's instruction.

"A-Ma, what are you doing out of bed?" I ask, hurrying over to usher her back upstairs. "You're supposed to be resting. The doctor said—"

She waves me off, hacking into her elbow. "That doctor is a quack, Sai. An absolute quack! What harm is there in stretching my legs from time to time?"

I sigh, swallowing down the frustration burning in my chest. "Come, come. Let's get you tucked in. Doctor Qi said not to put stress on your joints."

My mother groans in irritation, but allows me to guide her back to her room.

We live on the top floor of the teahouse. It was supposed to be used for storage, but since Father's passing all those years ago and Mother falling ill, money has been exceedingly tight. The few months following the funeral were particularly hard. More often than not, I found myself fretting over my choice between paying the rent and buying my mother's medicine. Our previous landlord didn't take kindly to my choosing the latter.

I'm thankful A-Ba left us the teahouse, at least, despite its disastrously red ledger. I know not how my mother would fare out on the streets, now that the nights are freezing. It's drafty and uncomfortably cramped up here, but I'm grateful we have a roof over our heads nonetheless.

My mother's pallet takes up the majority of the space, covered in all the blankets and pillows I have managed to collect from our more generous neighbors. We are surrounded on all sides by tall cabinets, jars of dried tea leaves stored away in each one of their drawers ahead of the slow trade season. The roads around the city become treacherous with winter storms, and merchants are far less willing to brave the weather. One of the first lessons my father taught me when I was a young boy was to stock up for the frigid months ahead.

Sometimes I wish A-Ba had been as good at squirreling away coin as he was with his beloved teas.

A-Ma settles in, but she does so with a pout. She was born in the Year of the Ox, so it makes sense that she's as stubborn as a bull. "I'm feeling better," she insists, then immediately coughs into her elbow. It sounds dry and excruciating, nails screeching across jagged bricks. "How did it go today?"

"It went well. We found him in the Pearl District. A councilman."

"Ah, good for her. I pray they have a happy and prosperous marriage."

I shrug off my outer robe, moving to drape it over my mother's tiny lap for warmth. She has been getting thinner and thinner, shivering at all hours of the day.

"I finally have enough to buy that new medicine from Doctor Qi," I explain. "He says his colleagues in the Southern Kingdom believe it to be one of the best remedies out there."

"He says, he says," my mother mutters bitterly. "Coins down the well, I tell you. You should be saving this money to fund your own search."

I sigh. "We've been over this. I'm not leaving you here."

"You should be married by now! With a house full of children." My mother grasps my forearm and gives the meat of it a squeeze. "Who wouldn't want someone as handsome and as strong as you for a husband?"

It's only natural for a mother to sing her son's praises. As I roll my eyes, I happen upon my reflection in the small upright mirror on the corner table. It's true that I'm almost five and twenty, though I don't look a day over nine and ten. Doctor Qi tells me my growth must be stunted. A-Ma has stood by her claim of my excellent genetics. I, however, prefer to think that I'm one of the Gods' chosen favorites, blessed with dashing good looks and a winning personality.

I mostly take after my father. Wide shoulders and strong arms, but slender legs. My dark brown hair looks almost black most days, but standing beneath the sun reveals its richer reddish hues. I'm admittedly a bit soft around the middle, about which I'm mildly self-conscious. Growing up in a teahouse has meant easy access to sweet treats at all hours of the day. A-Ba was a fiend when it came to sneaking me an extra almond cookie or two—or five—while A-Ma was busy tending to guests. She would later scold us, the crumbs at the corners of our lips confessing to our crimes. It was a wonder we didn't lose the teahouse to debtors, the way we ate into our profits.

My mother shakes her head. "You have been blessed with this wonderful gift by the Gods! Are you not curious at all about your Fated One?"

I glance down at my mother's hand. Her red thread is no more. Instead, a closed black loop is wrapped around her little finger. The day my father passed, all I could do was watch in horror as the thread connecting my parents—two halves of a whole—disintegrated before my very eyes, their connection broken only in death.

It's not a pleasant thing to dwell on, the death of one's parents. But there are days that I think it cruel that they did not go together. While A-Ba passed on and his thread fell from around his finger, A-Ma's turned black. These are a common sight when I am out and about. A mere glimpse is enough to make me hurt for others.

My mother has not been the same since my father passed on ten years ago. Her light has dimmed. She doesn't laugh as hard as she used to, doesn't smile as wide as I remember. Of course, I have to wonder if her grief is exacerbating her failing health.

All the more reason to see Doctor Qi as soon as possible.

"You could have found them three times over by now," my mother continues. "You must seek out your other half before it's too late."

"Too late?" I echo her words, amused. "I'm still young; there's no need for such dramatics."

"What if they decide to settle and marry the wrong person? A tragedy for the ages, I tell you. Take the money you've earned today to fund your trek. There's only one present, Sai. Follow your own thread and find them before your bones grow too weary for such a journey."

I shake my head and laugh. "And what about you?"

"What *about* me?"

"Who will take care of you if I'm gone?"

"Your Auntie Ying."

"I've been led to believe that Auntie Ying hates you."

"She does, but she's still obligated to help out her sister-in-law—"

A-Ma breaks into a sudden coughing fit, hacking and wheezing hard enough to rattle her bones. I'm quick to grab her a cup of water from the pitcher I've set just off to the side of her pallet, holding it to her lips so that she can take a long, careful drink.

I rub small circles against her back just as she did for me when I was a child, quietly troubled at how frail my mother has become. It feels like just yesterday she had all the energy in the world, nagging me about the teahouse as I giggled with glee. I might have been four or five then, though the memory is hazy. Now it's my turn to do the nagging—*drink more water, stay in bed, take your medicine.*

"Get some rest. I'll be downstairs preparing congee."

"Will you add some ginger and soy sauce? I can't taste it otherwise."

I kiss the back of my mother's hand and layer several blankets on top of her. "I'll do just that. I even splurged at the market and grabbed us some eggs."

My mother huffs, her lips thin and her eyes watery. "You're too sweet, my boy. Always taking care of others. When will you let someone take care of you?"

I shrug easily in lieu of an answer.

I head downstairs to tidy up in our small kitchen nook, then prepare my mother's dinner with the utmost diligence. One part rice to ten parts water. In go a dash of salt, a bit of diced ginger, some finely chopped green onions—exactly how A-Ma used to make rice porridge for me when I was sick as a child. I would spring for a bit of chicken to place on top, but meat has become increasingly difficult to come by since the emperor's decree. Rationing for the army, now that we're deep into wartime.

As I scoop the porridge into a big bowl for my mother and a smaller one for myself, I cannot help but glance down at my hand. The truth of the matter is, I *am* curious. But I have my own reasons for not setting out after my Fated One. I've thought of doing so many times before, yet I can't seem to find the courage. It's hypocritical of me, I know. A-Ma's failing health just happens to be a convenient excuse to stay home.

Threads of fate are red, unbreakable, and linked to the other half of a person's soul—destroyed only in death.

But my thread is a dull gray and fraying before my very eyes. It's been in this state for as long as I can remember, lacking the warmth and crimson shimmer of magic that I see with so many others. I have never seen anything else like it before, nor do I know what it means.

Frankly, I'm too afraid to find out.

2

According to legend, they were a family of three.

Rare, considering how their kind was known for their solitary and distrustful nature.

And yet, as the story goes, these mighty creatures adored and protected the lands and all those who resided within.

His Majesty, the red dragon, king of the mountaintops and the endless skies above, bestowed upon the people fortuitous rains in the dryer months and plentiful sunshine in those that were colder.

Her Majesty, the green dragon, queen of the bamboo forests and golden wheat fields, graced her people with bountiful harvests and plenty of game.

His Royal Highness, the blue dragon, young prince of the sparkling seas and iridescent rivers, gifted the people with calm waters, endless schools of fish, and rare pearls for those brave enough to dive down and claim them.

For centuries, the dragons lived their lives in peace and prosperity.

And then a stranger arrived from the lands beyond the horizon.

3

Finding customers in want of my . . . *unique* service is a surprisingly difficult affair. Most people don't believe me when I say I can help them find their Fated One for the low, low cost of ten bronze coins or a quarter of a silver nugget.

Any higher, and they claim I'm a charlatan.

Any lower, and they claim I'm a charlatan.

Even when they agree to my price, some still call me—surprise, surprise—a charlatan.

I receive referrals from time to time through my happy customers, but it's hardly a steady stream of income. I've only just started matchmaking as an official business, and my reputation has yet to truly precede me. There are many who doubt my capabilities, scoffing at the mere mention of magic and threads of fate. *Tall tales for children,* they say. And why should they take me at my word when they could simply go to the local matchmaker, who has a proven track record and sway within the community?

But I digress.

The sun has not yet risen when I wake the following morn. My mother sleeps soundly, lying on her side. She claims it's easiest for her to breathe that way. Carefully, I abandon my blankets and drape them over her brittle body for warmth before pulling on my outer robe to combat the frigid morning air.

I head downstairs, collect the four full coin pouches from my secret cache beneath the floorboards. It's where my father used to hide the teahouse's earnings from would-be thieves. I have since adopted it as my own. I count out every bronze coin and silver nugget as I hastily brush through my long dark brown hair and pin it back in a high bun tied by a thin piece of red ribbon.

In the Northern Kingdom of Xuě, most men and women alike wear their hair in such a way, for cutting a single strand would be a slight against the beloved parents who gifted us with our healthy locks. It's why the most popular hauls of the traveling merchants are of sparkling hair clips and pins. The merchants make an enviable profit, certainly more so than my teahouse. The richer folk up in the Pearl District can afford to dress their hair with gold and silver, rubies and jade. The rest of us settle for lengths of ribbon; the more vibrant the color, the more expensive the dye—and therefore the more you have to pay for such a luxury.

Once every coin is accounted for, I set out to see Doctor Qi before first light.

His shop is on the other side of the city near the markets, located in a rickety old shanty house. The whole structure leans slightly to the left, its foundation having been chipped away by decades of exposure to wind and rain, slowly sinking into the muddy, frozen remains of the emptied lake. Two small dragon figurines carved from bamboo sit atop his doorframe, diligently warding off evil.

I spot the doctor inspecting the rickety hinges of his shop's front door.

"Ah, just the man I was looking for," I say with a big grin. "How are you on this fine day, Doctor?"

Doctor Qi glares up at me, his one dead eye pivoting slightly to the left in its socket. "Must you always be so loud, boy?"

He's a little stump of a man, coming up no higher than my chest. I have been told that the doctor was once incredibly handsome, with long black hair and the strength to move mountains. But I've always known him to be bald, scowling, and hunched over so severely his back is practically folded in two. Were it not for the cane he carries around, I doubt he could manage even two steps without falling over his own feet.

"But just the other day, you said I had a lovely voice. Who am I to deny you the sound of my golden pipes?"

"Grating," he corrects. "I said you have a *grating* voice."

"Ah, a great voice? That may be too much of a compliment."

His good eye twitches. "Cease this unnecessary chatter and tell me what you want."

"What I want? To spend some quality time with one of my wisest elders, of course."

Doctor Qi snorts, knocking the side of my head with the handle of his cane. "Hurry up and come in. I have a long list of patients to see today; there's a small outbreak of the pox in a village northeast of here, and I would prefer to head out as soon as possible."

The inside of Doctor Qi's shanty is a chaotic mess, every available surface covered in unfurled scrolls, vials of ointment, dried herbs, and other small items that I can't even begin to name. It smells overwhelmingly of crushed gingerroot and dried mushroom, ingredients he no doubt bartered for down in the markets. In the corner, I spot the doctor's wife quietly tidying, a large broom in her small hands. She gives me a polite bow, but she doesn't seem to be in the mood to speak.

It's hard for me not to notice their red threads leading in opposite directions from one another. Not a love match, then. Those are few and far between up here in the North—or anywhere, truly—since marriageable women are scarce, eligible bachelors are far too plentiful, and matches are decided between families with the strategic shifting of dowries top of mind. With the chances of a blissful marriage being so slim, I can understand why it's preferable to at least aim for a tolerable one.

"Do you have the money?" Doctor Qi asks gruffly.

I reach into my outer robe and untie the pouches. They're hefty, each weighing a good four or five pounds, packed full with the bronze coins and silver nuggets I've laboriously earned over these past few moons.

"It's all there," I assure him. "I triple-checked, just for you."

The old man simply grunts and turns to pull a heavy trunk out from under his workbench. It's sealed at three different points with thick iron locks, the keys located on a chain around his neck. He unlocks them one by one before finally pushing the lid back, exposing the small glass vial seated securely amid a bed of yellow straw. Doctor Qi picks the vial up, pinching it between his thumb and forefinger, and holds it against the light streaming in through the window.

Sitting at the bottom of the glass are two reptilian scales, shimmering like starlight despite their deep greenish hue. I can't explain the warmth that blooms in my chest as I stare at them, transfixed, nor the way my heart drums loudly in my ears. These trinkets, more beautiful than emeralds and jade, are supposed to be A-Ma's medicine?

"Crush these into a fine powder," Doctor Qi whispers conspiratorially. "One scale in the morning and the other at night. Mix it in with your mother's breakfast and dinner. It should provide her relief for at least a month."

"A month?" I echo, taking the vial from him. "You told me this would cure her for good."

He shakes his head. "I said it *could*, but only if I secured a higher quantity. Dragon scales aren't the easiest thing to come by. Count yourself lucky my contact in the South managed to sneak it past the border at all."

My eyes go wide.

Damn it, he really is *a quack.*

"Dragons don't exist," I state.

"*Anymore*," he counters. "They were once as real as the air we breathe. Our ancestors have been using what remains of them for centuries. Their claws forged into weapons, their teeth sawed into jewelry, fragments of their scales"—he gestures toward the vial I now hold in my possession—"used as the most potent of medicines."

A laugh bubbles past my lips. "You can't expect me to believe this, surely."

"There are a great many things your simple mind will never understand, boy."

"Well, *that* was uncalled-for."

"Like I said, dragons and magic might now be a myth, but that was not always the case." Doctor Qi harrumphs. "Do you have any idea the lengths I went through to procure these? If one of the emperor's soldiers caught me smuggling them over the border, they would've had my head on the spot. You think I hobbled all the way down there and back for nothing?"

I pause. Is this what I sound like when I try to convince people of my abilities? Wild and brazen and downright impossible? I feel foolish for even considering it, but something stirs in my stomach.

Slowly, I rub my little finger, staring down blankly at my gray thread. It drags upon the ground: my Fated One is somewhere far, far away, perhaps forever beyond my reach. Perhaps Doctor Qi is correct. There are a great many things I don't know, but there's one thing I'm certain of: magic *does* exist.

Perhaps dragons did, too.

I pocket the vial and take a deep breath. I have little to lose at this point, desperation clawing at the nape of my neck. If I can help my mother feel even the slightest bit better, then this whole endeavor will be worth it.

"Do you offer receipts?" I joke lightly, doing my best to mask my unease. "In the unlikely case that I should require a refund."

Doctor Qi waves his cane at me, but this time I manage to duck out of the way. "No refunds. Now, away with you!"

I leave with a light chuckle, a sliver of hope rising within me. What I wouldn't give to see a true smile upon A-Ma's face once more.

As I make my way home, I can't help but feel like I'm being watched. There's an almost palpable weight on my back, the heat of someone's gaze trained on me as I move through the streets. When I throw a cautious glance over my shoulder, I see no one.

How curious, indeed.

I decide to cut through the markets on my way home, not to glimpse the day's wares, but because it will shave a few minutes off my route. There's no time to leisurely peruse the stalls and their lovely trinkets, and certainly no time for small talk with the merchants.

When I was a little boy, much to A-Ma's chagrin, I would spend hours upon hours listening to their colorful tales, too enraptured by them to keep track of the day. Very little has changed since then—my imagination would only run wild if I stopped to listen. Yes, it is best that I keep going.

As I slip past the crowd, the heavy presence of armored soldiers doesn't go unnoticed. Many of them appear fresh-faced and wide-eyed, likely recent recruits from the smaller towns farther north. There's a good chance they're only filtering through Jiao-shan on their way to the military base of Shéyǎn several hundred li south of here.

"Please, good sir. I must be on my way."

It's a young woman who speaks. Her silk robes are plainly colored, but still far too vibrant for her to be a mere peasant girl. Her short nails and dried-out hands are my next clue, while her lack of jewelry and hair ornaments is my third. A maid for one of the noble houses in the Pearl District, if I had the coin to wager.

"Please, sir, I have so very much to do," she says timidly.

A gaggle of soldiers block her path forward, though the largest of the bunch stands at the front, keen on gaining her attention. He's far more of a brute than his compatriots, sporting an ugly scar that bisects his right cheek. His armor is similar to theirs, except that it's run-down and marred by all manner of dents and scratches. The badge on his shoulder signifies that he is a captain.

When I look down at their hands, I notice that his thread stretches off into the distance. Hers is a closed black loop.

"What's your rush, little miss?" he asks, teasing. "Will you not join this honorable soldier for a cup of tea before I go off to war?"

"My madam has asked me to run a number of errands on her behalf. I really must away."

"I'm sure you'll have time to do them later."

One of the captain's compatriots pats him on the shoulder in the way one would dust off a prized trophy. "Do you have any idea who this is? Captain Tian was awarded his title by the emperor himself."

The ruckus begins to draw the eyes of the market, though no

one makes a move to help the poor girl. The bystanders are all too slack-jawed to move an inch. Curious whispers and hushed murmurs reach my ear, the mere mention of the emperor raising the fine hairs on my arms.

Emperor Róng—a name that, rather befittingly, translates to "glory." No one dares speak it aloud, but not just because we commoners are unworthy of it gracing our tongues.

When I was a boy, A-Ma would tell me stories about the emperor when I couldn't sleep. He was said to have brought fresh water to the people of the North, banished wild beasts to the shadows, and ruled the lands for thousands of years. Preposterous, of course, but it always made for a fantastic bedtime story. I was usually out cold by the time A-Ma got to the part where the emperor was said to have been crowned by the sun itself.

He is almost more myth than man, and perhaps that's why I feel so unsettled by the soldier's mention of him. No one has laid eyes upon the emperor in many years. I hear he has isolated himself in one of his many palaces scattered throughout the Northern Kingdom of Xuě. The rumor often floating around the teahouse is that he moves among these residences on a whim to keep his enemies at bay. The fact that Captain Tian has not only seen, but *met* our elusive emperor in person? It defies belief.

The young woman sighs, exasperated. Her attempt to sidestep the captain and his goons fails miserably. "*Sir*, I really must—"

"Don't be difficult. Come and keep me company."

I can't listen to this nonsense any longer. I may be in a hurry to return home, but I can't let this come to pass. Swiftly, I sidle up to the young woman and place myself between her and the soldier.

"There you are," I say, putting on a mildly frantic tone. "The madam has been asking after you. Do you really mean to keep her waiting?"

She blinks at me, stunned. "Who are—"

"Quickly, we must leave at once."

I'm about to turn away when a hefty hand claps me on the scruff of my neck.

"Hey!" the captain snaps. "You got a problem?"

I set my jaw and regard him calmly. "No problem at all, my friend. *Mèimei* and I were just on our way."

He snorts, nostrils flaring like those of a horse. "Why are you not in armor? Where's your sword and shield, boy?"

"I have no need of them. I've not been conscripted."

"Then you must enlist with this next draft. We're to leave for the South by week's end."

"You misunderstand me, sir. I have an exemption."

The captain's lip twists up into a sneer. "What's the meaning of this? It's every man's sacred duty to serve the emperor."

"I understand, but—"

"Are you a cripple?" he asks dryly.

My fists ball up tight, my nails digging sharply into my palms. "No."

"Infirm?"

"No."

"A monk?" The captain takes a step forward, leaning into my space. His breath reeks abhorrently of garlic and sour milk. "Or, perhaps, are you a coward?"

Anger bubbles just below the surface of my skin. "I'm no monk," I answer.

And then I promptly strike him across the face.

The captain stumbles back, clutching his jaw in surprise. He trips over his own boots, flailing as would a newborn goat, landing with a weighty thud.

"How dare—"

We run too quickly for him to finish his sentence, leaving the soldiers in our dust. The young woman and I don't stop until we round the corner and are well out of view. She gives me a bow, her cheeks a light pink.

"Thank you, *gēge*. That man wouldn't leave me alone."

"No need to thank me," I reply with an easy chuckle. "Best be on your way now."

"Right, of course."

With one last quick bow to one another, we go our separate ways.

Where did you sneak off to this morning?" my mother asks from the other room.

I'm in the kitchen preparing the leftover congee from last night, which I kept simmering above a low flame as we slept. It's as tacky as it is tasteless, but at least it's filling. I was unable to treat A-Ma to a helping of quail eggs today, as the purchase from Doctor Qi cleaned out my pockets. I won't complain about having to resort to plain porridge, however, if it means my mother will finally get a reprieve from her constant coughing fits.

"Just to the markets," I lie, keeping my tone light. The last thing I want is to worry her. "I thought I'd grab us a snapper for dinner, but I learned the fishermen won't be bringing a fresh haul until tomorrow. Figured I should wait until then."

"Good thinking," she replies. "No sense in paying for week-old trout." She sits at one of the teahouse's many empty tables, a flat cushion beneath her as she pours us both a serving of tea. Her thinning black hair, oily and in need of a wash, is pulled up into a loose bun. I would take her to the public baths if only she had the energy to walk there and back.

I busy myself over the counter, my back facing toward her, as I quietly and quickly shake one of the scales out of the vial and into the base of a stone mortar. It's an enchanting thing, truly more akin to a precious gem than a medicinal ingredient. It seems a pity to reduce such a thing to dust. Alas, I still pick up the stone pestle and grind away, holding my breath as small, brilliant sparks crackle inside the mortar.

Magic.

"Sai?" my mother calls. "Do you need a hand?"

I have no time to marvel at the glittering green dust. I hastily dump everything into her bowl of congee and mix it in thoroughly, topping both our meals off with a bit of green onion to disguise any discoloration. I join her at the table, kneeling on the bamboo floor as I set the food down before her.

"Enjoy," I say. "Make sure to eat every bite."

"You know I rarely have an appetite these days." She picks up her spoon and takes a sip of her congee.

And then another, and another, and another, until—miracle of miracles!—she has polished off the entire bowl.

The effects are immediate.

Her sallow cheeks are awash with a pink, dewy complexion. The deep, dark circles beneath her eyes fade completely. Her hair now looks thick and shiny. My mother's trembling hands finally still, her posture straightening as strength returns to her muscles and bones. In mere minutes, she looks twenty years younger.

"I thought I taught you that it's rude to stare," A-Ma teases lightly.

Picking my jaw up off the floor, I blink away my astonishment. "How are you feeling?"

"Famished. Is there enough for seconds?"

"You can have mine," I say, willing my heart to remain calm as I slide my breakfast across the table.

Triumph rises in my chest. *Could it be? Could it really, truly be?*

My silent celebration does not last long, however, because the front doors to the teahouse slide violently open. The force is hard enough to rattle the rickety walls and knock the few framed calligraphy pieces we have askew.

A group of five heavily armored men step in—the very same ones I had the misfortune of running into not even an hour ago at the markets.

"You there," the closest man snaps. I recognize him by the blooming purple bruise that my knuckles bestowed upon his jaw. Captain Tian. He points an accusatory finger at me, a vicious snarl exposing his crooked front teeth. "In the name of His Imperial Highness, I am placing you under arrest."

My mother gawks, quickly moving to her feet. "Under arrest? On what charges?"

"Dodging the draft, and the assault of a ranking officer this very morning."

"What in the nine suns are you talking about? My son would never do such things!"

"Stand down," a second soldier declares, roughly pushing her away. His hand hovers over the hilt of his sword, his threat unspoken.

Before I have a chance to protest, three of the men surround me, forcing me to my knees as they bind my arms behind my back. One of them searches my pockets and pulls out the small glass vial that Doctor Qi gave me, the remaining scale clinking around at the bottom.

"Looks like we can add the purchase and possession of an illegal substance to your list of crimes," the guard says with a dark look in his eyes. "We might get to see a hanging tonight."

My mother cries frantically as they drag me off, swearing that this whole thing must be a misunderstanding. I consider fighting back, but I'm not a betting man, and a five-on-one fight isn't the fairest of odds.

Tears streak A-Ma's cheeks as I'm thrown into the back of a waiting wagon. It's designed with tall metal bars to keep prisoners locked in. There are people out and about now, some of them gathering in wide-eyed shock and sharing scandalized whispers.

"Isn't that the—"

"Probably swindled the wrong person."

"To the ice fields with him, says I."

My mother grasps desperately at me through the bars, tugging at my outer robe. "Sai! Sai, what's going on?"

"Please, don't worry, A-Ma," I reply, keeping my voice as calm and gentle as possible despite my rabbit heart. "Go back inside where it's warm. I'll have this whole affair sorted and be back by evening."

"But Sai—"

With a startling crack of a whip, the two horses up front lurch forward with disgruntled whinnies. The wagon's wheels squeak in protest as it is dragged over the uneven dirt streets.

My gut tells me to try to escape, knowing something terrible is coming. But between my bound hands, the iron bars, and the sword-wielding soldiers now following on foot, I know that would be a guaranteed death sentence. The only thing I can do for now is let them take me.

And pray I can talk my way out of this mess.

4

The prison smells of sweat, piss, and shit.

They drag me through the winding labyrinth of stone, nothing but flickering torchlight to illuminate the way forward. The prison sits at the very edge of Jiaoshan, well hidden from the general public's view. I can't tell how deep we are underground, but there's a stale dampness in the air that clings to my skin, chilling me to the bone.

The anguished groans and whimpers of prisoners, along with the haunting rattle of their chains, echo loudly off the walls. My eyes have not yet adjusted to the darkness, though I can still make out the bloodshot whites of their eyes as they grip the bars of their cells, desperately begging for water or food—or a merciful death.

The soldiers cut my bindings and throw me into a cramped cell like a sack of flour, dumping me upon a rough bed of moldy straw. It's uncomfortably slimy, smearing my hands and knees as I scramble to my feet. They slam the cell door shut, the sickening scent of rusted hinges flooding my nose.

"Please," I say hurriedly, "this is all a misunderstanding. You have to let me out. My mother needs her med—"

The captain surges forward and slams the scabbard of his sword against the bars. They ring out angrily, rattling my eardrums.

"Silence!"

"Listen, my friend, what happened between us earlier . . . I'm terribly sorry. Perhaps we can put this entire incident behind us? I'll give you free food and drinks at the teahouse forever. What do you say?"

"I say I'll cut your tongue out if you utter another word."

Desperation claws at my throat. "My mother is very ill. I'm her only son, so I'm charged with her well-being. Please, find it in your heart to understand!"

"Listen here, you backwater degenerate—"

"That is enough, Captain Tian."

The voice belongs to someone I can't see, resonating from the safety of the shadows. Whoever he is, I figure he must be of great importance, because the captain's whole body goes rigid before he bows deeply.

A man steps out, his features highlighted by the shifting orange glow of the torchlights.

He is, in every sense of the word, overwhelming.

Dressed in flawless silk robes whose threads are dyed in the rarest of golden pigments, the man is a walking tribute to all the kingdom's splendor. The intricate pattern of a snarling five-clawed blue dragon is embroidered into the silk, starting with its tail on the bottom right corner, then wrapping all the way around his back, and over the shoulder to rest upon the man's heart.

His hair is well-maintained and shiny, even in the dim lights of the prison, pulled into a regal bun held in place by an ornate pin sculpted of shimmering gold. His fingers are adorned with thick jade rings, and his fourth finger and pinky on each hand are protected by sharp, clawlike nail guards.

While most people would gape at his obvious and exorbitant wealth, the only thing that catches my eye is his thread.

It's gray, just like my own, except his thread has been completely severed, dangling loose just inches from his little finger.

How is this possible? If his Fated One were dead, then he would have a closed black loop. The cut looks almost deliberate, as if he took a blade to it. I know this cannot be, however. Our threads are indelible, gifts granted to us by the Gods to help link two ardent souls. I have never been able to physically grasp hold of one—they might appear like living things, but they can only be seen, never touched or altered by those who possess them. The act of cutting a thread should be impossible.

I know I have been staring too long, because Captain Tian's arm shoots through a gap between the bars and grabs me by the hair, forcing me down into some semblance of a bow.

"Insolent wretch!" he growls. "Have you no respect for your emperor?"

My heart thuds anxiously. Did I hear that right, or has the deafening roar of blood past my ears somehow caused me to hallucinate? Keeping my eyes glued to the floor, I realize that I'm at a loss for words. It's not something that happens very often. I dare not speak, for the possibility of losing my tongue is suddenly very real, should I displease His Imperial Highness.

Unsure of what else to do, I risk a glance upward. The emperor reaches into one of his sleeves and pulls out the vial the soldiers confiscated from me. The long stretch of silence that follows makes me squirm. I find the emperor studying the scale with the slightest of amused grins.

I take a moment to study his face. He looks surprisingly young for a man who has ruled the Northern Kingdom for longer than I've been alive. Strip him of his ostentatious garb, and we might even pass for brothers. His eyes, however, give me pause.

They are ancient. Wise beyond centuries and dripping with something . . .

Cruel.

Nearby prisoners break out into frantic whispers.

"Is that—"

"No, it can't be," someone else murmurs. "He should be nothing more than a decrepit old man."

"He has shamans," whispers another. "I hear they use blood magic—they sacrifice virgin concubines, and it grants him eternal youth."

"He's the Son of Heaven, appointed by the Gods. A god himself! What need has he of such nonsense?"

Captain Tian bangs his scabbard against the bars of my cell door again, the metallic twang shocking everyone back into silence. "The next to speak loses their head."

I suck in a sharp breath. A terrible chill scrapes its way down the back of my neck, leaving goose bumps sprawling in its wake. The emperor takes another step forward, unperturbed by the senseless gossip.

"Do you know what this is, boy?" he asks me, holding the vial up to the dim torchlight. His words are clipped, succinct.

I'm unsure how to answer. If I tell him the truth, will he think me a lunatic? A fool? I can't think of anything more humiliating than having His Imperial Highness laugh in my face.

The emperor furrows his brows. "If you do not wish to answer, perhaps your friend will provide something more enlightening. Bring him in."

A prisoner is brought out from around the corner, propped up on either side by an armed guard. The man's small body is slumped over, his feet dragging upon the stone floor. His face has been beaten to a near pulp. Both his eyes are swollen and purple. They have broken his nose, and a trail of dried blood stains his lips and chin. I'm surprised the man still has enough strength to look up at me. When he does, I recognize him in an instant.

Doctor Qi.

The air pulls itself from my lungs.

"Wh-what do you want with him?" I ask, my teeth chattering uncontrollably.

The emperor regards the doctor with general disinterest. There's a darkness in his gaze, an air of superiority. We are all but cockroaches beneath his embroidered shoes.

"Where did you get this?" he asks Doctor Qi, holding the vial up before his battered face. "Answer honestly, and I may let you live."

The doctor's head hangs low, a mix of drool and blood dripping through the gaps of his broken teeth. I think his lip has split. "The South," he rasps. "F-from . . . the South."

"You had it smuggled past the border, correct?"

Worry weighs heavily on Doctor Qi's features. "Yes, Your Highness."

"And you know what this is?"

The doctor gulps heavily. "A d-dragon's scale."

"Do you know where to get *more*?"

Doctor Qi casts his eyes to the cold, hard ground. "I c-cannot say exactly, but I know who might. My contact in the S-South. A huntress. She believes a dragon may yet live. She claims to have been tracking it f-for some time."

My ears burn. I can't begin to comprehend what's happening. All I have the strength to do is kneel there, clinging to the bars, my mouth slack in disbelief.

A living, breathing dragon? No, that can't be. Could the woman have mistaken a snake or some other beast for it?

The corners of the emperor's lips curl upward. "Where is she now?"

"Last I heard, the huntress w-was spotted in the jungles just past the mountain border."

"Does she go by a name?"

"I believe she goes by Feng, my lord."

"You will find her for me."

"With all due respect, Your Imperial Highness, my legs . . . They—they aren't as strong as they once were."

Emperor Róng hums in contemplation. "You're quite right. I thank you very much, Doctor, for your cooperation in this matter."

Doctor Qi lifts his head, a glint of hope in his eyes. "Does this mean I am free to g—"

He doesn't finish his sentence. The emperor raises his hand and brings it down like an axe; his command silent, yet plainly understood.

Captain Tian moves swiftly, drawing his blade with alarming speed. He raises his sword above his head, and the sharp edge slices through the air with an abrupt whistle. In one fell swoop, he cleaves the doctor's head clean from his shoulders. It goes tumbling, rolling toward me, Doctor Qi's face forever frozen in shock.

I'm racked with uncontrollable tremors. My skin is feverish, and yet I have never been so alarmingly cold. The world spins around me, dizziness plaguing my mind.

I vomit, hunched over on my hands and knees.

I barely have enough time to wipe my mouth clean on my sleeve when I see it. The thread of fate tied around Doctor Qi's finger shifts from red to black, fading away like a candle's wick left to burn until nothing remains. Then it disintegrates completely.

The emperor clicks his tongue, looking upon me with obvious disappointment. "You look to have two strong legs," he says. "Tell me, boy, do you wish to live?"

There's only one answer to his question, and yet I can't find my voice.

He steps over the doctor's still-warm corpse without a fuss, the fabric of his long robes soaking with blood. The emperor crouches before me on the other side of the cell. He smells of rich perfumes, though they do little to mask the stench of the prison.

"I have heard of you," he murmurs softly. "They call you the Thread-Seeker."

My throat closes up, choking what little air I have managed to swallow. His eyes are dead and soulless.

"Is it true?" he asks me. "Can you truly see red threads of fate? Or are my informants mistaken?"

I nod shakily. "I can see them, Your Imperial Highness."

He lifts his hand for me to inspect. "Speak, then. Tell me what you see."

Confusion washes over me. I'm hard-pressed for an answer. I stare at his severed gray thread in dismay. If I tell him the truth, this will surely upset him. Everyone despises the bearer of bad news. Would it not be better to wax poetic about how a great love awaits him?

In the end, I choose honesty.

"I'm sorry, Your Imperial Highness, but it seems that your connection with your Fated One is . . . no more."

His face hardens, suddenly impassable. For a moment, I fear Captain Tian will strike me down without remorse. My chest is on the verge of bursting, my lungs blazing from lack of air. All is still and suffocating. And then—

The emperor smiles. It doesn't reach his eyes.

"What news have you heard concerning the Southern Kingdom of Jian?" he asks.

"Only that the border has been closed, and your Imperial Army has, erm . . . met great resistance in recent moons."

"But do you have you any idea as to why we're at war?"

"Not really," I confess.

"Resources, boy. Great empires are only as strong as they are wealthy. I've already liberated the Kingdoms of Lang, Fen, Min, and your Kingdom of Xuě, and look how the people flourish under my guidance."

Liberated? I nearly laugh in the emperor's face, but manage to hold back. Only one head needs to roll today. I hadn't even been born when the empire swept through and claimed my homeland, though the way A-Ma describes it, the people are no better off than they were before. It's true that we share the same language, the same currency—but with such a large swathe of territory comes innumerable problems.

The Kingdom of Lang is known for their droughts, its farmers struggling to meet annual harvest quotas set out by the emperor's own advisors. In the smaller Kingdom of Fen along the eastern coast, bandits roam the roads and pillage towns. The Kingdom of Min, located just to the west and bordering the Wastelands, is barely inhabited now. Most flock to Jiaoshan in the hopes of starting a new life, though life here is hardly a springtime walk, either. The year-long trade embargo has made normally plentiful goods difficult to come by. And the seemingly endless waves of conscription orders have made it near impossible to find capable workers.

But even with all these unchecked problems, the emperor still wants to claim the Southern Kingdom for himself?

I'm no ruler. I'm content with my simple life, making tea and serving cookies. Maybe matching a happy couple or two. I would never claim to understand politics or economics or the art of war, but this much I know: the emperor's campaign in the South will serve no one but him.

"It seems you managed to escape the conscription order," the emperor continues, one of his thick brows arched in a question.

I bite on the inside of my cheek, the memory of that day pulling to the surface. I heard the army officers approaching well before I saw them, the sound of their war drums announcing their approach. I remember their bright red banners flying overhead as they gathered at the city's center, fanning out to cover as much ground as possible while delivering their ordinance.

"I was granted an exemption," I answer tiredly, "in order to take care of my mother. She's in poor health and cannot work. As her only child, it's my duty to remain behind."

"Ah, that would explain this, then," the emperor replies, holding the vial up to the torchlight. "You do know what this is, yes?"

I swallow, my throat unbearably dry. "That I do."

"The dragon this belongs to . . . It's the last in existence."

"How do you know?"

Emperor Róng observes me carefully, a dark glint in his eyes. I can't fathom what devious plot might be stirring in his mind. "I wish to propose a deal," he says, ignoring my question.

"What sort of deal?"

"Head south and find this huntress. Seek out my dragon and bring it to me. In return, you will receive my full pardon."

My heart beats too quickly for me to distinguish each individual pulse. Has the emperor gone mad? I can't deny the possibility of the creature's existence now that I've seen its magic at work with my own two eyes, but—

"I'm no scout," I insist. "And I don't mean that to be humble, Your Imperial Highness. I have a lousy sense of direction."

"Would you prefer death?"

I stare up at him, still on my hands and knees. No argument there. "How long would I be away?"

"However long it takes you."

"But I'm free thereafter?"

"You have my word. I will even grant you a boon."

"A boon?"

"Find my dragon," he says, "and I will allow you to harvest as many scales as you should require from it to heal your dear mother."

My guts are tied up in impossible knots, the precariousness of the situation coating my tongue with something sour. Of course I want my mother's health to improve, but while I like to play the part, I'm no fool. When the emperor makes a request of you, it's only ever a command. There is no denying him. My answer is predestined.

"What do you want with it?" I ask hesitantly. "This dragon."

"That is none of your concern, boy. Answer me now: Do we have a deal?"

I take a deep breath. "As His Imperial Highness ordains."

He nods just once and pockets my vial. "Excellent. You shall embark immediately."

Concern jolts through me. "But I must inform my mother. She requires the last of her medicine, or else—"

Captain Tian slams his scabbard against the bars once more, cutting me off. "The emperor has spoken."

5

Captain Tian and I ride through the night, keeping to the main road. He has me on the saddle behind him, my wrists bound by a length of rope that he's attached to his waist so I don't make a run for it. It's near pitch-black, save for the moonlight and the glimmer of stars across the sky. Captain Tian has a paper lantern balanced on the end of a stick, held just in front of his steed on a bracket attached to his saddle. We make good time at a consistent trot. The serpentine mountain pass that separates North from South slowly but surely approaches, growing larger and larger until the rocky formations loom overhead like giants.

At the foot of the mountain, I spot an encampment roughly five thousand men strong—only a fraction of the Imperial Army. The military base of Shéyǎn—Snake Eye, named for the way it sits at the head of the snaking mountain pass.

Canvas tents are arranged row upon row, sprawling out from the center of the camp, where a massive fire pit sits for warmth and light. There is a surprising amount of activity at this late hour. Soldiers are already dressed in full suits of armor, some busy sharpening their blades, while others kneel in quiet corners of the camp with their hands pressed together in prayer.

Captain Tian tugs on the reins, bidding his steed come to a halt. He removes the rope from around his middle before throwing a leg over to hop off the saddle. I jump down, too, though my landing lacks any semblance of grace. I grit my teeth together and groan. My thighs are chafed and sore.

The captain tugs at the knot locking my wrists together, freeing me after several long, uncomfortable hours. "With me," he snaps.

He all but shoves me toward a makeshift forge near the edge of the encampment. It's far larger than the rest of the structures, the protective canopy above it a deep red. Within is a treasure trove of armor and weaponry. I daresay I have never come face-to-face with this much gleaming metal.

A team of forgemasters flit about their workstation, all sporting a thick layer of sweat and grime on their haggard faces. They work with the utmost diligence, stoking the fire with a shovelful of fresh coal. They appear to be working on several blades at once, a few placed into the flames to soften their steel, while a handful of others hang just off to the side for sharpening. A nearby blacksmith is in the middle of quenching a red-hot blade in a bucket of cold water when he spots us.

"What do you want?" he snaps.

Captain Tian gives me a good push forward. "A new recruit. See to it that he's fitted with a set of armor and a blade."

I frown. "Is that not the armorer's job?"

"Armorer's dead," the blacksmith grumbles, spitting onto the ground. "The buffoon tried to desert his post. You can see him, if you'd like. They have him strung up by his neck near the latrines."

I swallow hard, unable to dislodge the sticky lump at the back of my throat. I make a note to ask fewer questions.

"Have him fitted and ready within the hour," the captain says before turning on his heel to leave.

Without anywhere else to go, I remain rooted in place as the blacksmith trudges forward. He scrutinizes me, clearly unimpressed. "Tall, but scrawny," he mutters to himself. "You're a Xuě boy, yes?"

"That I am, sir."

"Why do you smell like vomit?"

My mouth has gone dry. I don't feel like answering. I haven't stopped thinking about Doctor Qi's gruesome execution since I left Jiaoshan.

The blacksmith harrumphs, stomping away toward a rack of lamellar armor. He grabs a set and all but throws it at me to catch. I'm no military expert, but I can tell that it was hastily made. Some of the plates don't fit quite right, and the stitching is sloppy and rushed, at risk of falling apart if placed under too much strain. Upon closer inspection, I realize that sections of the breastplate are scuffed and scratched.

"This has been used before," I point out.

"Waste not, want not," he answers indifferently.

"What happened to its owner?"

"Trampled to death beneath his horse, the poor bastard."

I chew on the inside of my cheek, my stomach churning at the thought of wearing a dead man's armor.

Sensing my unease, the blacksmith scoffs. "Would you rather go without?"

As with the emperor earlier, his question doesn't require an answer.

I frown as I slip the breastplate on. The armor doesn't sit quite right, just shy of too tight around the neck, but much too spacious around the belly. I'm also provided with a set of pauldrons bearing the sigil of the Imperial Family, along with boots that are a tad too small, resulting in an uncomfortable pinching of my toes.

The blacksmith holds out a finished sword, too. I take it

awkwardly, holding my newly assigned weapon out to the side like a rake. I have no idea how to use the blasted thing, let alone draw it from its scabbard.

I take my leave stiffly, shifting uncomfortably beneath my repurposed uniform. I feel ridiculous, merely a child playing dress-up. The more I take in of the encampment, the more I realize I'm not the only one feeling uneasy. Most of these soldiers are no older than I, likely recruited from the northernmost territories—perhaps even the ice fields, where the convicts are banished. The youngest looks no older than four and ten. He should be home playing with his siblings, not with sharpened swords.

I find the captain not even a few feet away, speaking to a fellow army officer. Their exchange is clipped and hushed, as though they are plotting a conspiracy. The other officer leaves the moment I step forth.

"I wasn't aware that the emperor's task required my enlistment."

"The army moves at dawn," Captain Tian says sternly. "We'll slip you past the border in the ensuing chaos."

"The ensuing chaos?" I echo, dismayed.

"Our enemy awaits just on the other side of the mountain pass. Those bastards have been using this pinch point to mow us down."

I look around, my unease growing by the second. "Is that why we're all gathered here?"

"The more of us there are, the more likely we'll force our way past those Southern bastards. Rushing them at first light increases our chances of success."

I shudder, the visualization not lost on me—five thousand men barreling down through a funnel to launch an offensive on a waiting army. The fact that I'm to go with them is preposterous. I'm more likely to be trampled underfoot by my own countrymen than make it to the other side unscathed.

"Surely there has to be another way," I insist, attempting to keep my voice level. I can't very well carry out my task if I'm killed before I'm able to begin my search. "Why don't we go around?"

"It's too long a trek. At least two weeks' journey. Heading straight through the pass will only take us a few hours."

"This is ridiculous."

"Scared?" the captain asks with a smirk, every ounce self-righteous and overconfident.

"Of course. I'm a sane man."

"I've been given express permission to spear you through, should you run. Just so you know."

Setting my jaw, I weigh my options carefully, only to realize that I have none. I'm trapped in a powerful river current, at the mercy of its flow. My head is above water for now, but one wrong move will see me dragged under. If I try to escape and run home, I'll be killed. If I march forward with the rest of the invasion, I have less than a razor-thin chance of survival, but at least there's that.

Near the camp's fire, people begin to gather, all of them kneeling before a man heavily clad in muted mulberry-stained robes. His mesmerizing headdress is what claims my attention, expertly crafted out of the long feathers of a silver pheasant. An Imperial shaman.

He has a bamboo calligraphy brush in hand, the fine hairs soaked through in red ink. As he recites an incantation in a dialect my ears fail to recognize, the shaman slowly works his way down the line, painting talismans directly onto the breastplates of the waiting soldiers. An apprentice follows closely behind, holding a clay bowl between his palms, thick plumes of smoke rising from it.

The shaman's work is sloppy, to say the least. The characters meant to ward off evil and bring good luck are barely legible. Some of them are missing crucial strokes, rendering the talismans useless.

The shaman does not stop to correct his work. There are too many soldiers to bless and not enough time before battle to do so.

Beside me, the captain makes no effort to join the line.

"Will you not ask for a blessing?" I question.

He scoffs. "The might of my sword will see me through."

I shrug and kneel at the end of the line. I'll take all the help I can get. Perhaps I will be one of the lucky ones with a working talisman charm.

The shaman finally makes his way to me, his brush hovering just above my armor. He doesn't make a move. Instead, he leans forward and squints, regarding me with an intense focus.

"You . . . ," he mutters slowly, his teeth and tongue dyed completely black with charcoal. The shaman's eyes glaze over as if he's in a trance. "You reek of magic."

Confusion swirls within my skull. Is he part bloodhound? He can *smell* magic? That's most peculiar, though I suppose I *was* handling dragon scales.

"I do? How can you tell?" I ask him.

The shaman doesn't elaborate. Instead, he throws a glance toward his apprentice, who stretches out his arms to present the bowl of what I now see are smoldering herbs and small animal parts. The foot of a chicken, the skeletal remains of a snake's head, along with sprinkles of silver shavings. The shaman breathes in the fumes, a low, animalistic groan escaping him as tremors rack his body. His eyes cloud over, a thick, opaque gray washing over the dark brown of his irises. He no longer seems present, staring through me rather than at me.

"*A broken son, a lover shunned,*" the shaman rasps. "*Three, now two . . . soon to be one.*"

The little hairs at the nape of my neck stand on end. "Sir?"

Behind me, Captain Tian snorts. He grabs me forcefully by the scruff of my collar and yanks me to my feet. "Are you finished? We're wasting precious time listening to this buffoon."

The shaman glares as he lifts a long, bony finger and points at the captain. *"A violent end you shall meet, your final breath drawn in the arms of His Red Majesty."*

Captain Tian huffs and rolls his eyes. "Ridiculous," he grumbles before stomping away, dragging me along with one strong hand digging into my bicep.

My heart hammers. I can't make sense of anything. I have no time to breathe, to process. As the captain drags me toward the mouth of the mountain pass, I catch a glimpse of the shaman one last time. He's deep in his trance, kneeling down on the muddy ground. He bends at the hips in a full kowtow, muttering all sorts of nonsense under his breath.

I cannot imagine the toll those fumes must take on the human psyche.

6

Soldiers prepare themselves, gathering their armaments be-fore falling in line. It's a long procession of infantry, followed by officers of higher rank on horseback. Supply wagons make up the tail end, largely unguarded. The captain drags me toward the middle of the army masses. He takes up the spot behind me, no doubt to dissuade me from thoughts of escape.

"Move out!" a commander somewhere in the rear ranks shouts.

I remain frozen where I stand, my legs heavier than lead. My throat is tight, my palms are clammy, and my guts twist with such ferocity that I worry I might get sick again all over my boots. There's no solace to be found in the fact that many of my neighboring soldiers already have. But then I think of my mother, waiting for me at home alone. If I'm to return to her, fear cannot overtake me—though it's certainly trying its best.

The front of the line marches forward first, and then the row after that, and so on. When it's finally our turn to move, Captain Tian gives me a hard push. I have no choice but to allow myself to be carried away by the tide of the army.

The mouth of the mountain pass is wider than its middle. The soldiers are quickly forced to break formation, the front line rearranging itself so that only four soldiers stand shoulder to shoulder. There's no room to turn, only to trudge on.

On either side of us, the jagged mountain walls scale high into the sky like silent sentries, blocking out any trace of sunlight and warmth. The sound of thousands of footsteps rattles against the stone, somehow both thunderous and distant. The air is still with the threat of death, heavy and cold upon our skin. Nobody dares speak.

The tension only grows as the hours drag by and we draw closer and closer to the end of the pass, the soldiers up front bracing for the ensuing onslaught. The pace of our march quickens, anxious battle cries suddenly erupting into the air. The exit is in clear view now, the sunlight a blinding beacon after so long spent engulfed in the mountain's shadow.

The march turns into a jog, the jog into a full-on sprint. I steel myself, my heart pounding louder than the war drums behind us. I'm buffeted on all sides by the storm of armored, angry men. There is no way for me to prepare for what might come next. I step out and—

My gray thread tugs to the left.

Never—and I mean *never*—before have I sensed my Fated One on the other end of the line.

But there's no time to marvel at it. Right now, I must survive.

My nose is bombarded by the bitter, stomach-churning scent of blood. I'm blinded by the sun, my eyes struggling to adjust in the sudden brightness. Desperate pleas of surrender and violent roars leave my ears ringing. The disorienting chaos of war encircles me while confusion swirls in my chest. It's mayhem, brutal and unforgiving.

We're a ferocious ocean wave crashing against a steadfast rocky shore. And it's upon this shore that we disperse, the soldiers ahead of me scattering as they're forced into battle by the surge at their backs. The clang of sword and armor rattles my eardrums. The sight of fallen bodies at my feet leaves me numb. Before I have the chance to catch my breath or gather my wits, I'm the next to find himself at the front of the line.

A soldier barrels toward me. I don't see his face so much as the color he wears. The pale blue of his armor clashes with my red. He charges forth with a murderous battle cry, spit spraying from his mouth as he raises his sword above his head.

I stumble back.

He swings.

The tip of his blade whispers past my eye, too close. *Much* too close.

I draw my sword in a hurry, my hands shaking so hard that I nearly drop the blasted thing. I parry the soldier's next blow—purely by chance—the force of metal clanging against metal sending vibrations through my bones.

"Stop!" I shout, tripping over my own feet as I scramble away, only to fall again over a small pile of bodies. "Please, I don't want to hurt you!"

He charges again, my plea for mercy ignored. There's no escape. Is this it for me?

The captain rushes forth, his sword slicing through the air with such tremendous speed that my eyes register only a blur. Blood spills forth, a red-hot spray splattering across my face and staining my armor. I gasp around the mouthful that washes over my tongue. The soldier's head lobs to the side. The cut isn't clean. I gag at the sight of ripped flesh, fatty tissue, exposed muscle, and the gritty bone of his severed spine sticking out from between his shoulders.

"Get up, you fool!" Captain Tian snarls at me.

I'm too scared to move.

"Have you lost your mind?" he hisses, stomping over to grasp me by the arm.

"This is madness!" I scream back. "I can't do this!"

"Fight or die, you coward!"

An arrow screams past my ear. It meets its mark, the tip so sharp and heavy that it pierces straight through the center of the captain's breastplate with a wet thud. He falls to the side, not quite dead, though certainly paralyzed from the shock.

The wall of Northern soldiers behind him doesn't stop, continuing forward as they charge their enemies with swords and spears raised. They shove their way past me, climbing over the captain without hesitation or regard for their fallen comrade. I'm close enough to hear his bones crack and crunch as he gurgles on the blood spilling from his mouth.

For the briefest moment, I contemplate running.

I could return home, away from this needless bloodshed and savagery. My mother needs me. I don't belong here, nor do I wish to be burdened with this search. My heart holds no love for the man now dying before me, and yet . . .

I drag him out of the way, grasping him under the arms to pull him off to the side. I lose my footing more than once, the soles of my boots slipping against the soil now muddy with blood. The smell is sickening.

"You f-fool," Captain Tian sputters. Every breath he takes is an arduous wheeze. "Leave me to die."

"Lie still," I snap. "Medic! I need a medic!"

The world spins. I can't begin to count the number of bodies. Our casualties are heavy, but our enemy's are heavier still. While we are at least clad in armor of questionable make, they appear to be nothing more than local farmers and last-minute conscripts. We outnumber them twenty to one. They're simply no match for the Imperial Army. But it's the cruelty of the emperor's soldiers that turns my blood cold.

Even when our Southern brothers raise their white flag, the fight carries on. Heads leave shoulders. Loose arms and legs scatter about, their owners lost somewhere in the clash. Young and old are stabbed through without remorse. Some beg for mercy, while others are resigned to their gruesome end.

All around me, red threads turn black and then disintegrate entirely. I swear in that moment I can hear thousands of souls cry out at once, all of them heartbroken. Fathers, brothers, sons, and lovers killed in the blink of an eye—never to return home.

I'm yanked from my sullen thoughts when the captain grips me by the collar. With shaking hands, he rips a scroll from the sash around his waist and shoves it to my chest.

"Your ordinance," he rasps. "See your mission through."

"Save your breath. I'll find you a doctor."

"Move, soldier!" he bellows.

"I can't leave you here like this."

An unexpected wave of calm washes over his features. He stares blankly up at the sky, his face bruised and swollen. "His Imperial Highness . . . promised me."

I lean down closer to hear. It's a miracle the captain has held out this long. "Promised you? Promised you what?"

"My family . . . will be looked after. I was to see you safely . . . across the border."

"Hang on," I tell him. "Just hang on. Those dragon scales . . . I can find you some. They can heal, and—"

Captain Tian's eyes may remain open, but they are dark, empty wells. His eerie stillness is my second clue, the transformation of his red thread to black and then to nothing, my third and final one.

I rise slowly, the emperor's ordinance in hand. My clothes are filthy, caked in dirt and drying blood. The soldiers finish off the last of the Southern Kingdom's army, too busy looting supplies and piling up bodies to burn in a single heap to pay me any mind.

One step after the next, I will myself forward. I clumsily approach a nearby warhorse. It's one of ours, a dark brown mare draped in the Imperial Family's colors, though her rider is nowhere in sight. Most likely dead.

I pat her neck gently, struggling to clear the murky haze clouding my mind. I must venture farther south to find out if this dragon really exists. Perhaps not to a city, but a smaller village that I can pass through discreetly. There's no doubt that news of the Imperial Army's advance will reach the major trading hubs faster than the towns far from the main roads. After witnessing the devastation firsthand, I shudder at the thought of the terrors my brethren will carry out in the emperor's name.

I mount the horse swiftly, grabbing her reins and digging my heels against her sides. I need to get ahead of the soldiers before they raze everything nearby to the ground. I can't gather information if there's no one alive to provide it.

"Hey!" someone shouts at me. The tall red feathers atop his helmet tell me that he's one of the higher-ranking officers. "Where do you think you're going? Our orders are to kill the survivors."

I look down at him in horror. "I'll have no hand in this madness."

"Dismount at once or you'll be tried for insubordination!"

"So be it," I say bitterly.

"Deserter!" he cries, brandishing his sword. "We have a deserter!"

I snap the reins to break the horse into a mad gallop, leaving the carnage far behind.

7

The warm winds that come off the Albeion Sea offer the Southern Kingdom of Jian a tropical climate. Its air isn't arid and thin like that of the Western Wastelands, but humid and uncomfortably thick. Even in these winter months, the moisture in the air clings to my skin in a film. I'm unaccustomed to the thick jungles and the nasty biting bugs that have made the leaves and branches their home.

My new equine friend has taken me far, at least a hundred li. My exhaustion finally catches up to me when the sun centers itself in the sky. I haven't had a chance to rest since the night before I visited Doctor Qi, and now my bones are weary from travel and the weight of all I've seen in the past two days.

The smell of blood lingers in my nose. The screams of dying men rattle within my skull even still. Every time I manage to close my eyes, I'm haunted by the memory of the captain's lifeless ones staring back.

Deserter!

I wipe a clammy palm over my chest, feeling the hard thud of my heart rattle my rib cage.

What if news gets back to my mother that I've gone missing? A-Ma would lose her sanity upon the discovery that her son was sent off and lost to battle; her nerves might not handle it well. First her husband, then her son . . . And with Doctor Qi dead, there's no one left to care for her in her condition.

I force myself to take a deep, shaky breath. No. No one, apart from Emperor Róng and Captain Tian—the latter of whom now lies dead, taking with him all his secrets—knows that I'm here. From what I can tell, my name was never officially added to any military roster. I have no rank, no regiment to belong to. I was only at Shéyǎn for a little under a day, so I doubt any of the other soldiers would even recognize me, let alone know that I abandoned them. My mission is a secret, as is my location. The sooner I find this dragon, the sooner I can return home.

My horse slows and veers slightly off the overgrown dirt path, drawn to the sound of trickling water somewhere nearby. We find a narrow stream slithering through the tall grass like a snake, barely deep nor wide enough to get my boots wet. Still, I suppose a short break could do us good.

She cuts through a low thicket of rich green ferns and dips her head down to drink greedily. I slide out of the saddle, sore in places I didn't think it possible.

I grunt when my feet hit solid ground. "I'm tempted to joke about how badly my misters hurt, but I fear that's not appropriate for the ears of a fine lady such as yourself," I say to the horse, stroking her tangled black mane. She snorts in response but appears otherwise unbothered.

I leave her side momentarily to turn in a circle, attempting to gather my bearings while stripping out of my armor, abandoning the heavy pieces upon the ground. If I fail to find food and shelter by nightfall, my chances of starving to death or being eaten by some ferocious jungle creature will rise exponentially. I would prefer not to die before I've even managed to catch a whiff of where this legendary beast could be lying in wait.

If, that is, it exists at all.

Now that I have, by some miracle, made it past the border into the Southern Kingdom, I must admit that I'm at a complete loss. I wasn't lying to His Imperial Highness when I said I have a lousy sense of direction. Even if I could tell north from south, I have little knowledge of this region, having spent all my life in Jiaoshan. The nearest town could very well be around the bend, or it could be several days of travel from here. I have no maps, no sense of the terrain. And where is this huntress that Doctor Qi spoke of? I would much prefer not to wander aimlessly through this jungle, but I have no clue where else to begin.

Despair creeps up on me.

But I can't just turn around and go home. Even if I somehow made it back past the massacre in the mountain pass, if I return home empty-handed, I will certainly lose my head and might even be risking my mother's.

My gaze mindlessly wanders down to my hand. The fraying gray thread around my finger hasn't moved since the battle earlier this morning. Could it have been a fluke? Perhaps machinations of my mind to distract me from my near-miss with death? No, that's not it. It was only for a second, but I have never been more sure—I was closer to my Fated One than I have ever been. I sensed them, which means maybe—just maybe—they were able to sense me too.

It's an exciting, terrifying thought.

"What do you think, my friend?" I ask my horse with a weary exhale, patting her neck. "I would wager all the emperor's coin that my beloved is the most beautiful being in all the realms."

My horse whinnies, lifting her head now that her thirst is thoroughly quenched.

"I hope they love to laugh," I continue to muse aloud while adjusting the straps of my saddle. My grumbling belly demands that we be on our way, and soon.

"I wonder how they pass their time. Do they enjoy singing? We would be well suited, since I can't carry a tune."

My horse stomps her front hoof.

"Not one for conversation, either?" I mumble. "Good thing I don't mind my own company."

Somewhere behind me, a twig snaps.

I whip around, alarmed.

There's nothing there.

I scan the thick jungle, searching for any movement. There's a chance one of the Imperial soldiers could have followed me, but I was careful to check for pursuers as I dashed away. Perhaps an animal, then?

Or . . . something worse?

The traveling merchants used to tell me all sorts of tales about the wild and dangerous animals that roamed the jungles south of the mountain border. I was only a boy when they filled my head with stories about fierce fox spirits who were said to have nine tails and bewitch their prey, luring them in so they could feed on their victim's life essence.

My favorite tales were about the yaoguai—creatures who were once Gods but were banished to the mortal realm for violating the laws of Heaven. It's said that they are unfathomably hideous beasts, intent on consuming everything in their path. If the dragons of lore are in fact real, it stands to reason that other monsters may also lurk in the shadows.

I search the jungle canopy, paranoid. Still nothing.

"Let's go," I whisper to my horse before climbing back into the saddle.

————

I am terribly, hopelessly lost.

The dirt road we were following ended almost two li ago. I'm convinced we're going in circles. It doesn't help that every tree I choose as a waypoint looks exactly like the last.

The sun will be setting soon. While I'm not concerned about temperatures dropping to unbearably low levels, I *am* concerned about starvation. I know the basics of pitching a tent, but hunting? Starting a fire without flint and a striker? Those were things A-Ba failed to teach me before he passed.

Snap.

I throw a look over my shoulder. A cold dread freezes my marrow. Something is out there, watching and waiting. I hold my breath and try not to panic. The last thing I want is for my horse to spook and toss me off.

Something rustles the leaves.

"Who's there?" I shout, praying my voice will scare whatever it is that's been stalking me. "Come out where I can see you!"

All of a sudden, something tugs my thread.

The air is knocked from my lungs. There's enough tension in the thread to keep it taut. My Fated One is near, but when I follow the direction of the thread—

It points straight up into the skies above my head.

Bitter disappointment stings in my chest, and my confusion knows no limits. How can this be? Surely it's some sort of mistake. I have long suspected my thread of fate to be broken, given its ashen color and frayed thinness. The impossible direction that my thread now points all but confirms my worst fear.

Is there something wrong with me?

Am I destined to be alone?

Out of the corner of my eye, something moves. Its silhouette is large and unfamiliar, shifting in front of and behind palm trees just to my right. Whatever it is, it moves with alarming speed. I'm only able to catch a brief glimpse at a time.

The winding tail of a serpent.

The body and legs of a stag.

The sharp, twisted horns and head of a bull.

The single red eye at the very center of its face.

An abomination.

My horse neighs frantically, tugging against her reins as she anxiously shifts her weight. The creature crawls forward from the underbrush, its dreadfully pointed teeth and razor-like claws now in full view. Its growl is deep, so loud that it feels like it's shaking the earth on which we stand. The beast steps forward slowly, its unfeeling eye trained on me.

"Hu . . . man . . . ," it rasps.

I'm frozen in fear. *It can speak?*

"*Filthy . . . human . . .*"

If I run, it will give chase. If I stay, I'll be devoured. The only option I have is to fight, but the monster is twice my size and no doubt thrice as strong. My heart springs up and lodges in my throat when the beast gets low to the ground, preparing to pounce.

I'm trapped. There's nowhere to run.

A part of me wonders bitterly if my luck has run out. If I have used up all my good fortune surviving the battlefield, and now my time is finally at an end.

The beast lunges toward us with a snarl, fangs and claws bared for a killing blow.

I bring an arm up to protect myself. Its teeth pierce my forearm, jaws snapping shut like a spring trap, dragging me off the back of my horse. I land with a harsh thud against the jungle floor. Branches snap under me, their splintered ends jabbing my back. A scream rips from my chest as I feel skin and muscle tear, the sticky warmth of my own blood soaking into my clothes and staining my flesh red.

The beast is close enough that I can smell its rancid breath. It yanks and it shoves, attempting to wrest my arm free from its socket. Death seems determined to claim me this day. The more I struggle, the more my vision blurs around the edges, giving way to murky darkness.

And then something even more terrifying happens.

Above, a deafening roar.

It frightens the birds from the trees and sends small critters skittering away. The sound spooks my steed, who rears back with a panicked whinny and kicks wildly at the beast before us with her front legs.

A shadow falls over everything around us, and something plunges from the sky.

The air whips through my hair and slices my cheeks as a great hulking creature arcs down and snatches the beast by the throat, pulling it off me. The red-eyed beast struggles only for a moment before its body goes limp. It dies with a pathetic whimper, suddenly lifeless on the jungle floor. Standing above it, its hunter feasts on steaming flesh, ripping through pelt and muscle and bone with rows of jagged ivory teeth.

The silence that follows is fragile.

I can't stop shaking, every inch of my body trembling. My racing heart pounds loudly in my ears. What *was* that bull-like creature? Have I gone mad? Slowly, I sit up, finally registering what just happened. I'm unprepared for the majesty of what I see.

My savior is serpentine in form, with four strong legs and five claws on each foot. The scales that cover every inch of its body are a rich emerald green that shimmer beautifully in the golden light of the setting sun. The mane that lines the back of its head and trails down its back looks as soft as springtime grass, flowing gently in the passing breeze. Its body is so large that it rivals the height of the trees, practically shoving them out of the way to make room for its intimidating presence.

A dragon.

My mouth drops open, but I can't find the will to speak. Especially not when I spot something peculiar wrapped around the divine creature's claw.

A thread of fate that is gray and fraying—its end connected to mine.

The dragon stares at me, an unmoving statue. Its eyes are a breathtaking emerald, hints of gold and amber flecks visible in the quickly fading light. I should be at my wits' end. For all I know, it could still choose to make a meal of me, and yet there's something . . . *familiar* about its gaze.

I can't explain it, this warmth that unfurls in my chest. I'm strangely at ease in the dragon's presence. This, despite the crimson dripping from its lips and the angry flare of its nostrils. Of all the things I could be feeling, safe and sound should not be among them. And yet . . .

And yet I know it will not harm me.

I slowly and carefully take a single step toward the creature. It hisses, flashing its teeth and flicking its long tail—a warning. I put my hands up cautiously as I approach.

"Easy, easy," I say gently. "I mean you no harm."

Genuine surprise washes over me when the dragon allows me within three paces of it. I extend my hand, the sensation of its breath tickling my palm a quiet marvel. We watch each other with an intense mutual interest, staring into each other's eyes as if all the answers from the Five Kingdoms to the Heavens above lie behind our gazes.

I know this soul, though I can't explain how.

I'm whole and complete and *home*.

But the cold, frightening realization washes over me. The dragon I have been tasked to hunt on behalf of the emperor, and my Fated One . . .

They are one and the same.

"How can this be?" I whisper, more to myself than to the dragon, my words soaked up by the surrounding foliage.

My questions are endless, but time isn't on my side. Honestly, when has it ever been?

Something behind us shifts in the underbrush, startling the dragon enough for it to roar. It bares its fangs, jagged like a serrated blade and just as terrifying. I turn, alarmed to find a lone huntress with a spear in hand.

"Get back!" she shouts, emerging from the underbrush. She winds back her arm to throw the weapon.

"No!" I cry, but it's too late.

The spear flies right into the dragon's front thigh. The creature bellows, whipping its tail violently to raise dirt and dust into the air. It launches itself into the sky without warning, disappearing into the inky gloom above.

My chest aches as I watch it go, my thread of fate shifting as it ascends into the night.

"You!" the woman shouts at me. She's a wild, bewildering thing. She pulls a knife and waves it before my face. "What do ye think yer doin'? Ye scared the blasted thing away!"

"Please," I mutter, lightheaded. "My arm . . . I need—"

"Oh, fer fuck's sake. Come with me before ye bleed out."

"Thank you, good madam."

She snorts. "There's nothin' good about me."

"Then what am I to call you?"

The woman shoots me a pointed look. "My enemies call me the huntress, but ye can call me Feng."

8

"Knowledge," the stranger explains.

He has traveled far and wide, his homeland ravaged by widespread famine, plague, and treacherous creatures of the night. Having heard tales of the dragons' generosity, the stranger set out in hopes of learning the secrets that might save his beloved people.

The stranger asks the red dragon, king of all that is above, if he might teach him how to control the rains to help the withering crops back home.

The red dragon shakes its mighty head. "The wind and rain and sun and snow cannot be tamed by any one man. No mortal shall possess the power to control the Heavens, lest he anger the Gods."

The stranger next implores the green dragon, queen of all living things, if she might instruct him on how to tame the violent beasts lurking in the shadows.

The green dragon denies him as well. "Beasts shall do what beasts always have. No mortal shall possess the power to impede their free will."

The stranger falls to his hands and knees before the blue dragon, prince of every refreshing river, mountain spring, and pond. The stranger beseeches the mighty beast for a way to ease the suffering of his dying people.

Believing his intentions to be noble and true, the young prince is moved by the stranger's words. The blue dragon shifts, his form shrinking down to resemble that of a man. He has a striking face and even more mesmerizing blue eyes.

"I will teach you how to heal and bring ease to your people," he says to the stranger.

For reasons he cannot explain, the young prince feels an unquestionable connection to the traveler before him. When he looks down at his hand, he understands why. He, just like all descendants of the ancient bloodline, can see the magic running between them.

They are connected by a red thread of fate.

9

I'm convinced that Feng has the worst bedside manner this side of the mountain border, but I'm nonetheless grateful for the salve of crushed roots and mixed herbs she's applied to my wound. It's nothing more than a dull ache and throb now, the poultice upon my forearm sealed beneath tightly wound strips of linen. There's no denying she's an excellent healer, her rough handling aside.

She's a striking woman, fierce and untamed, possibly a few years older than myself. Her clothes are stitched together from the pelts of different animals—a boar, a tiger, and what I assume was once a snake. Her complexion is darker than mine from her hours spent outdoors, her black hair cropped just above the shoulders, the wild strands framing her face curtaining over her dark brown eyes.

"How much farther?" I ask.

"If ye ask me *one* more time—" Feng groans. "I already told ye, we'll arrive by midnight."

Feng has me on horseback while she leads on foot by the reins, navigating through the twists and turns of the jungle with impressive ease. Though I was hopelessly lost in this maze of never-ending green, I quickly learn the markings Feng uses to find her way. I hadn't noticed them before: different symbols carved into the bark of the trees, some highlighted in heavily pigmented paints.

A column of three horizontal slashes accompanies the sound of rushing water up ahead. A large red cross warns of the dark thicket just around the bend, angry beasts growling louder as we pass their territory. There are triangles, too, pointing us in the direction of smoke—a campfire some distance away. It's not long, however, before the etchings give way to more permanent path markers.

Small statues carved of stone sit atop fallen stumps or deliberately placed rock piles. It's clear that they're well looked after, for though the statues are easily decades old and visibly worn from wind, rain, and time, none of them are covered in moss or leafy debris. In fact, many trinkets have been left at their feet, ranging from melted candles to small bits of jewelry and pieces of fresh fruit.

Every single statue is in the shape of a dragon, its mouth open in mid-snarl, its long tail curling behind it, with a front paw raised to brandish a fearsome claw. They're not unlike the dragons we carve upon our doors back home in Jiaoshan. It seems some superstitions transcend borders. Perhaps we're not so unlike our Southern brothers.

"How long have you been tracking it?" I ask Feng, shifting slightly in my saddle. My inner thighs are chafed and throbbing. "How did you know where to find the dragon?"

"Didn't," she confesses stiffly. "A happy coincidence, but I was trackin' the fei."

"Bless you."

"No, ye moron. A fei beast. That's what attacked ye."

My palms grow clammy at the memory of the creature's vile form. The echo of its voice—not quite human, but not entirely animal—clatters inside my skull. I've heard of fei beasts, just as I've heard of evil spirits, forlorn ghosts, demons . . . and dragons. All of which, until recently, stood in my mind as nothing more than the imaginings of ancient myth and superstition.

"Do you hunt them often?" I ask.

"Only when they cause problems for my village."

"What sort of problems?"

"Fei beasts're harbingers of rot. They kill every plant they step on and poison the waters they wade in."

I chew on the inside of my cheek, half tempted to tell her that *any* plant is likely to die when stepped upon, but I decide against it. The knife at her hip looks dangerously sharp.

"Haven't seen one in years, though," she continues. "It's bad luck. Somethin's changing in the air, I fear. And now there's a dragon."

Holding my breath, I lean forward slightly in my saddle. "You didn't seem as surprised as I was to see it. Have you encountered one before?"

Feng shakes her head. "Never directly, but I've found this one's scales littered all over the jungle floor. Bright like emeralds, I tell ye, but worth much, much more."

"And you know this how?"

She squints at me, suspicion washing over her features. "I sold a couple to an old Northern bastard a few moons back. Some doctor. He paid an arm an' a leg for the pair I had. It was a right pain in the ass tryin' to sneak it past the border patrols."

My heart skips a beat. Doctor Qi. So *this* is the woman he spoke of in his final moments. I can't believe my luck in finding her so quickly, although she was bound to remain somewhat close to the border if she routinely sells such goods for Northern coin.

Death has followed me lately and weighs heavily on my mind. I try not to think of the wet sound of Captain Tian's blade slicing through skin, muscle, and then bone in the name of conquest. I fend off the memories of the captain trampled beneath his own soldiers, his rank doing nothing to stop the awful gurgling of his dying breaths. And then I think of A-Ma, too close to death before that precious dragon scale I slipped into her food. I must complete my mission and see to it that she remains in good health.

With Feng's knowledge of the jungle and her skills as a huntress, I stand a better chance of finding the creature again. But how am I to convince her to bring me along? And even if we find it, I'm not quite sure what to make of the thread I share with the same beast I am meant to hunt. I can't let her harm it before I find out, but I'd stand little chance in a physical fight with the huntress, even without my injuries.

Before I have a chance to broach the subject of accompanying her, Feng leads us around a final bend. She pushes aside a large palm leaf, exposing a village hidden at the heart of the jungle.

The homes are made of brown clay and have straw roofs; strings of peppers, garlic, and local herbs hang from doorframes to be left out to dry. The area is relatively flat, beaten down from decades of foot traffic, and a tall fence of sewn water reeds encircles the entire village to keep predators at bay.

Her village boasts no more than fifty members, all of them dressed in similar patchwork pelts from hunts gone by. They have all gathered by a large fire at this late hour, sharing stories over bowls of stew. Movement and chatter fade as Feng and I approach. I quickly notice that in this sea of faces, not one appears happy to see us.

"What's *she* doin' back?" someone mutters under their breath.

"Is 'er banishment over already?" gripes a young woman near the back of the crowd.

"Who's the man? A trader from the North?"

"Can't be. They don't come down this far no more."

"What's she doin' draggin' him here, then?"

I carefully dismount my steed, affectionately patting her neck. "Popular with the locals, I see," I say softly to Feng.

She gives me a pointed look. "Keep yer trap shut and let me take care of this." Feng turns to her people. "Where's the Matriarch? I wanna speak t' my grandmother."

Everyone in the crowd turns their heads to face an elderly woman among them. She stands slowly, wearing a grave expression. She may be small, no taller than my chest, and yet the respect she commands is clear. People bow their heads as she circles around. The woman's hair is stark white, loose columns of snow flowing over her shoulders. The drastic sag of her jowls and the deep lines upon her brow give her a heavy quality, matched by the drag of her every step.

Even I feel compelled to bow my head. I know not what to say. The tension in the air is wet and sticky, clinging to my skin and weary bones. The Matriarch doesn't even bother to glance at me, her cloudy gray eyes focused on Feng alone.

"Ye dare show yer face?" the old woman croons. "Does this mean ye slayed it?"

"No, Grandmother. But I've seen it. We both have." She nudges me in the ribs with the tip of her elbow. "The dragon. Ain't that right?"

My mouth goes dry. "Yes, it's true."

The Matriarch's expression hardens with obvious disapproval. "Have ye not learned yer lesson? Do ye really still intend to kill it?"

"Yes, Grandmother."

"Then yer not welcome here."

Feng steps forward. "Grandmother, just listen—"

"They're otherworldly, made of magic. Gods among men. To kill one would rain their wrath upon us."

"They're like any other mindless beast," Feng protests.

"Ye dishonor them, child, and therefore dishonor us. Get out, the both of ye, or ye won't survive the next time we meet."

I have clearly stepped into a problem that's not my own. I fear it may be my greatest weakness, sticking my nose where it doesn't belong, but I can't help myself.

"Good madam," I say, stepping forth. "There must be some sort of misunderstanding. We have traveled a long way. Might we rest here for the night and leave in the morning?"

The Matriarch sneers. Feng really must be her granddaughter, for the resemblance they share is uncanny. "Hold yer tongue, stranger. We don't take kindly to Northern spies."

"I'm no spy," I insist. "I may be from the North, but I'm just a humble teahouse owner, nothing more."

Feng groans. "Leaf water? Disgusting."

I ignore her comment. "Please, madam, a night's rest is all we ask. We'll be gone by sunrise."

"What's this 'we' business ye keep yappin' about?"

I wave Feng off, keeping my gaze locked on the Matriarch. It goes without question that a night spent out in the middle of the jungle is rife with dangers. If fei and dragons are indeed real, what other horrendous beasts await us out there in the dark?

The Matriarch remains silent in contemplation. She doesn't strike me as an unreasonable person. I'm proven right when she says, "Use the abandoned hut at the edge of the village. No one'll speak to ye, no one'll help ye. Begone at first light."

The villagers disperse without a word, though that doesn't stop a few of them from spitting at our feet. Feng doesn't react. Instead, she stands a little taller, her head held high and her chest proud. It's only once everyone has left that she stomps off.

"With me, Leaf Water," she calls.

The hut in question is in a state of grotesque disrepair. The walls are cracked, the thatched roof full of holes. It's no small wonder that it remains standing. I sit gingerly on a bamboo cot in the corner. Feng seems unbothered, both by the terrible conditions and her poor treatment in the village.

Her presence almost feels too expansive and grand to reside in this tiny abode, even for a night. Feng moves about the space with familiarity, easily navigating around low furniture in the dark. My suspicions are further raised when she stops precisely over one wooden floorboard, crouches, and lifts it to reveal a hidden cache of ointments and medicinal preserves. After a moment of rummaging, she tosses me a small clay jar.

"Poultice for yer wound. Change it before ye sleep."

I tilt my head to the side in curiosity. "Is this place yours?"

"My parents'," she answers, though her tone is clipped.

"And where are they now—"

"I'll leave before ye tomorrow," Feng interrupts. "The villagers'll be more inclined to feed ye once I'm gone."

"We're parting ways?"

"I've got a dragon t' hunt. Yesterday was the first time I caught a glimpse of it in ages. I need t' get after it, and yer only deadweight."

I shift uncomfortably upon my bed of straw. "What did the Matriarch mean before? About raining down wrath and dishonor?"

Feng snorts. "Idiots, the lot of them. My people think them beasts Gods."

"And you don't?"

"Gods don't bleed. They can't be harmed, but I've harmed it. It's proof."

Strangely, I find logic in her reasoning. I lean back against the wall, taking in Feng's face in the moonlight. She's nothing but rough edges and sharp corners, a fearsome warrior from head to toe.

"Just because you *can* harm the beast doesn't mean you should," I insist. "Perhaps your people have a point."

"Rocks for brains is what they have," she snaps. "D'ye have any idea the name I could make for myself? Just imagine it: Feng, the Dragon Slayer!"

I furrow my brows. "It's fame you're after, then?"

"Not just that, but fortune, too. Did ye know they used to sell dragon bones fer jewelry? Their scales for medicine? That kinda money could feed the whole village for years."

My breath catches at the mention of dragon scales. "How interesting."

Feng nods. "They'll see. One day soon, they'll all see how wrong they were."

"So you would kill it even if it were the last of its kind?"

"All the more reason to gut it first! I would've done it by now, but no one in the village will help me track it."

"Why don't you just leave?" I ask. "They don't treat you very kindly."

"Ye got family, Leaf Water?"

The muscles in my jaw twitches. "Only my mother."

"Do ye ever argue with 'er?"

I shrug. "Sometimes."

"And ye love 'er anyway?"

"Of course."

Feng nods slowly. "We may be at odds, but they're still my family. When I kill that dragon, fame and fortune're as good as mine. I'll be able to provide for 'em all. They might not understand yet what an opportunity this is, but they will."

She makes camp beside the old remnants of a hearth, collecting up bits of dried grass and small branches. Feng goes about starting a fire wordlessly, likely having grown accustomed to long stretches spent in silence. She produces two pieces of flint from one of the many pouches attached to her belt, striking them together again and again until a spark finally appears. She's so consumed in her work that for a moment, I wonder if she's forgotten that I'm here.

"You're very resourceful," I comment. "Hunting. Making your own medicine. Starting a fire . . . It's quite impressive."

"A three-year-old could do this."

"I can't."

"Then yer an idiot." Feng hits me with a hard glare. "But I could tell that just by lookin' at ye."

I huff. "No need to be rude. I have a great many talents, too."

She arches a brow but doesn't press further. Her disinterest is palpable.

This is the chance for me, I suddenly realize, to ingratiate myself to this prickly huntress and learn about the Southern Kingdom. I stare at my gray thread, once again lifeless on the ground. Even if I could follow it to the dragon, there's little chance I would survive the journey without Feng's skills as an outdoorswoman.

"My lady," I say after a while. The fire crackles to life, the growing flames melting the chill from my bones. "Please, allow me to accompany you on your search for the dragon."

Feng sneers. "Why in the hell would I do that?"

"I'm an excellent cook. I can keep us well fed. Whatever you hunt, I can roast."

"It's not that hard. Ye stick it over the fire and yer done."

"I can tell you stories and keep you entertained."

"Yer chatter'll only scare the beast off."

I sigh. "Many hands make quick work?"

"Ye just want to kill the beast and hog the glory for yerself."

That's untrue—I wish the creature no harm, even if it could well devour me in a single bite. As brief as our connection was, it was undeniable. I have so many questions—all of which will go unanswered if Feng manages to find and slay the dragon first.

"I confess that I could make use of a few scales," I answer, a partial truth. "For my ailing mother back home. I care not for the hunt. But you know as well as I do that it would be foolish for even you to take the creature on alone. I believe our meeting was fated. I can . . . I can fight."

"I thought ye said yer a teahouse owner."

"A man can know how to do two things. Besides, this is clearly an intelligent creature to have evaded mankind for so long. Wouldn't it be wise to have someone watching your back?" When Feng doesn't answer, I add, "I'm indebted to you. For saving my life. The others don't seem keen to join you, so let me. You can even use me as bait. With a helping hand, you will certainly achieve greatness."

Feng is silent for a while. The shadows grow long as the silver moon climbs yet higher into the sky. After a seeming eternity, she finally speaks.

"Fine, Leaf Water. I'll let ye come with me. But mark my words—if ye get in my way or steal my kill, I'll cut ye from throat to stomach."

I nod slowly, trying not to look at her knife. "Of that, I have no doubt."

10

We *travel for four days* and three nights riding double on horseback, headed farther south toward the Bo Shan Peninsula.

I have heard a great many tales of Longhao, the Southern Kingdom's capital city. It's said to be a fortress within a fortress. At the very center lies the Jade Palace, once home to the Southern Kingdom's own imperial dynasty, carved from peak to foundation of the greenest jade, from which it received its name. That was several centuries ago, however. An uprising saw to the end of their rule, or so I've heard.

Now the Southern Kingdom is governed by a handful of provincial ministers, though I hear they fight among themselves more often than they work together. Too many captains aboard the ship, as it were. It's frankly no wonder Emperor Róng decided to launch his war. It's far easier to conquer your enemies when they already stand divided.

Now the Jade Palace lies empty and rotting, haunted by the wandering souls of kings of old, their concubines, and eunuchs alike. It's not uncommon to hear tales about would-be thieves who sneak onto the premises in the dead of night, bringing along with them the tools they need to chip away at the walls and escape with handfuls of jade to sell under the table, as much as they can take before being frightened off by the strange noises in the palace. Some say a pair of nine-tailed fox demons roams the halls, searching for souls to devour—not that anyone is brave enough to prove it.

That's what the traveling merchants have told me, at least. I was an impressionable young lad when they recounted these tales in town. Everything beyond the mountain border is a mystery to me. I might have enjoyed all this as some grand adventure if my heart weren't so rife with concern for my mother.

I wasn't always such a worrywart. I can remember the exact moment the world shifted around me, the easy days of my childhood vanishing overnight. It was the day after A-Ba's funeral. My mother was normally the first in the family to rise. But that morning, I entered her room, my stomach grumbling and eager for breakfast, startled to find her curled up with one of A-Ba's old robes. They still smelled like him, she said. For days, she didn't eat, nor did she sleep. A-Ma didn't *move*, too overcome by her grief to lift a finger. At five and ten, I suddenly became the man of the house. I was determined to take care of my mother at all costs.

Within the span of a week, I taught myself how to cook. I would stand by the food vendor stalls and watch them prepare hot meals over roaring woks, studying every spice and noting each step of their recipes. Some would shoo me away, calling me a nuisance, but most took pity on me.

Poor boy lost his A-Ba. Let him learn.

It was the teahouse I was most intimidated by. I feared attending to guests. I didn't have A-Ba's easy charisma, nor his lighthearted humor. I couldn't talk to the grown-ups about politics or philosophy, and I had little interest in making small talk about the weather. But I knew I had to do something. A teahouse with a bad host couldn't hope to survive for long.

So I began spending more of my mornings at the markets, listening intently to the tales of the traveling merchants. It was an education, in a way, exposing me to every corner of the Five Kingdoms without ever having to leave Jiaoshan. I would return to the teahouse every day with a new tale to share, and when I recounted it to my mother, I would do my best to imitate my father's animated confidence.

I knew I was doing something right the day I finally made A-Ma laugh. It was many moons after the funeral, late at night, just as we were finishing dinner. I can hardly remember the story now—something about talking fish griping in the belly of a whale. She laughed so hard that it brought tears to her eyes, the sound hugging me like a warm blanket in the dead of winter. I swore I would have more of it.

I decided then that if it was a fool she needed, a fool I would be.

I hope A-Ma is well and doesn't become even sicker with worry. I fear Emperor Róng may take his ire out on her if I don't return promptly, but I hope even he won't resort to such monstrousness. I wonder if I might be able to get a message to A-Ma over the closed border. The fastest way would be by carrier pigeon, but there will be no way of knowing whether the bird makes it home. Still, I must try. My first stop will be the post, should Longhao boast one in the first place.

I can't wait to tell her all that has happened. My encounter with the emperor, my terrifying ride into battle—and my encounter with a *living, breathing dragon*.

It's late afternoon by the time Feng tugs on the reins and brings the horse to a full stop just outside the city gates. She elbows me in the stomach as she throws her leg over and dismounts. I follow suit, eager to stretch my legs. It's never been more obvious that I would have made a very poor horseman.

"Here, take this." Feng throws a hooded cape over my head. It smells musty and sour with soil and sweat. My nose curls at the stink. I don't dare ask where she had it stored.

"I take it you wish for me to put it on?" I ask, pinching the rough fabric between my fingers with a grimace.

"Ye look too foreign," she tells me. "Try not to draw too much attention to yerself. People're skittish around these parts. We're at war, after all."

Feng guides the horse through the city's main gate. The outer walls show signs of recent work, stone slabs layered together with dried, cracking mud. The main road leading into the city is in an equal state of disrepair, though one glance at Longhao's unique design is all it takes to understand why.

It is a city built upon water.

Narrow canals cut past buildings in a grid formation, arching gray moon bridges offering pedestrians safe passage over the murky river flow. Wilting wisteria trees droop along the water's edge, their branches thin and bare, their shriveled purple petals floating away with the current. Long flat-bottomed boats made of smooth wooden planks line the sides of the canals in disorganized rows, their hulls filled with empty woven baskets. It's a water market, though goods for purchase seem scarce and far between.

The border closure has taken its toll. The people here are starving. Perhaps this is a part of Emperor Róng's strategy. The Empire stretches from east to west, trapping the Southern Kingdom of Jian on the other side of the mountain pass. Without direct passage for trade to move freely, imports can arrive only via the rough, unforgiving waters. Merchants who pass through Jiaoshan frequently bring with them the news of yet another capsized ship, lost to the unpredictable nature of the Albeion Sea. A year without proper access to food has left the people weak—too weak, even, to put up a proper fight.

"We need to restock before headin' out on our hunt," Feng states. She slaps a small pouch of coins into the palm of my hand. "I'll find a stable fer the horse and get us supplies fer the trip. Yer in charge of food. Meet me back at this here main gate by nightfall."

I nod hesitantly, sincerely hoping I don't lose my way. Pulling my cape's hood over my head, I set out in the opposite direction from Feng. I'll find food just as she has asked, but first—the pigeon post.

The paths of Longhao are narrow, the waterways taking precedence over the walkways. There's just enough space for two people, the grazing of shoulders inevitable when trying to pass someone in a hurry. It's not the lack of space that concerns me, though—it's the stark decay and poverty around every corner.

I was always led to believe that Longhao was a vibrant, thriving place, despite its abandoned palace. Instead, I find myself surrounded by a sea of beggars. Men, women, and children, all clad in soiled clothes, with their hands outstretched in the hopes that they might be spared a few coins. Pity sits cold in the well of my stomach. They're everywhere, the poor and the forgotten, so weak and thin that they cannot lift their heads to look at me as I pass.

Something tugs at the hem of my cloak. A child's little hand clings to the bottom corner.

"Please, sir," he says in a barely audible whisper. "Have ye any food to spare?"

Feng gave me only enough coin to purchase food for the two of us, so I have little to offer besides my intentions. Still, I cannot in good conscience ignore the boy. I can almost hear A-Ma's words.

Always do the right thing, Sai, she would say. *Besides, it's good karma. You don't want to come back as a dung beetle, now, do you?*

I'm just about to reach for my money pouch when someone grasps me by the shoulder.

"Stop."

I turn to find a man in saffron-dyed robes, the simple cloth wrapped around his slender frame. His head is shaven down to the scalp, and his sandals are crafted with dull leather straps. An Albeion monk. A curious sight, indeed, given how reclusive their kind are said to be. I once heard that in order to become a monk, initiates must meditate for three moons without a bite of food or even a sip of water. Survive, and they're ordained. If not . . . well.

In one hand, the monk fiddles with a necklace of smooth wooden beads. In the other, he holds a large bowl for collecting alms. "Yer charity is better spent with the temple," he tells me. "Please, good sir, might we rely on yer kind donation?"

"But the child—"

The boy I've been talking to rushes over to the monks, hiding behind them like a shield. The mischievous, self-satisfied grin he wears makes me uneasy.

"My brothers and I use the givings we collect to buy and distribute food to those in need. I've seen too many squander away the generosity of strangers on poppy sap. Yer coin is in safer hands this way."

He speaks in a convincing manner, and I know I should take a holy man at his word. Yet there's something *off* about him. His expression is too perfect, too practiced. And what's a monk doing collecting alms in the backstreets of the city, anyway? He showed up seemingly out of nowhere the moment I revealed my coin pouch.

I slowly take a step back and away. Something's amiss.

"I must be off," I mumble, attempting to keep my tone breezy. "There's only so much daylight."

The monk's friendliness instantly melts away, replaced with a menacing scowl. "Where d'ye think yer goin'?"

Out of the corner of my eye, four lumbering figures emerge from around the corner. They, too, are dressed in monks' robes, but their smug expressions and bruised knuckles suggest they don't adhere to the teachings of pacifism.

The five of them block the path forward and back. I have no escape.

"Hand over yer coin!" one of the imposters growls, his Southern accent so thick that his words come out a near-indecipherable jumble.

For a moment, I consider it. Perhaps it's wisest to follow the path of least resistance. If I explain why I lost her money, Feng might understand. Or, more likely, she'll stab me through. It's the choice of being beaten to a pulp now or later. I slowly reach for my coin pouch—

And scramble up the rickety wall of the low shanty house beside me, throwing all my momentum into the jump. The men curse and race after me. One of them manages to grip my ankle just as I clamber onto the roof, but I end up kicking him right in the mouth and using his face to boost myself up. He falls back with a hard thud.

"Sorry!" I rasp, purely on instinct.

"Don't let 'im get away!" the first imposter monk shouts.

I roll clumsily off the opposite slope of the roof and land awkwardly on the narrow street on the other side. It's less crowded here, but nowhere near safe. With no other options, I run. My pursuers give chase, following so close I swear I can feel their labored breaths raking down my spine. They spit slanders at me, taunt me mercilessly, but still I flee.

I take a left and then a right, squeezing through narrow side alleys in the hopes of shaking off my would-be robbers. And here I thought I might enjoy a break from all my running. I end up taking a turn so sharply that I almost fall into the canal—a near-fatal move on my part, since I can't swim.

I don't know where I'm going, the layout of Longhao's labyrinthine footpaths unreasonably difficult to navigate. One wrong turn, and I could fall into the water. Even worse: I come to a full stop, trapped in a dead end. Out of breath, I turn slowly to see that the awful charlatans once again have me pinned.

"Gentlemen," I say as evenly as possible. "Let's just forget this whole thing ever happened, hmm? I won't tell anyone if you don't."

One of the monks draws a knife, flashing his teeth with an ugly sneer. "Hand yer coin over, and I promise to gut ye nice and clean."

Sweat beads across my brow as I attempt to ignore the ache of my lungs. This is all so hopeless. "Come on, then," I hiss, bracing for the worst. "You'll have to pry it off me!"

"With pleasure, you little—"

Someone kicks the monk forward, cutting him off. The impact is so violent that I swear I hear him swallow his own tongue. He lands on his face, nose crunching in and teeth shattering against the hard ground. His partners in crime whip around in confusion, rage painting their expressions a vibrant red.

"Who—" The pretender who tries to speak is gifted with a swift crack of knuckles against his jaw. He stumbles back with a sharp grunt.

All eyes are on the stranger standing at the mouth of the narrow alley. They have a mask on their face, and are clad from head to toe in a hooded dark green cape, so dark that it appears almost black. Confusion lances through me. Is this another thief, hoping to take my coin? Why do I feel like I'm being . . . *pulled* toward them, as if there were a strong wind behind me?

The newcomer moves swiftly, so nimble that their movements are an almost-imperceptible blur. A powerful kick sends another monk careening into the wall, his skull smashing against the jagged bricks. A terrifying strike knocks the last of my attackers out cold, the crack of his ribs echoing loudly in my ears. One after another, the thieves meet their brutal defeat, but my savior doesn't stop.

They charge at me next with such alarming speed that I stumble backward and raise my hands in surrender, heart hammering against my rib cage.

"Wait, please, I—"

The stranger's hand flies out. But instead of reaching for my coin purse, they snatch my ordinance scroll from my belt. I stare in awe as they quickly unroll it, revealing the three different paper talismans stuck to the inside. They are thin yellow bits of parchment covered in expertly drawn red-ink calligraphy. I do recognize the symbols, but the characters are too ancient for me to comprehend.

Before my mind has the chance to spiral, my attention is pulled elsewhere. As the hooded stranger wordlessly rips my ordinance scroll to shreds, I see their hands.

Tied around their right little finger is a fraying gray thread—its end connected to mine.

My mouth falls open. I can hardly believe what I'm seeing. I try to get a better look at their face, but it's completely covered by their mask and hood. *"You."*

They toss the bits of the ordinance to the ground and give my chest a hard shove. My back slams against the alley wall. The contact is brief, but there's no denying the sudden heat that flickers over my skin where they've touched me. It's an explosion of firecrackers, alarming at first, then oddly pleasant.

"Leave," the stranger hisses. The voice of a woman, of my *Fated One*.

"Wait!" I exclaim, winded and shaking. "Wait, I beg you!"

She turns on her heel and sprints away without a word. My heart sinks. No, this isn't right. I can't let her go. Not without answers.

I've nearly lost her by the time I round the corner, but thankfully see her fleeting silhouette out of the corner of my eye. I give chase right up until the canal's edge, deterred only by the deep, dark water. All I can do is watch as she jumps from the embankment and leaps from river boat to river boat, vanishing into the thick fog rolling in to blanket all of Longhao.

I watch in confusion and dismay as my gray thread of fate tugs weakly along after her. Any remaining thoughts I have of giving chase evaporate the moment the thread changes direction, pointing directly into the now-raining sky.

II

"There y'are!" *Feng huffs in* frustration. She stamps her foot like a petulant child and brushes her wet hair back with one hand. The light rainstorm is already passing, but it leaves the air sticky and smelling of petrichor. "What in the nine suns took ye so long?"

My mouth drops open only to shut again. How am I to explain that I have come face-to-face with my Fated One—a *dragon* who can somehow take human form? There was certainly no such detail in the legends. Could I have imagined it somehow? I could have sworn that the end of my thread was connected to that green dragon earlier.

"My head hurts," I mumble, rubbing my temples with a sigh. The pounding pressure behind my eyes threatens to crack my skull open like a chick bursting from its egg.

"Did ye at least get the food?"

I toss a burlap sack full of food rations in her direction. Feng opens it up, examines the contents, and scrunches up her face.

"That's it?" She pulls out a half-rotten onion. "Do ye Northerners have no sense of taste?"

"This was all I could find at the market. It'll be fine if we cut off the slimy outer bits," I insist. "The vendors have had an unsteady supply of food since the start of the North's embargo."

She rolls her eyes. "That, or they're keeping the good shit from ye. Lemme guess—no spare coin?"

I shake my head, pulling the pockets of my robe inside out. "Not even a bronze piece."

"Fine. If we run low, we'll hafta barter fer supplies in the next town," Feng tells me as she mounts my horse. My steed has taken a far greater liking to the woman than me, nipping at my hair whenever I stand too close. She offers me a calloused, dirty hand and helps pull me onto the saddle behind her.

The journey is arduous. I'm not yet accustomed to the ever-present humidity of the South, sweat soaking into my robes as heat radiates off my skin despite the fact that we're in the beginnings of winter. We ride for hours, the city of Longhao now just a dot on the horizon. It will be dark soon, the air growing chillier by the hour.

"How much farther?" I complain.

"Would ye quit yer whinin'? You Northerners are a prissy bunch."

"I prefer 'delicate and refined.'"

We travel along the perimeter of the thick jungle on a dirt road made soft by the afternoon's light rainfall. The skies above are gray and cloudy, the threat of a more violent storm brewing in the distance.

The wind whistles by, bringing along with it the scent of something . . .

Burning.

"Do you smell that?" I ask.

Feng tugs on the horse's reins, turning her head from side to side to survey our surroundings with a suspicious squint. She sniffs the air, just as concerned as I. It's not until I look up once more that I realize those aren't rain clouds I see, but clouds of smoke.

"Silence from here on out," she says before shooting a pointed glare in my direction. "I know that might seem an impossibility for ye, but it's for yer own good."

I put my hands up in mock surrender, pressing my lips into a thin line. Contrary to popular belief, I'm capable of taking things seriously at times.

We continue forward down the beaten path until an obstacle halts our advance, lying strewn across the dirt path.

A body.

I dismount the horse, approach with caution, and crouch down to examine the corpse. It's a fresh kill, the man's flesh not yet cold. His end must have been a traumatic one. Cuts and bruises mar his face, nothing about his visage recognizably human. His nose is a broken clump of cartilage dangling from the center, his eyes gouged out, the front of his skull caved in. Shards of his teeth stick to his bloodied cheeks, his long hair shorn down to the scalp in an act of pure hatred.

There's no thread around his finger; it has dissolved in the arms of death.

He looks to be a mere peasant, his ragged tunic covered in dirt and crusted blood. The man has no valuables on him, his pockets purposely ripped from their lining. One of his shoes is missing, knocked clean off. His left arm is bent the wrong way at the elbow, and bone pokes out of the front of his right calf.

This can't be the work of an animal.

Or perhaps it is—the worst animal of them all.

Ahead, the piercing cry of a woman in distress.

My body moves before my brain has a chance to register what I'm doing. Feng shouts something, but her commands are lost on me. We can't just stand idly by when someone's calling for help.

I hear them before I see them—the voices of at least ten imposing men, speaking my own Northern dialect. I quickly throw myself into the cover of the jungle underbrush, watching with bated breath as a troop of Imperial soldiers surround what appear to be innocent civilians.

They've set up some sort of checkpoint, forcibly confiscating goods and trinkets from those attempting to pass. Several wagons have been set ablaze, these people's whole livelihoods along with them. The soldiers show no mercy, punching and kicking the men and corralling the women and children as they beg for a reprieve.

Anger licks at the nape of my neck. "Bastards," I hiss.

The huntress joins me in my hiding spot, keeping a watchful eye out. She's momentarily left the horse behind so as not to attract any attention. "We'll go around," she whispers. "Another two days' travel, but we should be able t' avoid the worst of it."

I frown. "You'd leave them to fend for themselves?"

"There's nothin' we can do, Leaf Water."

"Do you mean to tell me that knife of yours is only for show?"

"This doesn't concern us. Besides, would ye really kill yer own countrymen?"

A heavy weight bears down on my chest. I've never harmed another person in my entire life; I've never felt the rage that burns within me at present. How dare they torture the innocent and downtrodden? War is one thing, but this is another.

"We have to help," I insist. "We can't let them get away with this."

"What're ye going to do, hmm? Charge in there like a bull, and then what? Ye'd be stupid to play hero."

The silence that lingers between us is punctuated only by desperate screams. As much as I hate to admit it, Feng has a point. I think back to when the emperor's men nabbed me at the teahouse. I was no match for the five of them. I sincerely doubt that a head-on bout with ten will prove more successful. I might be a man of good intentions, but I am just that—a man.

I kneel there in the underbrush, stewing in my helplessness. I'm not strong, and I have no idea how to fight. The only thing I may boast to my credit is my inflated sense of wit and a sharp tongue—both useless against the threat of a blade.

"Please!" one of the women wails, clutching onto her husband's arm. She places herself between him and a soldier, her tiny body a makeshift shield. "Take what ye want, but please, leave us be!"

The soldier strikes her across the face with a harsh crack, then moves in like a viper to snatch the man by the upper arm. "Out of the way, you swamp-water whore."

"Wh-what're ye going to do with him?"

"He'll be joining us on the front lines to fight for His Imperial Highness."

The woman seethes through heated tears, desperately trying to hang on to the man I see her thread of fate is bound to. "Fight fer that madman? Ye'd have him kill our own?"

The soldier draws his blade and stalks toward her. "Enough of this nonsense! Release him, or I'll have your head."

"I beg ye, please—"

He grabs her roughly and starts to tear at her robes. She screams even louder.

Damn it all.

Good sense and self-preservation tumble out of my head as I spring from my hiding place. I charge the soldier with a yell, throwing all my weight against him as I tackle him to the ground. His sword flies from his hand, rattling against the dirt road as his body goes crashing. Dazed and confused, he swings at me wildly.

I'm only successful in blocking one of his blows. The other hits me in the jaw hard enough that I hear my molars crack against each other inside my skull.

"Run!" I shout at the woman and her husband. "Get away from here!"

It takes me all of thirty seconds to realize what a bad idea this was. In doing the right thing, I have signed my own death warrant. All at once, the soldiers are on top of me. My own compatriots. We may live under the same flying banner, but they still treat me as scum beneath their boots.

And yet, I don't regret it.

Even when I'm being kicked and punched and spat on, I find some semblance of relief when I see the couple escape into the jungle together. The soldiers stomp on my chest, swing at my head. My body is merely an outlet for their unchecked fury as they pummel me into the ground.

I'm not sure when it's over. All I know is that I'm somehow breathing and lucky to be alive. For how much longer, it's impossible to tell.

My bones are likely broken. Blood coats my teeth. Black encroaches on the edges of my vision. Lying on my back, I stare up at the gray sky, suddenly envisioning myself in flight. I can't tell if it's a memory or a hallucination, but I can see it as clear as day. Soaring through the soft clouds, wind sweeping through my hair—

Two dragons fly on either side of me, one a beautiful green and the other a dazzling blue.

I blink once.

Twice.

Definitely a hallucination.

The tips of my fingers and toes are numb, the rest of my body growing freezing cold. Exhaustion weighs heavily on my eyelids, but the feeling in my gut tells me to remain alert and awake. I struggle to stay conscious, wheezing for air. I worry one of my lungs has collapsed inward.

"This is what you deserve, maggot," one of the soldiers curses at me.

I snarl at him. "This maggot'll feed upon your body when it decays in the ground, heathen!"

"Rot in Hell."

He raises his arm, sword in hand.

My thread tugs upward.

Above, the roar of a colossal beast.

The dragon.

Our connection sings, a sudden warmth flooding my veins. I can't move my head to see—my neck is sprained and my collarbone fractured—but I know it's here. While I suddenly find myself at peace, all around me are the bloodcurdling screams of the men who hurt me for interrupting their cruelty.

I can only assume the worst, lying here paralyzed on the ground.

I hear the wet tear of flesh, grown men crying for the same mercy they dared not grant me, the metallic crunch of armor being pierced and weapons being thrown. At some point, I stop listening. I can't find any sympathy for these loathsome men. As sleep pulls me under, I wonder if that makes me as bad as them.

Another minute passes. Or is it an eternity? I no longer have the energy to process time.

Just as I feel myself slipping away, a woman appears above me, kneeling at my side with her hand pressed gingerly to my chest.

She's beautiful.

Concussed as I may be, I know she's the most stunning woman I have ever laid eyes on. Her sparkling green eyes remind me of thick bamboo forests in the summertime. She smells of dewy grass after a fresh rain. Her soft black hair streams over her shoulder in one long, loose braid. She's dressed in light green robes, the silks embroidered with a subtle floral pattern. The faint scent of jasmine floods my nose, a welcome change from the dirt and blood and ash that surround us.

"Sai?" she whispers, her voice concerned, yet still somehow angelic to my ears. Her brows are knotted in worry. I would reach up to soothe her expression, if only I could feel my arms.

"I . . . know you," I rasp, my throat squeezing so tight that I choke.

I have no idea why I'm saying this. I've never seen her face before, and yet it feels as though I have known this woman many lifetimes over. And then it hits me. She's the one from Longhao, the hooded stranger who saved me from those thieves.

But it runs deeper than that. I felt this strange familiarity then, too. Her presence is the salve to my wounds, a fire on a cold winter's night. The very air around her seems to vibrate, a tangible force that ghosts across my skin. The blinding pain radiating through my broken body is nothing compared to the comfort she brings.

A million questions race through my head—*What is she doing here? Where did the dragon go? Has Feng harmed it?*—but the darkness pooling at the edges of my vision makes it difficult to ask.

She shakes her head. I can almost *feel* her disappointment, a cold, heavy sensation crossing our shared gray thread of fate. I don't understand how it's possible, and yet there's no denying the pulsing of my heart. It sits heavy in my chest—though that could very well be my broken ribs piercing holes into my lungs.

"You're a damn fool," she says, placing her hand on my forehead. Her fingers are lovely and cool and soft.

"Who—"

"Rest."

I don't have the energy to argue. My eyes drift closed, too heavy to open again. The last thing I register is the sensation of being lifted into the air.

The world falls away a moment later.

12

I *wake up.*

And immediately start screaming.

I'm not only in an unfathomable amount of agony, but have suddenly found myself thousands of li up in the air, which is enough of a fright to make me lose consciousness all over again.

Wind screams past my ears, deafening me. It's difficult to appreciate the beauty of the lands below when I could plummet to my death at any moment. Craning my neck to look up, I discover that I am tightly wrapped in the grip of a creature's massive claw.

"Please . . . don't . . . eat me," I wheeze out, genuinely surprised I can speak.

The dragon doesn't respond, doesn't give me so much as a glance. I doubt it can hear my pathetic croaking over the rush of air around us anyway. But for the briefest moment, I can feel its fear.

That fear washes over me in waves, pulsating from the center of my back and licking up my neck to weigh heavily in my skull. It's cold and frantic, mixed with an overwhelming anguish. I wish I could calm its worry somehow, but my body is in rough shape. It's frankly a miracle I've even opened my eyes.

I'm unsure where we're going or how long we've been airborne.

All I know is that the winds are terribly hot and dry, which tells me we are no longer in the warm, sticky climate of the Southern Kingdom of Jian. I panic for a moment. Is the dragon flying me to its lair? Will it devour me whole while I'm at my weakest?

Before I can think more on it, sleep drags me under.

I 'm in and out of consciousness for Gods know how long. Days? Weeks? Full moons? I have no sense of my surroundings, no idea what time of day it is. I'm barely coherent enough to register the soft blankets upon which I lay, plus the gentle hum of a woman's voice.

It's a beautiful sound.

Magical and otherworldly and again so *familiar* that it causes my chest to ache. I know this voice, and yet I do not. I know this song, and yet I swear I have never once heard it in my life. It's a wordless tune, pulling directly at my heartstrings. Its sweet notes resonate, vibrating in my very bones.

I'm caught somewhere between waking and a dream. I see them again, visions of myself free and in flight. The clouds are cool and refreshing against my body, the wind warping around me as I move through the skies with abandon. I'm proud and brave and strong, protecting everything between the mountaintops and the Heavens above. And at my side, my beautiful wife.

"*Jyn,*" I wheeze, delirious.

I don't know why I say the name. Surely it's the fever.

And yet it feels so comfortable on my tongue, as though I have said it a thousand times before.

I feel the cool press of a damp cloth on my forehead. My skin erupts with heat, yet my frozen core makes me shiver. The humming ceases, the woman's song interrupted. Even though my eyes are swollen closed, I can sense movement beside me.

"Drink," her voice orders, and the solid rim of a cup is tucked between my lips.

I obey but gag around the sharp copper taste now trickling down my esophagus. Surely it must be poison, for it's so disgustingly bitter that it makes my tongue swell and my lungs seize. The longer the taste lingers, the sooner I begin to realize what it is I'm being fed.

Blood.

I pry my eyes open, then thrash about, my broken body shuddering in protest. "Unpleasant" doesn't even begin to describe it. This is disgusting, made ten times worse by the fact that I can barely see.

Beside me, I can just make out the silhouette of a woman.

"Relax," she says, calm but firm. "You must drink every last drop."

Protests die at the base of my throat.

"Where's the dragon?" I rasp around a mouthful of her horrifying concoction.

"Be at ease."

"No, tell me where—"

My caregiver—or perhaps captor?—tilts the cup steeply, dumping the remaining blood into my mouth. My reflex is to spit it out, but before I can, the woman forcefully grasps my face and crushes her lips to mine.

Stunned, I swallow it all down.

I blink several times, desperately attempting to clear my blurry vision. Something strange is happening to me. Not moments before, I was in so much agony I could have sworn I was approaching death's door. The memories of the roadside attack come rushing back to me. Those soldiers beat me within an inch of my life and would have delivered the final blow, had it not been for . . .

I sit up abruptly, looking down at myself. I have been stripped of all my clothes and am as naked as the day I was born. What confuses me more than my indecent exposure is my lack of injuries.

Bones that I felt break are no longer broken.

Deep cuts and open wounds inflicted upon me have healed over without a trace.

My fever is gone in an instant, along with the ache of my muscles and general fatigue. I feel like a new man: my vision is clear, my breathing steady, my strength returning in full force. I am healed, almost as if by—

Magic.

I take in my surroundings. We appear to be beneath the shade of a rocky overhang in the middle of a glittering oasis. On all sides, we are surrounded by luscious plants and tall palm trees, a deep pond at the center of it all. Beyond our little paradise are the endless dunes and hot golden sands of what I can only assume is the Western Wastelands. The merchants of Jiaoshan always speak of how taxing it is to go around the desert plains rather than endure a straight path and subject themselves to the unforgiving climate.

I look to my side, marveling at the radiant woman kneeling beside me. It's the same woman I saw on the roadside, though I was so sure I imagined her. Now that I have my wits about me, I can appreciate the full extent of her beauty.

I can't place her age—A-Ma used to tell me it was a rude thing to ask a lady—but if I had to venture a guess, I would say she's no older than five and twenty. Her long black hair is silky and thick. Her skin is as fair as porcelain, rivaling the elegance and grace of the most expensive tea sets we have at the shop back home.

She is by no means delicate or dainty. Her body is strong and lean, the hard curves of muscle evident beneath her pale skin. It's her eyes that do me in. A vibrant, stunning emerald green that sparkles in the noonday sun. They leave me breathless, my heart skipping with unbridled glee when I find myself the object of her gaze. I can't explain why looking at her makes me feel so wonderfully at peace. Like Emperor Róng, she has an ancient quality about her. Wise, but troubled with an indescribable burden.

And then I glance down at her hand.

It wasn't a dream, then. We really are connected by the same gray thread. It has shortened in length with our proximity, but it still hangs loose, lazily dragging down like a boat tied to a dock with too much slack, rather than changing in color or tautness, as is normally the case when two Fated Ones draw near to each other.

"You," I whisper, at a complete loss for words. *My Fated One.*

Very slowly, I reach for one of the blankets beneath me and place it over my lap to cover my indecency. This woman has seen me naked and kissed me in a matter of two minutes, and I am, to be perfectly frank, overwhelmed.

"Are you feeling better?" she asks me, her tone and expression flat. A far cry from the person I heard humming just a while ago.

I nod. "Yes, thank you."

"Good." She stands and turns to stalk away. "Now, please leave."

Her sudden about-face leaves me winded. I'm so full of questions that I may well fall apart.

"Wait!" I gasp, clambering to my feet like a newborn colt. "Please, wait—"

"Now!" she bellows. "I will not be saving you from your recklessness again."

I give chase, no longer concerned by my state of nudity. I'm desperate to know more about her, desperate for answers.

I attempt to take her hand as I plead, "My lady, please—"

She lunges at me with ferocious speed, her sharp nails grazing past my cheek. I barely have time to pivot out of the way before she backhands me across the side of the head and sends me flying to the sandy ground.

The woman leaves no time to breathe, to think. She throws all her weight behind her next strike, missing my head by only an inch. The rock wall behind me crumbles beneath her mighty blow, pulverized dust billowing into the air.

I stumble out of the way, heart pounding in my throat. "I'm not trying to hurt you! I only wish to talk! I think you might be my—"

Faster than I can blink, the woman whips around and sends me flying with a hard kick to the chest. I land on my back, wheezing for breath, though I'm surprised I'm not as tender as I could be. Considering her inhuman strength and speed, she could decimate me within seconds.

She's holding back her attacks . . . They're only a warning.

But why save me, only to harm me?

Holding my hands up in surrender, I glance at our weak gray thread. This certainly was not how I imagined meeting my other half, but I refuse to let the opportunity pass me by. I have spent all my five and twenty years wondering if I would ever find her, and now that she's here, I'm equal parts terrified and in awe.

"Please," I rasp. "I think you're my Fated One."

"I know I am," she says. Her green eyes are cold. "Now leave me the fuck alone."

Part 2

The
Green
Dragon

13

She grumbles to herself under her breath, her words inco-
herent. The woman steps out into the oasis, anxiously pacing
around the sparkling pond of crystal-clear water while rubbing at
her temples.

"Damn it! Why am I such a fool?"

I hastily throw on what little remains of my clothes. My outer
robe has been torn to shreds, and my tunic and pants are heavily
stained with crusted blood. *My* blood. It's no wonder she stripped
me bare.

"My lady?" I ask as I follow her around the edge of the water.

She doesn't hear me, too absorbed in conversation with herself. She curses in a language I don't quite understand—a dead
dialect?—but I don't need to know the words to feel her distress
pulsating over our thread.

It leaves me nauseated, my guts tying themselves up in sickening knots, causing my stomach to lurch. Is this what she is feeling?
Why is it that I can sense her emotions so clearly that I almost
confuse them for my own?

"My lady?"

"What?" she snaps, turning on a point.

My Fated One is so spellbinding that I can hardly find any words. I fixate on the severe press of her rosebud lips, the curl of her long lashes framing her icy glare. I'm especially fascinated with the small beauty mark just below the corner of her left eye. I won't do her the injustice of comparing her beauty to the stars, for she is far more radiant than anything in the Heavens, the earth, and the spaces between.

"I—I wanted to thank you," I say, heart hammering in my ears. "For taking care of me. And rescuing me, too. That *was* you, was it not?"

She grinds her teeth, her fists clenched. When her lip curls back in a snarl, I can't help but notice how her teeth are the slightest degree sharper than most humans'. She looks terribly upset. "You . . . need to go," she says, shoulders trembling with tension. There's a note of hesitation in her tone, but force in her words nonetheless. "Right now! As far as your legs can carry you."

"As far as my legs can . . ." I shake my head. "But we're in the middle of the Western Wastelands. I'll certainly die of thirst before I make my way home. And I have so many questions, besides."

"Not my problem."

"My name is Sai," I say quickly with a hand over my heart, desperate to have her hear me. "Might I know your name?"

Her hands fly to her hair. Instead of answering me, she returns to her agitated pacing. "Bringing you here was a mistake."

I follow without hesitation. "All I want is your name. Is that so much to ask? I would very much like to know it, so that I might thank you properly."

"And I would very much like for you to piss off."

"I'll remind you that it was your choice to strand me here, my radiant sunshine."

She whips around, one finger pointed at me like a dagger. "Do *not* call me that, unless you have a death wish."

I beam at the glimmer of her gorgeous eyes in her frown. Even angry, she's the most beguiling creature who ever breathed. Her words sit low in her throat, but I'm confident her threat is an empty one. Again, why go through the trouble of saving me— thrice now—just to do me in?

"But I don't have anything else to call you, my succulent pork dumpling. Unless you bestow upon me your name?"

"If you call me by one more nickname, I'll bite your face off."

"If it should please you, my lady, I wholeheartedly give my consent." I bend forward slightly. "Here, now you can reach it better."

She presses her hand to my face and pushes me away forcefully. "I should have left you to die."

"You wound me, my mooncake—"

This time, she shoves me straight into the pond.

My whole body plunges beneath the surface of the water. My skin is immediately cooled by the plunge, but it's far from relaxing.

Instinct tells me to panic. My limbs flail about uselessly as I sink like a boulder. I accidentally inhale water, and a burst of adrenaline rushes through my veins. An unfortunate tumble into a stream when I was a child ensured my ever-present fear of deep water.

And yet the water is so clear and pure that I can see the very bottom, sunlight dancing over the gray rocks beneath my feet. It's a welcome sensation against the hot desert sun, colorful pupfish swimming about in small schools between the ribbonlike blades of underwater grass.

I once again get a flash of something across my mind's eye. It feels too real to be a daydream, but too spectacular to be a memory. Clear as day, I see a serpentlike dragon with shimmering blue scales swimming around me. It's much smaller than the green one I have come to know, youthful in its movements as it joyfully chases its own tail.

When I blink, it's gone. Nothing more than a vision.

A hand breaks the water's surface. I'm dragged up for air.

"What are you doing?" my Fated One shouts. "Are you trying to drown yourself, you idiot?"

"You're the one who pushed me!" I cough around a deep gasp for air, hacking up water.

She shakes her head and walks away as I climb out, my clothes fully soaked. An effective way to wash the blood out, I suppose. I pull my tunic off and wring it out, sunshine beating down on my skin. In this heat, I'll be dry within a few minutes.

"Why are you always such a pain?" she mutters.

"Always?" I echo. "What do you mean by that? You've just met me."

She pauses on the other side of the pond, casting me a look that is equal parts anger and . . . grief? "Never mind. Please, just *go*."

Anxiety turns my palms clammy. How can I possibly go, now that I've finally met my Fated One? Does she not feel what I feel, this inexplicable pull?

Why help me when she seems to want nothing to do with me?

I purse my lips, swallowing down what little blood remains coated on my teeth. I don't believe her words. They're an attempt to put distance between us, but why? The notch between her brows signals something else—vulnerability, or even fear.

"Fine. If you wish me gone, so be it," I say slowly, "but only once you answer my questions."

The woman sighs. "Fine. But make it quick."

I pause for a moment, unsure where to begin.

"I thought I was a dead man," I say. "What was that you gave to me earlier?"

"It was blood. My blood. It has . . . healing properties."

"How's that possible? Unless you're . . . part dragon?" I feel ridiculous asking such a question aloud, yet here I am, sounding like a madman.

"I'm not *part* dragon," she utters, her tone indignant. "I *am* a dragon. I have the ability to transform."

"How?"

"Just as the Gods may choose their form to suit their desires, I, too, can change on a whim."

"You said before that you knew you were my Fated One. How?"

The woman shifts her weight from foot to foot. Her mouth opens for a moment before she closes it again. Even from across the water, I can see that she's choosing her words carefully. "Next question," she says.

I stride around the edge of the water and approach her cautiously. "Please, answer me."

"I can see them, too."

My brows knit together. I now have more questions than I started with. "The threads? How is that possible?"

"It's complicated."

"I'm willing to listen."

"Even if you do, it will do you no good."

"And why is that?"

"Because . . ." She trails off, her eyes glassy with the threat of tears.

I take a step closer, my fingers itching to touch. There's barely a pace between us now, the tension thick and heavy in the air. I reach up slowly and carefully, genuinely surprised when she allows me to graze her cheek with the back of my hand. It's fleeting, but electric.

Now I know exactly what all my customers have experienced the first time I bring them to their Fated Ones. It's unlike anything

I've ever felt before. My skin tingles with a pleasant warmth, my soul is wrapped in a restful peace. It's the same feeling I get when I lay my weary head on my pillow at night, soothing and comfortable and secure.

And then she pulls away, and I'm adrift once more.

"You can see our thread, then?" I ask hastily.

"Yes."

"Why is it gray?"

She stares at me, then exhales deeply before her eyes flick away. She's still being very deliberate with her words; I can't say that I like it.

"I don't know," she replies.

"But you must have some idea—"

"Enough questions," she says. "You'll get no more answers from me."

"Just one more," I barter. "And I'll let the issue rest."

"What is it?"

"What's your name, my lady? At the very least, please grant me that."

She glares at me, but the anger from behind her eyes is barely there anymore. Her resolve is dwindling. "You already know it," is her vague reply.

I stare at her, my mind reeling. How could I already know her name?

Then it hits me out of nowhere, breaking free from a locked-away box in the back of my skull.

I see that brilliant green and her smile and fragments of our lives together. I hear her voice and her wordless songs and the rush of wind howling past my ears. I smell the ocean spray and the damp springtime earth after heavy rains.

When I look at her, I swear I can hear my own voice—older and rougher somehow—calling out her name.

"Jyn," I say without meaning to.

She nods but doesn't seem nearly as elated as I am. Instead, she begins to cry.

"I'm sorry, I didn't mean to upset you. If I've offended you in some way—"

She wipes at her eyes, her deep-seated anguish magically seeping through our connection. "Enough," she snaps, trudging off toward the shade of the rocky overhang. "Leave me be."

I have no plans to do such a thing. If I can convince Jyn to let me stay—just for a little while longer—perhaps she'll open up, even a little. Looking around, I formulate a loose plan.

"Very well," I say with my best feigned huff. "If you wish me gone, then say no more. Have a pleasant rest of your day."

I set off due . . . east? The sun is blazing hot, and I have no water or other necessary supplies. There's a good chance that I'll be fried to a crisp within an hour or two, should I continue in this direction. I push past the last of the leafy green oasis and step out onto the hot sand, scorching the bottoms of my feet.

"Not that way!" Jyn shouts after me.

"This way, then?" I head in the opposite direction and try again. This time, she lets me get half a li out before stomping after me.

"No, you idiot!" she exclaims, grabbing me by the wrist.

"You know, you could just fly me out of here."

"I can't."

"Why not?"

"Because I need time to rest—*argh!* Stop talking. I'll draw you a bloody map. You can stay the night and leave in the morning."

I beam, pleased with my efforts. It's not as long as I would like, but it's a start. Being in Jyn's presence is a much-needed relief after all the death and carnage I've witnessed since crossing the border.

"As you command, my lady."

14

This place, *I quickly realize,* is more than a desert sanctuary.
This is her home.

Traces of domesticity, albeit simple ones, are everywhere. Handwoven baskets made of dried leaves sit out by the water, a collection of ripe mangoes and red berries that I can't name sitting inside. There's a thick line made of spun grass tied between two large palm trees, clothes hung over the top to dry. It's what is beneath the low rock overhang that impresses me most.

Arranged against the back is a nest of blankets and soft pillows. It's a comfortable heap of colorful silks and soft cotton and woven yarn—big enough for a dragon to curl up in, bigger still for a woman to spread out comfortably in the lazy desert heat. Not too far off is a fire pit, the earth beneath baked into a hard clay from constant use. Stacked up in the far back corner of the overhang is a pile of wooden crates, their contents unknown to me.

Jyn hasn't said a word to me in hours. I hate it more than anything.

Here I am, a normally enthusiastic—and dare I say, sparkling—conversationalist, with a Fated One who prefers grunting in response rather than speaking. The lunar gods who matched us must have an ironic sense of humor.

"How did you find me that first time?" I ask her. "When I was being attacked by the fei?"

Jyn doesn't answer. Instead, she sits by the water, dipping her toes in as the sun slowly sinks in the distance. I'm seated a stone's throw away on the other side of the fire. Given her obvious coldness, I fear trying to get any closer might not bode well for me and our tenuous acquaintance.

I decide to forge on; perhaps I can pester a response out of her. "I sensed you for the first time when I crossed the mountain border. Did you sense me, too?"

I receive no response.

"Well, I'm grateful you came to my rescue. I would be dead otherwise."

Jyn rises to her feet and makes her way silently to the fire pit. She gathers dried leaves and grass from a nearby basket to use as kindling, expertly piling it high before producing a piece of flint and a striker.

I get up, too, watching her from a few paces away with my hands tucked respectfully behind my back. "A little warm for a fire, is it not?"

"It gets cold at night in the desert," she mutters, annoyed.

"Do dragons suffer from the cold?" I ask, thrilled to finally hear her voice after so many hours. "And what is it that they eat? How do you spend your days? Do you take on your human form often?"

Jyn glares at me. "The fire is for you. Anything. I enjoy sleeping. Yes, it's easier to hide that way. Now, kindly cease your jabbering so that I may work."

I sit back down on the other side of the fire pit as the first few flames flicker to life. "Interesting."

Her pretty green eyes glance up at me. "What is?"

"Do you not breathe fire?" I lean back on my hands. "I was told dragons breathed fire."

"What idiotic trout told you that?"

"The traveling merchants," I say. "When I was a little boy, they filled my head with stories. One told me that in the lands past the Moonstar Isles, well into uncharted territory, dragons have massive wings and breathe fire from their gullets."

Jyn snorts. "That sounds awfully painful."

"I'll take that as a no, then?"

"I have no need for anything so destructive," she mumbles quietly, her gaze far off and her mind seemingly somewhere distant. "I have seen more than my fair share."

"What was that?" I ask, straining to listen. "You always speak so quietly."

Jyn turns. "Perhaps you have shit hearing."

I pick at my fingernails, growing more and more unsure of our bond with every passing minute. Why does she dislike me? What must I do to get her to *talk* to me? In this moment, all I really want is to make her laugh, to ease whatever burden she's carrying. Cracking jokes always worked with A-Ma; maybe it can help with Jyn's mood, too.

"What can you put in a bucket to make it weigh less?" I ask her lightly.

"A hole," she answers without missing a beat.

"You've heard that one before, I take it?"

"No." She doesn't sound amused in the slightest.

"How about—"

Jyn shoots me a hard glare. I shut up immediately. So much for that plan.

My attention gradually shifts to the crates piled high beneath the overhang. Curious, I hop to my feet and mosey over, fascinated by the black markings painted on the sides. It's a foreign language, one that I have never seen before. One of the crates at the very top is open, revealing small white linen sacks. I pick one up, my nose immediately greeted with a familiar scent.

Tea.

"Longjing tea," I say with a light chuckle. "Also known as Dragon Well."

"What of it?"

"Did I mention I own a teahouse?" I continue, breathing in the lovely sweet scent of the dried leaves. "It's a humble establishment, but I brew an excellent pot. This is a favorite among our customers. Or rather, was, back when they came in droves. Business has been dwindling as of late. I suspect it's because of the war. No sense in spending coin on frivolous things, though I would argue tea is a necessity. A way of life, even."

"I don't remember you being this chatty," she says under her breath.

"Pardon?"

"Nothing."

I shrug a shoulder. "Do you know the legend behind Longjing tea?"

"I have a feeling you'll tell me, whether I request it or not."

"Once upon a time, there was a severe drought," I start with a grin. "The lands were so parched that the ground would crack underfoot, and all the plants and trees had long since withered away. Desperate for a solution, a young man climbed the highest peak of the tallest mountain, where they said a well sat at the very top, a benevolent dragon sleeping just inside.

"It took the man three days and three nights to make the journey. When he arrived, he prayed to the dragon to bring the rains. So moved was the dragon by the young man's determination that he blessed the lands with a storm. The rain was so pure that the tea trees drank up every drop and took on a sweet and gentle taste. From then on, the tea was known as Dragon Well to honor the creature and his kindness."

I turn to study Jyn's expression. She clearly does not share my fondness for the tale.

Floundering, I say, "If a story isn't what you are after, perhaps I can attempt another riddle?"

"No."

"A song?"

"Absolutely not."

I cross my arms. "I take it you don't have many guests."

"Prefer it that way." Jyn works her jaw before letting out a frustrated sigh. "Your story was fine, though incorrect."

"Please, enlighten me."

"It was not a young man, but a little girl who climbed the mountain to beseech the dragon for the gift of rain."

"And you know this how, exactly?"

Her lips press into a thin line. "I was there."

My mouth suddenly goes dry. "But this tale is said to be nearly seven thousand years old. It predates the written word. If you were there, then that means you'd be . . ."

Jyn glares. "Yes. Your point?"

"You look, um . . . well, very good for someone so . . ."

"Old?"

"I would never call you such a thing."

She snorts. "Must be the tea. Keeps me looking youthful."

The corners of my lips tug up into a small grin. "Was that a jest? And here I thought the effort would kill you."

"Are you going to stand there all night, or are you going to brew us some tea?"

My heart skips excitedly. "How would you like it, my lady?"

"Strong."

"A woman after my own heart. Er, dragon after my own heart? You'll have to forgive me, I'm unsure how this works."

Jyn grows silent again as she rummages through her small collection of things. She doesn't have much—a few chipped plates, a couple of cracked cups. It's hardly a dragon's fabled treasure hoard, but I'm pleasantly surprised when she retrieves an old teapot made of brownish-red clay. She quietly collects fresh water from the pond before setting it near the fire, but not over it. I'm glad she knows we need hot water and not a rolling boil, lest we oversteep the leaves and ruin the flavor.

"Why *do* you look so young?" I ask after a moment.

Her lips remain sealed for so long that I fear she may not answer. I attempt to ignore the awkward silence by busying myself with the tea. I pour us each a cup, and push it toward her, careful not to spill anything.

She accepts the cup and lifts it to her lips. After a contemplative sip of her tea, Jyn finally replies, "I've never given it much thought. I suppose dragons age quite slowly once we've reached maturity. To the human eye, it looks as though time has stopped altogether."

"How long do dragons live for?"

Jyn raises an eyebrow. "Sometimes too long, and other times not long enough."

"I don't understand."

"Never mind."

"Which of the other stories are true?" I ask, taking the first sip of my own tea. It's delicious, the flavor earthy and rich.

"How should I know?"

"If you've been around long enough to see the invention of writing, you've surely experienced many other monumental events. All legends start from an inkling of truth, do they not? That's how myths and superstitions are ingrained in our bones."

Jyn shrugs. "Some. Not all."

I refill her cup of tea as I search my memory for my favorite childhood tales.

"The legendary archer, Houyi?"

"What of him?"

"Was he real? And did the Gods reward him with a potion of immortality for shooting down the stars?"

Jyn tenses. "He was real. And yes, they did."

I lean forward, intrigued. "And his wife, Chang'e. Did she really steal it from him and escape to the moon?"

"Is that what you were led to believe?"

"Am I wrong?"

"I knew Chang'e to be a devoted wife. She drank his potion of immortality to keep it from falling into the wrong hands. She did the right thing but was banished to the moon for it."

I frown. "I don't like this version. It's far more tragic."

"You were the one who asked," Jyn grumbles, unsympathetic.

"What of the three dragons and the stranger?" I ask before I'm able to stop the question from tumbling out.

Like the untouchable night sky, Jyn is suddenly still and distant. I can't explain why the air around us goes cold. The flickering flames of our modest fire cast shadows upon her face; her exhaustion is evident in the deep, dark circles beneath her eyes.

"I hate that story."

"But why? It was one of my favorites growing up. 'According to legend, they were a family of three—'"

"I know how it goes!" she shrieks, rising to her feet so quickly that she drops her cup and the tea soaks into the thirsty ground. Jyn turns on her heel and walks off along the water's edge.

"I'm sorry. I didn't mean to—"

"Go to sleep. You'll leave at first light."

"But—"

"Leave. Me. *Alone!*"

She transforms before me, becoming both magnificent and terrifying. Her fingers grow and stretch into thick, piercing claws. Her teeth elongate and harden into two rows of razor-like fangs. Her skin grows dazzling, iridescent green scales that cover her from head to toe, her size doubling and then tripling into the dragon's mighty form.

She is a haunting beauty, with undeniable power and strength beneath the mesmerizing sparkle of her emerald hide. I can't look away, entranced in my slack-jawed awe. Her emotions hit me like a tidal wave over our bond, so cold and crestfallen that they knock the air from my lungs. I've never felt a distress like this before, so deep-seated that I feel it clawing with unforgiving violence through the hollows of my bones.

The sensation grips me by the throat, a phantom hand squeezing my windpipe so tight that it brings tears to my eyes. It frightens me to my core. It's grief and madness and agony wrapped up in one desperate outburst. What is this heartbreak, this hopelessness? Did I bring this upon her?

Before I have the chance to blink, to try and apologize, Jyn disappears into the sky.

My thread of fate points upward, where I cannot follow.

15

While the king and queen tend to their domains, the stranger and the young prince set off for the seaside, taking in the salty winds and call of waterbirds. This stretch of beach is just for them, a place to hide away as they share sweet smiles at sunrise and tender kisses beneath the silver moon. The warm thrum through their bond sets their hearts ablaze. It has been only a few days since the stranger's arrival, but the love they share is pure and true.

"Tell me, my prince," he says, "how might I use magic to heal my people?"

The young prince hands the stranger a single sapphire scale. He instructs the stranger to place it at the bottom of the nearest mountain spring. "The magic imbued in the scale will cleanse the waters," he explains, "purifying not only those who drink, but so too the plants and the animals who call the land home."

The stranger thanks the young prince profusely for his kindness. "Come with me," he urges, "to the lands beyond the horizon. We may help thousands yet!"

The young prince shakes his head. No, his honorable, doting parents would never allow such a thing.

As determined as ever, the stranger promises to return one day *soon with tales of his adventures. After a parting embrace, he sets off with the dragon scale in hand, determined to save his people. The blue dragon is so full of hope and integrity that he cannot help but feel sure in his decision to share his secrets.*

The red thread of fate between them stretches beyond sight, but does not break no matter how far the stranger goes. The blue dragon looks out to the glimmering seas, longingly awaiting his Fated One's return.

16

I awake to the sound of . . . nothing.

    Exhausted from my travels, I wound up falling asleep by the fire shortly after Jyn's departure. The fire has long since gone cold, and there's not a trace of movement anywhere within the oasis. It appears that the dragon has not returned.

I sit up slowly, rubbing the sleep from my eyes with the heels of my palms. As I blink away my grogginess, I anxiously rub my little finger and stare mindlessly at my gray thread. Pressing questions sit on the tip of my tongue, threatening to crush me down. I force myself to remember the reason why I agreed to set out in the first place.

My mother is no doubt waiting for my return.

She was a force to be reckoned with back in the day. At least, that's what A-Ba used to tell me. She was one of the prettiest girls in all the North, and as the daughter of a successful silk merchant, her dowry was said to have been so immense that it filled twenty heavy coffers. The line of suitors waiting to ask for her hand in marriage stretched across the Five Kingdoms and back. A-Ma turned away every single one.

Except for my father.

One look was apparently all she needed to know he was her

Fated One. She described it as a feeling, like coming home. My grandfather was furious that she'd chosen a penniless commoner with no proper education or steady job. If she went through with this match, he said, he would cut her off. Without a coin to her name, she was no doubt dooming herself to a hard life. But A-Ma defied him all the same, content to have found true love.

I think of her now, sitting alone in the teahouse A-Ba built for her with his bare hands, all because she happened to mention her love of Longjing tea, and my heart aches. If I can convince Jyn to part with a few of her scales to be used for A-Ma's medicine, then at least I have one fewer problem to concern myself with. *If* Jyn decides to return, that is.

But what of Emperor Róng? He's a thorn in my side that I can't dislodge. He has me in a chokehold. If I return without Jyn, will he harm my mother? That, or let her illness take her. But if I *do* bring Jyn back to Jiaoshan, there's no question that he will harm or perhaps even kill her. I let out a frustrated sigh. No matter what I do, someone will get hurt. What I need right now is time to think. As long as I remain with Jyn, I'm sure I can come up with a plan.

Caw! Caw! Caw!

The boisterous call of a crow pulls me from my thoughts. I look up to find a curious sight among the large palm trees. The black bird rests on a long branch, but even from this distance, I can tell there's something peculiar about the creature.

It has three legs, and its eyes glow red.

"Hello, friend," I say, rising to my feet, watching the little beast curiously. "How did you come to find yourself so far from home?" We are surely nowhere near a crow's nest here in the desert.

The crow swoops down and lands just before me by the water's edge, its movements jerky and abnormal. It drinks greedily from the pond, then grooms its black feathers and taps its third foot on the soil.

"What a strange little thing," I mumble to myself, making a quick study of the creature. "Come for a bit of rest, I see. Well, that's all right. There's plenty of space for the two of us."

The three-legged crow continues to tap its middle foot on the ground. It squawks at me, red eyes glued to my form with unusually rapt attention. The longer I watch the crow, the colder and darker the feeling in my gut grows. Its eyes are too . . . aware. I don't like it one bit.

As the minutes tick by, the crow stares and stares and stares—
And then flies right at me.

It pecks at my forehead, my nose, my eyes. It scratches me with its talons, mincing my forearms when I bring them up as a shield. The bird screeches at me as it goes for my jugular, but I manage to grab it by its wing and tear it away. I throw the blasted thing to the ground with a sharp cry, my torn flesh searing.

The crow recovers, hopping to its three feet and stretching its wings to their full span. It's there beneath the creature's primary feathers that I spot a thin piece of yellow parchment marked in red ink.

A talisman?

My heart lodges in my throat. What in the nine suns could that mean? I can't allow this creature to escape. Something tells me that could spell disaster, and I'm frankly very tired of having things go wrong.

I hastily throw off my tunic and charge the little beast, tossing the fabric over it before it has a chance to fly off. It frantically struggles against my makeshift net, crying out loudly as it tears at the linen with its sharp beak and even sharper claws. For something so small, it's terribly strong. I have a difficult time keeping it contained as I gather up the fabric in my clenched hand.

"What do you think you're doing?"

I turn just in time to see Jyn descending from the sky, transforming back into a woman before my eyes. The shift is seamless and takes not even a full second, her body shrinking down and her features morphing into those of the heartbreakingly beautiful woman I still yearn to know. I probably look a fool with my jaw on the ground as I hold out my catch.

"It attacked me," I mutter lamely. "And where did you disappear to?"

"Kept watch while you slept," Jyn grumbles flatly, avoiding my gaze.

I smile, still struggling to keep my fabric parcel down. "Were you worried about me?"

Jyn ignores me outright and reaches into my tunic, grasping the crow by the neck with one hand. She frowns deeply when she spots the talisman beneath its wing. Jyn swiftly yanks it off and studies the red-ink markings.

"What is it, my lady?" I ask. "Can you read it?"

She doesn't need to speak for me to get my answer. I can sense her mood turning frightfully cold over our connection. It's almost like taking a deep plunge into a cavern, no light or hope to be found.

"A tracking spell," she hisses. Jyn stares the crow dead in the eye. "Like the one on your scroll earlier."

My breath catches in my throat. "Was that what that was? But how did you even know it was there?"

"I could smell *his* scent."

I frown. "Whose scent, my lady?"

"Come after me again," she says not so much to the bird, but through it to its sender, "and I will devour you. Don't forget—a heart for a heart."

The crow pecks at her hand, its sharp beak piercing her flesh.

Jyn grunts as blood drips from the shallow wound. Overcome with fury, she snaps the crow's neck without hesitation, squeezing it tight in her fingers, and tosses its corpse to the ground.

I stare at her, alarmed. "What was that for?" I demand. "Who were you just talking to? Who's tracking us?"

Jyn turns her head to the sky, looking out for something my mortal eyes can't comprehend. She sniffs the air, her tongue flicking out subtly at the corner of her mouth to taste the breeze. "We can't stay here any longer. I don't know how, but he's coming for me."

"*Who* is coming for you?"

She grits her teeth in a snarl. "The man you call Róng."

My heart rails against my rib cage. "The emperor is coming here? How is that possible? I was led to believe he didn't know the location of the dragon—"

Swift as lightning, Jyn whips around and grasps me by the shoulders. "You've spoken to him?" she growls.

"That I have, my lady, but I swear I meant you no harm. He sent me to find you, that's all."

Pure fury spreads across her features. "And you agreed to work for that monster?"

"I wasn't given much of a choice," I reply.

"I thought it odd when I sensed you passing the mountain border, and now I know why. What did that beast offer you?"

"He didn't—"

"*Do not lie to me,*" she seethes, digging her fingers into the flesh of my shoulders. Her hand hasn't stopped bleeding, the red staining not only her palm but my skin as well.

"My mother's sick," I blurt out. I can't bring myself to lie to her. "My mother is sick, but once I fed her a dragon's scale, her condition immediately improved, and—"

"A dragon's scale?" Jyn rasps. "What color?"

"I beg your pardon?"

"What. Color?"

"Green. It was green, my lady. Why does that—"

Jyn pulls away, hiding her eyes, but I already see the edges are red with the threat of tears. "Oh," she whimpers, choking on the sound. Her torment screams at me through our thread, so raw that it almost makes me sick. Her agony is my agony, her sorrow my sorrow. I'm suddenly overcome with a vast, terrifying emptiness that nearly tears me in two.

"I'm sorry," I whisper, clutching my chest. I fear that my heart may burst. "I didn't mean anything by it, Jyn. I was told it was medicine. I would never do anything to harm you."

She takes a deep, shaky breath. "No, I . . . I know that." Jyn wipes at her eyes. "So, this is what he promised you? The promise of medicine?"

I nod slowly.

"So you led him to me."

"Not knowingly. Believe me, my lady, I would never have—"

"Does he know who you are?" Jyn asks.

"Who *I* am?"

"Yes. Does Róng know who you are?"

I stare at her blankly. "I'm afraid I don't understand your question."

Jyn stands still as stone, her thoughts a mystery to me despite her emotions pouring into mine. What new map is unraveling inside her head?

After a moment, she clicks her tongue. "Make haste. Grab what you can."

"We're leaving?"

She busies herself about her home, hastily grabbing what few supplies she can—canteens filled to the top with water, dried fruit, a bit of spiced jerky—throwing everything into an old supply bag.

Her urgency is so contagious that I find myself helping her, anxiety buzzing between us like an army of ants crawling on my skin.

"Where shall we go?" I ask.

"Far from here."

I pause. "But my mother . . . I need to return to her."

"We don't have time."

"Jyn, I beg of you—"

"Your mortal mother is of no concern to me, Sai. She will pass on, just as all humans do."

I swallow hard. I can't abandon my mother, but I can't abandon my Fated One, either, no matter how hard she endeavors to keep me at arm's length.

"She needs me," I say firmly. "I must return."

Jyn pauses her gathering and narrows her eyes at me. "Then you will do so on your own. I will not join you in that monster's lair."

"What do you know of the emperor?" I demand, fed up with her roundabout way of telling me things.

"What do I—" She stares at me as though I have stabbed her in the heart. Jyn throws her hands up with a frustrated huff. Something untamed ebbs across our bond, a feeling so heavy and ancient I feel it crushing down on my shoulders.

Then her expression hardens. "I can't do this anymore, Sai. *I cannot.* All mortals die, and your mother is no exception. Either go to her, or don't. It doesn't matter to me."

My jaw drops open, but no words come out to rebut her cruel ones. As I stand there in stunned silence, Jyn grabs her things and rushes out into the desert alone.

My head tells me to return home. I've been gone too long, and venturing any farther into the Western Wastelands could spell my end. It's easy to die of starvation and thirst out here.

But my heart tells me to follow. I must know more: about Jyn, my Fated One, our fraying gray thread. All my life, I have wondered about her. Now that she's within reach, how can I possibly let her go?

Choosing my heart, I set out after her beneath the unforgiving sun.

17

I *have never fared well in* the heat. My pale skin burns far too easily, and my dark hair soaks up all the sun's rays. I've thrown on my tunic, but the crow's sharp claws have slashed through the fabric. There's no doubt in my mind that I'll wind up with awkward burn marks by night's end.

We have been walking for hours, not a single other soul to be found in the arid wastelands. To make matters worse, the air is irritatingly dry and still, and it teams up with the blazing temperatures to bake my tender flesh from the outside in. We trudge on, nary a cloud in the sky as the sun beats angrily down on us.

"My lady," I rasp. "Why do we not take to the air, as we did before?"

"Crows fly" is her simple, perplexing answer.

I swipe my forearm across my sweaty brow. "Right. Crows fly," I echo, resigned and very dehydrated. "Of course."

"He'll be watching the skies," Jyn goes on. "We'll better outpace him on foot."

"'Outpace' implies an intentional direction. You have yet to tell me where we are headed."

She doesn't grace me with a reply.

Annoyance licks at the nape of my neck, the tension in my shoulders building to the point of cramping. I catch up to her brisk pace, ignoring the chafing of my thighs and the needles stabbing into my feet. The footprints we leave in the sand are a peculiar thing. Jyn's are far heavier and deeper than my own, despite her smaller human stature. The wind wipes them away regardless, any evidence of our passing existence smoothing away with time.

"Jyn, you should rest," I say. "We have been walking for hours."

"The more distance we put between ourselves and that terror, the better," she replies, keeping her eyes ahead.

She appears unaffected by the blazing heat, though something about her hunched shoulders and the hand she's keeping cradled against her chest gives me pause. Upon closer inspection, I notice the piercing wound the crow inflicted on her.

"You're still bleeding?" I ask, alarmed. I take her hand to inspect it. Without thinking I immediately rip part of my tunic to wrap it around her delicate palm. My clothes were ruined anyway, so it might as well serve a purpose. "Why didn't you say so earlier?"

Jyn attempts to pull away, but I'll have none of it. I hold her arm steady as I tend to her injury. "This is nothing. I've survived far worse," she says.

I tie off the bandage with a sigh. I know how much stronger Jyn is than myself, and yet she doesn't fight against what I do next: allow myself the indulgence of gently grazing my fingers over the curve of her wrist.

She looks surprised, but I can feel her thrill of delight through our connection. I have noticed that the more time I spend with her, the easier it is to tap into her thoughts and sensations. It's only ever a fleeting glimpse, but that's more than enough.

Right now, I know that she's happy—happier than she has been in a very long time.

"Where are we going, my lady?" I ask softly, the distance between us closing.

"Somewhere far from that monster," she whispers.

"You would be hard-pressed to find land the Emperor Róng hasn't claimed for himself. Save for the Moonstar Isles and the Southern Kingdom, though the latter may well fall to the Imperial Army within a matter of moons."

Jyn's lip curls. "Yes, I heard of that vile snake's attempt to wrest more land for himself. That leaves the isles, then, though the journey won't come easily."

"Is there no other option? I could take you to my city and hide you there."

"That won't work."

"Whyever not?"

"Because if evil has a face," she says, her eyes growing dark, "then that man has carved it off and worn it around as a mask. He won't stop until we're . . ." Jyn trails off, her eyes growing distant.

I've noticed in my short time with her that she does this often, escaping into some unseeable corner of her mind. She talks to herself often as well. The result of being alone for so long, perhaps? Whatever the answer might be, I wish to ease her worries—it's just a shame that I don't know how.

Jyn withdraws her hand and keeps walking. "To the Moonstar Isles it is, then." She chews on the inside of her cheek, much the same way I do when lost in thought. "We must put as much distance as possible between us and the emperor. Every second wasted is a li he draws closer."

"And every li we travel, the farther I am from home."

Jyn simply stares at me, as she always does when she is at a loss for words. In these moments, she is made of stone—hard and indifferent. "There's nothing we can do for your mother."

"You would have me abandon her completely?"

"I've said as much."

Her bluntness hits me like a strike across the face. "I didn't think you were serious."

"Be logical about this, Sai. You have two options: return without me and surrender yourself to the emperor's mercy—and trust me, you will find none—or escape with me and live out what little remains of your mortal life."

"What little remains?" I echo with a disbelieving chuckle. "You make it sound as though I have mere days to live."

"Why are you always so . . . ," she mutters to herself, pulling at her hair and gasping in a full breath. "I shouldn't have done this." Jyn squeezes her fists at her forehead, shutting her eyes tight. "This time will be no different. Why did I think it would be different?"

This time?

Her anguish is disheartening to witness and even more traumatizing to feel. It makes my skin chill, despite the blazing desert heat. There's also an unexpected rage, making for a violent concoction that almost causes me to gag.

I take up her hands, alarmed and desolate to see her in such a state. I need to help her calm down, not just for her sake, but also for mine. One more minute of this sensation will see me sick all over the sand.

"Jyn, look at me. *Look* at me."

Her eyes find mine, but not without a pause.

"I'm here," I assure her, a gentle whisper. I gingerly press her palms to my chest and keep them clasped there beneath my own. "I'm here, Jyn. You needn't worry any longer."

As her breathing steadies, she grows sullen, though her cheeks are beginning to redden.

"If you're positive that we can't fly," I say, "then let us travel by night and rest during the day. The sun is too harsh. We can journey by moonlight." I hold my breath as I carefully stroke my fingers over her blushing cheeks; she leans into my touch just so. "I don't wish to see you burn up. Allow me to make us a camp here, where the sand is flat. Besides, your hand still needs to heal, and I'm, uh . . . Well, let's just say I'm not used to walking this much. I need a break."

"I suppose there is . . . some merit to this plan."

I break into a grin. I can't help it. "Would you do me the honor of saying that again? I do love hearing that I'm right."

Jyn rolls her eyes and huffs, then sits down right on the spot. "Go on, then."

"As my lady commands."

It's a trial and a half to create some semblance of shelter, but I make do with my determination and wit. We're surrounded on all sides by blazing hot sand, without a tree or cloud in sight for shade. It dawns on me at some point that there's no need to build a structure when I can simply dig *down*.

The work is nowhere near as arduous as I anticipated. The sand is soft and easy to pile up into tall mounds, the tiny grains slipping through my fingers like fine silk. Within a few minutes, I have managed to create a shallow trench just big enough for the both of us.

"After you," I say as I offer her my hand.

When she takes it, I swear I can feel our connection *sing*.

The contact is brief but life-changing. For just a moment, all is right with the world. The soft press of her fingers against my own keeps me grounded, an anchor to thoughts adrift. Each and every one of my insecurities and doubts evaporates into oblivion the moment I take her hand in my own. My breath catches in my throat, a giddy lightness rising in me with such force I feel as though I'm floating.

Best of all, I know she feels it, too.

It's in her soft inhale, her full lips parted just so. It's in the way her eyes find mine with ease. It's in the way time stops, granting us a fraction of infinity to just *be*. This peace that washes over me is unlike anything I have felt before. My soul is calm, my place in the world suddenly as clear as the sky above.

Then she pulls away, and again I'm lost.

"We should . . ." Jyn clears her throat. "We should get in."

"Right, of course," I say quickly.

I shrug off my tunic and place it over the top of the trench, placing generous amounts of sand around the edges to create a weighted anchor. Pulled taut, the fabric provides just enough shade and protection for the both of us. A makeshift canopy. The shade it provides only covers three-quarters of the trench, leaving a wide enough space near the end for us to crawl underneath. The air is stuffy and the space is cramped, but the relief of finally getting out of the sun is immediate.

Jyn and I lie there together, barely an inch apart in our shelter, the warmth of the air amplifying my exhaustion. Only my toes stick out from beneath the shade, but I grin and bear it. It's better than nothing.

"Where did you learn to build things like this?" she whispers.

I bury the tips of my fingers into the sand beneath me, feeling the coarse grains rub against my skin. "I'm not sure," I admit. "Instinct, I suppose?" I stare up at the underside of my tunic-turned-canopy as memories surface. "I recall one particularly terrible summer, when it was so hot you couldn't step foot outside without sweltering. The only way to escape the heat was to remain indoors. When I was a boy, I would venture out to a stone well I had found atop a mountain. I would climb down and sleep away the days at the bottom where it was coolest . . ."

I trail off, confused.

What am I saying? *Why* am I saying this? There was never any well, and summers in the North were always mild at best.

And yet I can so clearly see the soft green moss against the cool gray stones, smell the damp earth beneath my feet. I feel the cool shade against my body, the stretch of my muscles as I curl up for a much-needed noonday nap before a little girl's voice reaches my ears.

. . . What *was* that just now? These visions are not only growing more frequent, but much clearer the longer I find myself in Jyn's presence. She has awakened something inside me, something I can't attempt to name.

Colors, sensations, smells—all vibrant and real. Could it be that I'm dehydrated? Highly likely. Victim to sun poisoning? Even more so. But if that's the case, why do these visions resonate so deeply within me? I don't understand how it's possible: they are my memories, and yet they are not—echoes of a life that may or may not be mine. Maybe they belong to Jyn, and I'm somehow privy to these brief flashes of a time long gone by.

Beside me, Jyn lies motionless, eyes closed, her chest slowly rising and falling. How she's managed to fall asleep so quickly, I will never know. I take a moment to admire the graceful curl of her long lashes and the serious press of her lips. She is just so . . . *close*. So close that I can't believe any of this is real.

I rub my little finger. Perhaps my hypothesis is correct. These visions I've been having must be the result of our thread of fate. If I can sense her emotions, is it not possible that I could sense her memories, as well?

I roll onto my side and hazard a direct look at the woman lying next to me. Words cannot do her beauty justice. There's an otherworldly quality to her, something that balances on the cusp of the ethereal. She lies so still that one could mistake her for carved marble, her pale skin smooth and soft. Her long dark hair flows over her shoulders in rivulets, pooling about her head like a shadowy halo. I can't fathom the seven thousand years she has claimed to live, for she looks not a day older than I.

She stirs, her eyes fluttering open. When our eyes connect, however brief the moment might be, I swear I can see it—the lifetimes upon lifetimes of wisdom, of wandering . . .

And *pain*.

Cold and insidious, it seems to seep out of her, overwhelming our bond to the point that I'm surprised it has not yet cracked through her fine marble skin. All that grief in a simple glance. In that moment, I feel it seep into my marrow. And while I'm fervid to know everything about her, now I'm also afraid.

What horrors has Jyn seen to look so haunted?

How much of it has she had to endure all alone?

Just as sleep tugs at my mind, I happen to peer down at our fraying thread. My eyes widen, a gasp rushing out of me. The center point of our thread of fate . . . is *glowing*.

It's the faintest hint of red. A persimmon, not quite ripe. Like the morning sun peeking out over the horizon. There's still slack between us, but nowhere near as much as before. Where our thread once looked moments away from snapping, now it slowly knits itself together. It happens at a snail's pace, one barely perceptible fraction at a time, but I know what I'm seeing is real. Our thread of fate is repairing itself, starting from the center and working its way out, winding carefully.

"Jyn," I rasp. "Jyn, our thread is . . ."

I glance at her, suddenly realizing that she's watching, too. But where I'm vibrating with excitement, her brow creases in a steep frown. Her jaw is tight, her lips a hard line. Whatever joy I felt drains when she turns away, rolling onto her shoulder to expose her back to me.

In an instant, what little progress our thread has made comes to a halt. The red bloom shrinks back to the center, its warmth dwindling like the final embers of a hearth, before it fades back to its usual gloomy gray. I can sense a divide between us, an intentional wall that stops me from sensing her thoughts. My Fated One is pushing me away.

And I want to know why. I *need* to.

"I have a request."

"What would that be?" she says suspiciously.

"If we're to head to the Moonstar Isles, allow me to send a message to my mother so that she at least knows I'm well. The last time she saw me, I was being dragged off to prison."

"You care about her a great deal," she says, as though it's a bad thing.

"Of course. I'm always thinking of the ones I love."

Jyn sighs slowly, sounding equal parts irritated and . . . resigned. "Very well. We'll send a messenger bird when we arrive."

Hope rises in my chest. There's still an icy distance between us, but I will gladly take her reluctant suggestion over outright rejection.

"Thank you, Jyn." I say her name slowly, carefully; as one would handle fragile glass. I'm overcome with the urge to say it ten, a hundred, a thousand times—but I settle for just this once.

"Go to sleep," she says, though not unkindly, before falling silent once again.

Waves of exhaustion gently tug at my senses. The steady rhythm of Jyn's breaths is more soothing than any of my childhood lullabies.

It's not long after that I, too, drift off. Sleep claims me as I study the length of her pretty hair, all the while attempting to ignore the gray thread that is once more slowly mending itself between us.

18

"S ai?"

Something brushes gingerly against my cheek. Fingertips? No, softer than that. Perhaps a pair of lips?

My eyes are too heavy to open. The sand makes for a surprisingly comfortable bed. My weight sinks into it, the fine grains molding around my form to provide the softest of cocoons. I'm tempted to remain here a while longer, but—

"*Sai!*"

Jyn raps two knuckles hard against my forehead. The sting jolts me awake, my hand flying to my head.

"What was that for?" I demand, suddenly awake and alert.

"It's nightfall," she says flatly, already shifting about to throw off my tunic-turned-shelter. "We're running low on water. We must find more as soon as possible, else you won't last three days without it."

Sand fills my mouth as we rise to our feet together. The air is significantly cooler, the gentle breeze a welcome reprieve. The moon is big and full, a bright silver disk illuminating the inky-black skies above. I gawk at the grand expanse of stars, bewitched by their dazzling beauty. It's a canvas of blinking lightning bugs, arranged in swirling patterns more intricate than the finest tapestries in all the Five Kingdoms.

"I've never seen this many before," I whisper to myself.

Jyn regards me with a barely perceptible smile. The sight of it nearly sends me flying. Oh, how I yearn for more.

"Have you been taught to use them for direction?" she asks.

"I can't say that I have."

She gracefully lifts a finger to point at the sky, drawing the outlines of constellations. "This one here," she says, "is the Black Tortoise, Xuan Wu. You can just make out the shape of the snake who rides on his back. He will point you north. And over there is the White Tiger, Baihu. Follow him, should you wish to go west."

"And that cluster there?" I ask, trying my best to visualize the shapes.

"That is the Red Bird, Zhu Que. Use her to guide yourself south."

"And what of that one?" I say, curiosity bubbling beneath the surface of my skin. I adore listening to Jyn speak. As a child, I was never considered a good student, too easily distracted to pay attention during the schoolmaster's lessons. And yet when Jyn instructs me, I hang on her every word, soothed by the soft lilt of her voice, which resonates deep within me.

Jyn pauses, looking at the final cluster of stars. "That is the Great Dragon, Qing Long," she answers slowly. "Follow him to go east."

"Are they true, the old stories? They say dragons were once born on the easternmost islands."

"Where did you hear such things?"

"My mother, I suppose. I always had trouble sleeping as a boy. Too hyper an imagination. She told me all manner of stories to help me doze off."

Her lips press into a thin line, her jaw tensing. "There's some truth in fiction, I suppose."

"Is that where you're from? The east?"

Jyn nods slowly. "Yes, but I left a very long time ago."

"And Qing Long, the azure dragon of old . . . Was he real?"

"My great-great-grandfather."

My eyes widen in delighted surprise. "Really? How did he end up in the stars?"

Jyn shakes her head. "It's said that he wanted to see how high he could fly . . . and got stuck there."

"Oh, that." Laughter rises out of me. No matter how hard I try to swallow it down, it bursts forth with twice as much force. "How *terrible*."

Miraculously, Jyn begins to giggle too. It's a quiet sound, but marvelous all the same. The corners of her eyes crinkle as she smiles, and I can't help but stare at her bashful delight. So sweet, so joyful. Eventually, though, her hard mask slips back into place, the sound of her laughter ceases.

"Come," she says, serious as ever. "Let's not waste moonlight."

"Lead the way, my lady."

Traveling across the sand dunes at night proves an ingenious decision on my part, if I do say so myself. It's far easier to traverse the Western Wastelands this way; without the sun baking us from the outside in, Jyn and I are able to keep a good pace.

Every now and then, I see her tongue flick out. It's a discreet movement, very much a quick lick of her lips, but I notice it all the same.

"This way," she says. "There's a small body of water nearby."

"How can you tell?" I ask.

"I can smell it."

"With your *tongue*?" I back away with a grin when she shoots me an irritated glare. "I'm only curious. Can you fault me for wanting to know more about you?"

"Yes," she grumbles, continuing forward with a sharp huff. Her long braid swings back and forth as she walks, silky locks pulled up high and secured with an ornate silver pin.

It appears to be the only extravagance on her person. I study it with great interest as we walk, the craftsmanship of the pin unlike anything I have ever seen. Flowers are carved into it, bits of silver expertly twisted to resemble delicate petals. No gems, but I think that fitting. Anything more would clash with her natural elegance. The longer I stare at it, the more fascinated I become. For some reason, I can't shake the feeling that I've seen it somewhere before.

A vision flashes before my eyes.

I'm surrounded by a lush bamboo forest, sunlight filtering in through the light green leaves. A woman sits before me, and I'm combing my fingers through her long black hair. I'm the one who sets the pin in place, carefully weaving braids in her hair as the noonday sun climbs higher. She turns, and although the details of her face are out of focus, there's no denying that brilliant smile.

A gift for you, my love.

I will treasure it forever.

It's all real, and yet it's not. Am I dreaming this somehow?

"Sai?"

The sound of Jyn's voice snaps me out of my trance. She's a few paces ahead of me now, looking back with a furrowed brow.

"Apologies," I murmur, quick to catch up. "I was lost in—"

The loud, grating sound of a bird's screech interrupts us.

At first, I ignore it. Surely it's just a desert scavenger flying overhead. But then the screeching grows louder and louder, punctuated by the sharp beats of many pairs of wings. Alarmed, Jyn and

I both turn and look up at the sky, now blackened with an incoming swarm.

A murder of crows, numbering in the thousands. Their bloodred eyes are trained on us, the sharp talons of their three feet poised to claw and stab. This is Emperor Róng's doing; of that I have no doubt. They have spotted us, several crows diving down to begin their assault. One of the creatures slices me across the cheek with its razor-sharp feathers: a warning.

Jyn grabs my hand.

"Run!"

No matter how hard we sprint, we can't escape the crows. The cacophony of screeches rattles my eardrums, surrounded by the red-eyed swarm. The sand is too soft, our efforts to flee useless. There's no hope for us, buffeted by the beating of wings, the pecking of sharp beaks, and the piercings of unforgiving talons.

It's a nightmare, one I can't wake myself from. The harder I fight, the more resistance I meet. The faster I run, the hotter my muscles blaze. The tighter I try to hold on to Jyn, the faster these damned beasts tear her away. The emperor's crows have us trapped in the center of their murder, the air growing thicker and harder to breathe with every passing second. They mean to suffocate us into submission.

A crow nearly pecks out one of my eyes, the sting of its beak scraping my bottom eyelid radiating a thousandfold within my skull. I lose my grasp on Jyn's hand, and her fingers slip from mine.

"No!" I choke.

Panic shreds through me. I have to get to her. I have to. And yet the harder I struggle, the more helpless I become. No matter what method I try, I can't reach Jyn. The birds have separated us, dragging her away and out of my line of sight. I can see nothing past the blood in my eyes, nor hear my own cries over the chaos.

A sudden shift overcomes me. My panic transforms into an all-out rage, their relentless attack causing my blood to boil over. I have felt this anger before, a force that threatens to explode from deep within my core. All I see is scarlet red.

And then I lash out, driven by a sudden, unexpected thirst for blood.

A crow drives its talons into my shoulder, the piercing of my flesh the catalyst I need to lose control of my other senses. With a swiftness I didn't know I possessed, I reach out and throttle the bird by the throat, yanking it free of my shoulder. There's no time to think, only to kill.

I surprise myself when I bite the damned beast's head clean off. The metallic tang of its blood gushes into my mouth. I spit it out, thoroughly appalled. Confusion storms within me. What's happening? What are we going to—

My thread suddenly tugs upward.

Jyn has taken to the skies.

With a mighty roar that shakes the earth around me, the emperor's crows disperse. They fly straight up, following the fierce dragon into the clouds above. She's a streak of emerald, twisting and looping in an attempt to shake them off. The three-legged beasts have all but abandoned me in pursuit of their true target.

Jyn shows them no mercy, snapping at them with her powerful jaws and frighteningly sharp teeth. They tear into her with just as much ferocity, ripping away scales and clawing at her mane until every other inch of her body is covered in wounds and exposed flesh.

All I can do is stare up at the violence, grounded and completely helpless to stop the madness.

The dragon roars again, this time plummeting hard and fast toward the sand below. Jyn is wounded, unable to keep up the fight. She falls and falls and falls. Just as she's about to crash—

She instantly changes direction, swooping horizontal mere feet from the sand.

The crows who were in pursuit are unable to change direction in time and smash into the sand all at once, their bodies bursting upon impact. Their blood soaks into the desert, feathers scattered about, carcasses lying broken in the middle of the wasteland. The heat will expedite the rot. My dragon manages to fly toward me, only to transform midair, Jyn's limp body falling at an alarming speed.

My body reacts before my mind does, my feet carrying me to her as quickly as they're able. It's the furthest thing from a graceful landing. I manage to catch her, but her momentum knocks me back. I sit up and anxiously check her injuries. Jyn's eyes are closed, her breathing shallow. Blood drips down from her face, her arms, her legs. It stains her clothes, the scent of iron weighing heavily in the air.

"Jyn?" I rasp. My hands shake. I'm horrified at the harm they've inflicted.

She doesn't stir.

I don't know why I look around for help, but I do anyway. Desperation twists at my heart. She's barely breathing. Surely there must be something I can do to help her. We've only crossed half of the Western Wasteland, but it's clear Jyn is far too injured now to walk.

Only three options present themselves: we head back and risk capture by the emperor, we stay here and die from thirst, or we go forth toward the Moonstar Isles and pray we find a doctor or someone who knows how to heal her.

I gingerly brush her hair away from her face. "Everything will be all right, Jyn. I promise. Please, just hold on."

Carefully, I lift Jyn and carry her on my back. I trudge forward despite the blunt ache in my eye and the spasms of my body. It has become abundantly clear that I'm no fighter, nor am I a healer. I may not be strong like a dragon, but I can try to be as brave as one.

One step at a time, I march forward. Determination courses through my veins.

Jyn carried me to safety once.

Now I will do the same for her.

19

Despite my best efforts, she doesn't stop bleeding. Blood drips from her mangled arm, leaving behind a dotted trail in the sand. Her breathing is shallow against my ear, her chin propped against my shoulder. Jyn slips in and out of consciousness, groaning in agony even in sleep.

I carry her through the night, and then all through the day. By noon, my skin peels back, burnt and blistered by the sun. No matter how much I pray for rain or the reprieve of a single cloud, my wishes go unanswered. I'm unsure of how much progress I've made, for each stretch of sand looks precisely the same as the last. Knowing my poor sense of direction, we may well be going in circles. If so, I've doomed us both.

My neck strains and my back cracks, every step a trial. To make matters even worse, I lost sight in my damaged eye nearly an hour ago, the surrounding skin swollen to the point of sealing my eye shut. Any other person would be concerned, but my only thought is getting Jyn to safety.

I would gladly lose my other eye if it meant she would be all right.

Behind me, Jyn groans. It's a soft, weak sound.

"A little while longer, my lady," I wheeze. There's sand in my throat, crunching between my teeth. My mouth is too dry to swallow away the irritation.

"Put me down, Sai," she rasps.

"Save your strength. I'll carry you the rest of the way."

"Hurts . . ."

"Just bear with me a while longer. Would you like to hear a story?" I ask, trudging ahead. "It's a good way to pass the time."

Jyn mumbles against my shoulder, "Fine."

"How about the tale of the first Fated Ones? My father used to tell me that story all the time."

Another step forward, another sharp jolt of electricity slicing through my bones and muscles. I keep going because I have to. I will not fail her.

"A long, long time ago," I begin, huffing a labored breath, "a boy was walking home one night after a day spent fishing by the riverside. The night was clear, and the moon was full and bright, stars speckled across the sky. The young boy crossed paths with an elderly man standing at the center of a bridge.

"'Boy,' the man said, tying a red thread to the little boy's hand, 'do you see that lass, just over yonder? She is destined to be your wife.'

"The young boy scoffed at this. Girls were abhorrent to him, you see. Covered from head to toe in maladies and insects. He was sure to catch something, were he not careful. The boy was quick to cross the bridge, pick up a stone, and hurl it at the girl in a fit of childish anger before storming away.

"It was not until many years later, on the night of his wedding, that he was finally able to meet the woman his parents had arranged for him to marry. When the woman removed her red veil, he discovered a scar over her brow. He asked her how it happened, to which she responded, 'When I was but a young girl, a boy threw a rock at me and left me with this scar.'

"It was in this moment the boy realized that what the old man had said was true. And that is the origin of the red threads of fate."

The end of my tale is met with silence—not that I was expecting jubilant applause. Jyn is barely hanging on.

"Fret not," I say, half speaking to myself. "There's a light up ahead. Do you see?"

I squint to get a better look. The sun is mercifully fading in the distance. Finally. I've been walking all day; our canteens of water are now depleted. The light in question appears to be moving, rocking back and forth as it eludes us. Could it be a lantern? Who in their right mind would be all the way out here in the middle of the Wastelands?

"You there!" I shout, my voice carrying over the sands with no echo. My throat is so torn that I could easily be mistaken for a toad. "Please, we need help!"

All of a sudden, the light goes out.

An indignant squawk escapes my throat. "We mean you no harm!" My words soak into the sand, my already weak voice dampened entirely. "Please, my"—*Fated One, destined soul, the other half of my being*—"friend is hurt!"

The light flicks back into existence, this time to my right at the very top of a rolling dune. I blink in confusion. How did it get there so fast? Brimming with newfound determination, I start toward the lantern, eager for assistance.

"Sai," Jyn rasps. "Sai, stop—"

"All will be well, my lady. All will be well."

The moment I climb to the apex of the dune, the light flickers out again. I see no footprints in the sand, no shadowy figure retreating into the distance. Just when I think I'm going mad, the light suddenly reappears on the other side of the dune, as if leading me down a trail. This is getting frustrating.

I strain my one good eye and take in the light's shape, gawking with a mixture of fascination and confusion when I realize what it is I am looking at. A white-blue flame, floating a few feet off the ground on its own, like the plentiful lightning bugs back home in Jiaoshan. The hairs on the back of my neck stand on end. What magic is this? This is no lantern light.

It is a *wisp*.

An entire row of white-blue flames suddenly illuminate the way forward, their fiery tendrils flickering back and forth in the arid breeze. I follow them one step at a time, my curiosity piqued. Could they be trying to help us?

I can't be sure how far I travel, or for how long. All I know is that my muscles are fatigued and feel moments away from snapping from their joints. Thirst is the only thing on my mind. That, and this seemingly endless trail of white-blue fire. My head pounds. I heave, but there's nothing to hurl from my stomach.

We're surrounded by a sea of golden sands, constantly shifting with the winds like waves upon the ocean. It's endless. How far have we come? How much farther do we have to go? Ahead of me, behind me, and to either side of me—it all looks the same. There are no mountains. No trees. No distant waters to use as markers. We are alone in this barren prison, a great and lonely distance in every direction.

Delirium sets in.

Where are we even going? Have I not passed this stretch of sand before? Is Jyn still there on my back?

Exhaustion. I want to lie down, but I'm already waist-deep in the sand. I sink farther with every step. Before I know it, the grains are up to my chest. I focus on the remaining wisps ahead. I'm sure they will guide me to safety, if only I could escape this pit. . . . Perhaps if I try harder, move faster.

I'm up to my chin in sand now. The person I was carrying . . . Who was it, again? I can no longer sense them with me. Have they been swallowed by the sand, too? Why is it that I can no longer breathe? My nose and mouth are covered. I'm suffocating.

Movement is unthinkable. My good eye strains in the dark. Is that a woman's hand I see sticking out of the pit, grasping fearfully in search of something to hold on to? Who could it be? How curious that she should have a gray, fraying thread just like—

Jyn.

I come to my senses all too late. My fear of water has now been replaced with a fear of being buried alive. Either way, I'm drowning. Desperate for salvation, I've been tricked into taking us to our own graves. There's nothing more horrifying than the awareness of my final dying moments.

Jyn and I are sinking, sinking, sinking. And just when I think I have met my untimely end—

I land on my back at the bottom of an underground cave.

Fire screams through my bones, a terrible pressure pulsating inside my skull. I wheeze and cough, hacking up fistfuls of sand from my throat. There's no light, only darkness and cold. Panic grips me by the throat. What is this forsaken place? Have we stumbled our way into Hell?

Somewhere in the darkness, a cough.

"Jyn?" I call out, my vocal cords shredded to bits. Gods, this night couldn't get any worse.

I fumble about helplessly, doing my best to follow the sound of her voice. When that fails, I instinctively follow my thread. Jyn's presence has a glow to it, though it's fading fast. I seek it out, tripping over my own two feet until I find her, curled up on her side. I fall to my knees and pull her into my arms, grazing my fingers over her cheek.

"Jyn? Please, say something!"

"Wisps," she wheezes. "Little bastards . . . Tricksters. Their magic . . . hypnotizes their victims."

I huff, exasperated. "Yes, well, I know that *now*. How do we get out of here?"

Something in the darkness hisses.

Jyn and I freeze. I hold my breath, fearing that even the faintest of noises will alert whatever beast is lurking in the darkness. Perhaps it will ignore us and move on if we remain perfectly still.

Another wisp suddenly ignites into existence before us, illuminating the dark cave with its soft blue flames.

I grimace. Little bastards, indeed.

But what horrifies me is not that the wisp has given away our position, but the fact that I can now see the creature responsible for the hissing. I have never seen anything more hideous.

A man, except he's the furthest thing from it. He's emaciated, with leathery white skin hanging loosely from his bones. His eyes lack any trace of color, his lids pulled back so far it looks as though they might pop right out of their sockets.

His nose is missing, as are his lips. Both have been torn off his face. He twitches, clawlike fingers curled and crusted with dirt and browned blood. He gnashes his yellow teeth, chewing on something wet and *fleshy*. His meal falls from his mouth and drops to the cave floor.

A nose.

Gods, is it *his* nose?

"F-friends . . . ," he croaks. "New friends . . . here for *dinner*."

20

I *stand slowly, a cautious hand* stretched out before me as I place myself in front of Jyn. "H-hello there," I stutter. "We, uh . . . seem to have lost our way."

Jyn drags herself to her feet, then clings to my back. I can feel her trembling. "Sai, *run*."

"Run, run, run," the man echoes, his whole body jittery like a jumping spider. He stands naked, his limbs shriveled and each one of his ribs prominent enough to count. He's more skeleton than human, whatever humanity he had having died ages ago. "Run from me? That . . . makes me so sad. So long since new friends came last. So long since dinner."

There's no calming my skittering heartbeat. Reaching back, I take Jyn's hand in my own. "Please," I say, trying and failing to keep my voice level. "We really must get going."

"Four moons," he croaks. "Four moons since the wisps trapped me down here. So . . . so hungry."

My mind reels. I don't understand how he's managed to survive down here. I can only assume that these cursed wisps have something to do with it, stringing him along with their magic long enough for him to make it to his next meal. In this case—*us*.

Jyn's fear runs so cold over our connection that it almost scalds my hand, like I've dipped it into a bucket of ice water. While I can't read her thoughts, I'm still able to sense her frustration scraping along the sides of our bond. She's still in a terrible state, lucky to be standing. I can tell she wants to shift, to transform into the mightier version of herself, but the rolling sickness in her stomach blocks the free flow of her magic. She's in no condition to fight after our disastrous narrow escape from the emperor's crows.

Her safety lies solely in my hands.

We take a deliberate step back. He takes a step forward.

Something crunches underfoot. Bones.

Human bones.

"Sai," Jyn says tightly.

The man takes another threatening step forward. Saliva spills from his lipless mouth, thick globs dripping down the point of his sharp chin. "Just a bite," he says with a maniacal laugh. *"Just a bite!"*

He lunges toward us with such alarming speed that we have no time to retreat. He latches onto my arm with force, digging his sharp nails into my flesh as he bites straight through my hand. A scream rips itself from my throat as he gnaws my forefinger off at the base knuckle. The disgusting crunch of my finger between his teeth leaves me sick with nausea, too dizzy to catch myself before I stumble onto my back.

He's on top of me in an instant, slicing through the skin of my arms, my chest, my throat. He smells so putrid that it makes me gag. I kick and punch, doing whatever I can to throw the monster off. My own blood drips from his mouth, coating my face with spit and the smell of iron.

"So . . . *juicy.*"

Disgust and panic swirl within me, but there's not a second to waste. I wrap my legs around the crazed man's hips and lock him to my body, screaming over his rotting shoulder.

"Jyn, *run*! Go!"

"I'm not leaving you here!" she yells, leaning heavily against the cave wall for balance.

"There's no time to argue! Find a way out while you still can."

The monster throttles me, wrapping his long, rotten fingers around my throat. He's missing a few of his nails, one or two of the remaining ones dangling by their nail beds. He squeezes so hard that I swear I feel my windpipe collapse beneath the force. Leaning forward, he licks a stripe up my cheek. Goose bumps break out across my flesh.

"I will save you for later—oh, yes! A nice big meal. The pretty one will be a nice snack—such a nice snack!"

"Take your hands off him!" Jyn shrieks, charging from behind.

She's grabbed a long bone from off the ground—a femur, I think—one of its ends having happened to be broken off into a sharp point. She lances him through the back, piercing him straight through the chest. The sound he makes is disgustingly wet, but he's nowhere near dead. I'm the one who must finish the job.

I throw him off me, clambering on top as quickly as I can to keep him pinned beneath my weight.

A blazing heat surges forth from my core, my fear unexpectedly erupting into uncontrollable anger. My mind blanks. Nothing matters except the crack of my knuckles against his jaw, the fading light from this monster's eyes, the twitch of his fingers as I beat him past the point of submission.

I'm not myself. This unshakable frenzy can't be explained. There's no way to describe the thrum in my veins, the fire that spurs me on. It singes down to the tips of my toes, builds in an enormous pressure behind my eyes, tastes like bitter charcoal on my tongue. Something inside me is changing, but I'm so consumed by this sudden bloodlust that I don't register anything except the sound of my fists beating his head in like a drum.

Even as his red thread of fate turns black and begins to dissolve away, I don't regain control. I can't.

And it feels *good*. To be the one on top. To let out all this rage and hatred.

Shouldn't he be with the other conscripts?

Probably weaseled his way out of it.

I have seen too much of it. Death upon death upon death.

Fight or die, you coward!

I have seen too much suffering, inflicted upon myself as well as others.

This is what you deserve, maggot.

How nice it is to finally be the one to strike. If I hurt him first, then he can't hurt me. I want to lash out at the world, to tear this man limb from limb. I'm so frightened of this feeling. All I wanted was to walk away. To protect Jyn. If he had only listened—why didn't he just *listen*?

"Sai!" Jyn's voice cuts through my thoughts with crystalline clarity. "Sai, enough!" She drags me off the dead man, staring at the mess I've made in abject horror.

I slowly come back to my senses. My hands shake, my knuckles are swollen and bruised. My fingers are stained crimson, bits of his flesh beneath my nails. I, too, am revolted at what I see.

"What . . . what just happened?"

Jyn collapses to her knees and reaches out with unsteady hands. She cups my face, a look of bewilderment on her own.

"Is something the matter?" I ask.

She pauses, shakes her head. "It's nothing."

I can't catch my breath. The clawing in my lungs returns. Now that the adrenaline is fading, every inch of my body aches. Dread crawls its way down my spine.

"I . . . killed him," I mutter. "I didn't mean—" I choke on a sob that catches in my throat.

The gravity of my actions bears down on me with a vengeance. I fixate on the sticky warmth of his blood on my hands, splattered across my face. It is the bits of bone stuck to my skin that break me. Tears well in my eyes, my heart twisting within my rib cage. I must look every bit as monstrous as I feel.

"Jyn, what have I . . . He had a Fated One. His thread . . . I saw it. Someone out there was waiting for him, and I—"

"Calm down, Sai."

"But it's my fault! We could have helped him. Why didn't I stop?"

Jyn looks deep into my eyes, our faces so close that I can feel her breath whisper against my cheeks. The tip of her nose bumps mine.

"It was a mercy," she tells me firmly. "A *mercy*, do you understand? You saw the state he was in."

"No," I rasp. "It was murder; I felt his life slip away at my touch."

"Do you really think his Fated One would want to see him like that?"

"And instead not know what happened to him at all?"

Anguish is etched into her expression. "Believe me," she murmurs, casting her eyes down. "Sometimes, when it's clear they are doomed for tragedy, it's for the best."

I want to ask her what she means by this. Her every word is colored with unspeakable grief, with an experience I can't see. What in her past haunts her so? Her melancholy subsides after a moment. Slowly, Jyn wipes my tears away with the pads of her thumbs. Her touch is so gentle that I can't help but feel soothed.

"It was him or us," she says firmly. "Don't let it weigh on your heart, Sai."

We remain there a while longer, my face cupped in her hands, our foreheads pressed together as we breathe in a matched rhythm. I stop trembling eventually, regaining some semblance of myself. I feel better. Just by a hair.

"Are you hurt?" I ask, breaking the silence. My voice feels far too loud for my own ears.

"My ankle . . . ," she admits. "I must have sprained it when we fell. But never mind me, let me look at your—"

Jyn reaches gingerly for my injured hand. When we both look down to inspect the damage, we stop. My jaw drops open. My missing finger has *grown back*. The skin is pink and tender, my knuckle throbbing where the man's teeth chewed clean through. I turn my hand over and back, reeling. Now that I think about it, the vision in my ruined eye has faded back in as well. If the emaciated underground cave dweller wasn't enough to send me over the edge, this is bound to do it.

"I don't understand," I murmur. "How can this be? It's as if by—"

"Magic," she finishes for me, thoughtful and perplexed.

"Is it a lingering effect of the blood you fed me before?"

Her brows furrow into a deep frown. "No, this . . . this is something else."

"Like what?" I tilt my head to the side, studying her. She holds something conflicted in her dark gaze. Contemplative. *Secretive.* "Do you know something?"

"We must find a way out of this place before hunger reaches us," she deflects.

I glance down at the dead man beside us. It would certainly be a cruel fate to end up like him. He said he'd been trapped down here for four moons; I shudder at the bones beneath us, wondering how many other poor souls were led here only to be devoured. Were it not for Jyn, I might well have been next.

If she notices the way our thread of fate has begun to take on more and more color, she says nothing of it. I don't draw attention to it despite my lightheaded reverie, fearing that she may once again cut the process short. The thread is nowhere near fully restored, but it's transforming with every passing second. It twists and it weaves, binding itself together where once it looked seconds away from breaking apart, the center of it becoming a richer, deeper crimson hue. The ends connected to our fingers may still be gray and unraveling, but with enough time . . .

"Do you have the strength to transform and fly us out of here?" I ask.

"We don't know how deep underground we are. If we're not close to the surface and I try to break through, there's a good chance the cave will collapse and bury us alive."

I sigh heavily. "Not ideal."

We help each other to our feet. Jyn slings her arm over my shoulder while I circle mine around her waist. She leans against me heavily, shifting uncomfortably on her injured foot. Silently, we both search for a way out of this hell.

A wisp appears before us, floating ominously a few feet away. A whole line of them appear, one by one, leading down what looks to be a long, narrow tunnel. There's another narrow tunnel next to it, our path forward forking into two. The wisps want us to go right.

"This way," I say, helping Jyn turn so that we stumble left.

They won't make a fool of me twice.

21

The winding tunnels are labyrinthine. Were it not for the wisps and their simpleminded nature, Jyn and I would have ended up going in circles. Every time we come to another fork, the wisps eagerly try to tempt us down a certain path.

We never follow them.

The walls are tight and the tunnel roof is low. I have to duck down more than once to avoid hitting my head on dangling stalactites. The air is thick and stale. More than once, intrusive thoughts of the walls caving in and crushing us to death skitters like a nest of spiders through my mind. This would be such a terrible place to die. Our very own tomb. The only reason I don't give in to full-fledged hysteria is because of the soft press of Jyn's body against my own, keeping me anchored to reality.

She limps along beside me, quietly gritting her teeth as we venture farther underground, judging by the downward slope beneath our feet and the growing chill in the air. It's alarming, to be sure, when we're so desperate to make it back to the surface, but what other choice do we have? I doubt Jyn and I will be able to climb out of the sand pit we fell through. I figure that whatever made these tunnels must have also made an exit for itself.

Jyn has not uttered a single complaint, but I can feel the agony she's masking. My own ankle throbs empathetically with every step we take. It makes me wonder if she can sense my bruised throat and splitting headache.

We wander for hours, the endless maze appearing to warp and shift. The first pangs of hunger cause my stomach to clench. When was it that I last ate? How I would love a meal of rice and steamed vegetables. I think of the roasted pork A-Ba used to make for us to welcome each new year. Everyone knew that his spice blend was the best, but he'd never divulge his recipe.

I swallow dryly, shoving the thought aside. None of that, now.

Eventually, those tricky wisps bring us to a sudden drop. They resorted to following us like insistent children tugging at their mother's hands for some attention. The soft breeze I detect whispering against my cheeks gives rise to a spark of hope. Fresh air. It can only mean we're getting close to the exit.

"Let me go ahead first," I say, using the light of the wisps to get a sense of the drop. I see ground. Not a leg-breaking plummet, but still a significant fall all the same.

I take a deep breath before sliding carefully over the edge, hanging on tight before letting go entirely. It *is* a long fall, but I manage to roll and disperse my harsh downward momentum to ease the landing. I groan as I pull myself to my feet. Everything is heavy—my body, my soul, my mind.

I turn, looking up. "This way, my lady."

"Are you sure?"

I extend my hands. "Trust me."

Jyn sits upon the ledge, takes a deep breath, and then allows herself to fall.

I catch her, my hands at the dip of her waist as she circles my neck with her arms. She is by no means light and crashes into me with the full force of a . . . well, a dragon. Jyn knocks me off my feet and I land hard on my backside, but I'm more than happy to take the brunt of the fall.

It feels like heaven. *She* feels like heaven. Jyn fits comfortably in my hold, the scent of her jasmine-scented hair filling my nose. For but a moment, I lose myself in the brilliance of her eyes and the softness of her skin. My gaze flits down to her lips, lingering there far longer than it should.

Perhaps I *do* hunger.

And apparently, I'm not the only one.

Jyn stares at me with just as much intensity, the tips of her fingers lightly grazing the line of my jaw. Her lashes flutter as she studies my face, her walls momentarily crumbling. Finally, I can sense her contentment. What I wouldn't give to stay with her like this, just for a while longer. What a shame our surroundings are far from idyllic.

"Jyn." Her name is a soft murmur on my tongue.

A mistake, for this breaks the spell we're under.

Her cheeks flush, suddenly a light dusting of pink. Jyn clears her throat, her brows knitting into their usual frown. "Let me go."

I do so, releasing my arms from around her. I struggle onto my feet first and offer my hand, biting back relief—and even a little glee—when she takes it without a fuss. Between us, our thread glows a soft crimson. Still not quite mended, nor as bright as I have seen in others, but certainly a welcome change from its usual dreary shade.

I take a single step forward on what I now realize is not the cave floor, but *tile*, and the sole of my shoe clacks against its cool surface. I look about, amazed to find that we have somehow ventured into what I can only describe as a forgotten library.

The walls are high and the ceiling domed. Rows upon rows of bookshelves fill the structure, stuffed full of old bamboo scrolls and books of leather binding. We're at the very top, at least a hundred levels descending below us. I can't see the bottom. A thick layer of dust covers every available surface, and our feet leave prints on the grimy floors.

"What is this place?" I ask. My voice carries across the bottomless athenaeum, echoing back at me. It sounds like an entire army of me, whispering in mirrored fascination.

Jyn limps toward the railing carved of granite and peeks over the edge. "The Lost Library of the Albeion Monks."

I stare at her, perplexed. "The old legend? But what's it doing all the way out here?"

"The Western Wastelands were not always empty. The last time I was here . . ."

She pauses, noticing me hanging on her every word.

"Please, go on."

She takes a deep breath. "They used to be everywhere, the monks. They built monasteries all across the lands. They were dedicated scholars as well as devout practitioners, determined to share their knowledge with the world. This is said to be their largest archive. Or at least, it was, once."

"Lost to time, it seems." I run my hand over the nearest wall, wiping away dust. My palm comes away black. "But how did it end up down here?"

"You tell me. What does the legend say?"

I search my memory, thinking back to a time when A-Ma was in the kitchen, busy cooking as she treated me to a story. She always liked to talk while she worked, unable to bear long stretches of silence. It's a good thing she happened to have such a chatty son.

"Many centuries ago," I recount aloud, "the lands were ravaged by war. It swept across the Five Kingdoms, bringing with it total destruction. The Albeion monks supposedly fled across the sea for their safety, but, unwilling to let their knowledge fall into the wrong hands, they cast a spell to make their library vanish." I glance toward her. "How much of that is truth?"

Jyn gives me a weak smile. "All of it."

I wonder about all the things she must have seen in her life. All the civilizations she's witnessed rise and fall. The hundreds of battles fought between kingdoms that no longer exist on the map . . .

All the people she's loved and lost.

We start down toward the winding staircase leading to the lower floors. It's a great and arduous task to descend, for her twisted ankle makes for clumsy steps. Jyn and I manage a single flight before I turn to her and ask, "Will you allow me to carry you?"

She hesitates. "You're injured, too, Sai. I can handle myself."

"I'm feeling better," I insist, and genuinely mean it. I don't understand why, but my rapid healing has me feeling like a new man. My finger is fully regrown, my throat is no longer sore, and my muscles are mostly refreshed. Apart from my overwhelming thirst, I'm right as rain. I suspect that the blood Jyn had me drink days ago is at the root of my miraculous recovery.

She licks her lips and sighs. "Very well."

She drapes an arm over my shoulder while I brace her around her back and beneath her thighs, carrying her close across my chest. I know there will never be a moment when I'm not thrilled by our proximity. I used to dream of holding my Fated One in my arms, though I never could have predicted it would be several li underground with the threat of death hanging over us. Not exactly romantic, but alas.

We continue down the steps, making it as far as ten floors before I am thoroughly winded.

"If I'm so heavy, just put me down," Jyn says with a huff.

I shake my head. I want to hold her forever. "You're as light as a feather, sunshine. That's not the problem. How many floors have we to go?"

"The legends say that the Lost Library of the Albeion Monks boasted a thousand levels filled with a millennia's worth of knowledge. If I had to guess, nine hundred and ninety remain."

I groan. "For the love of the nine suns—"

"Let's stop here for the night," she says. "We could both use the rest, and my ankle should be healed by morning."

I arch a curious brow. "So quickly?"

"I heal faster than most."

"Because of your magic?"

Jyn nods. "Set me down. We can sleep a few hours and continue our trek."

As luck would have it, there's a seating area in the very center of the library floor, complete with a few low tables, cushions—now rock-hard with centuries of dust buildup—and a few wooden chairs. I help Jyn take a seat before making my way through the bookshelves.

Wisps float around me, still very much attempting to lead me astray. I ignore them, figuring that we can at least use them for a bit of illumination. I peruse the stacks, intrigued by what I discover. Forgotten histories of kingdoms long since vanquished. Detailed accounts of scientific experiments in the fields of medicine, astronomy, and agriculture. There's a treasure trove of stories, too, myths and legends from times gone by and lands well beyond our own.

"Perhaps we can use those over there for blankets?" Jyn suggests, pointing toward the far wall. It's covered with several large, intricately woven tapestries.

I make my way over. They're beautifully crafted, the colored threads woven to form stories with their shapes. Some of the threads are dyed in colors I have never seen before, the methods behind their creation likely lost to time. I run my hand over the surface, brushing away a thinner layer of dust, intrigued to find the image of ten suns and an archer pointing his arrow toward them in the sky.

"The legend of Houyi," I tell Jyn over my shoulder. "They say there were once ten suns in the sky. It was too hot for humanity to bear. Crops shriveled and died, the rivers and oceans dried. So Houyi expertly shot nine out of the sky and was forever hailed a hero. The Gods rewarded him with an elixir of immortality, but his wife . . . Well, we all know how that one goes."

"Yes, I know," Jyn mumbles quietly. "Poor woman."

I pull the tapestry down, gathering the heavy fabric in my arms, before I move on to the next one. I'm fascinated by all the glorious, painstaking details. It's clearly the work of a master weaver. "And this one . . ." I say, looking over the thread-woven story. "It's the legend of the nine-tailed fox. This was another one of my father's favorites."

"Why would that be?" Jyn asks.

"He liked the moral of the tale, I think. That even the most un-expected of us can be heroes." I smile at her. "Have you ever seen a nine-tailed fox?"

Jyn takes a moment to think. "Once. Nearly five thousand years ago, but we gave each other a wide berth."

"Why?"

"Out of respect. Kings may clash over territory, but queens know better. Besides, I remember her having her family close by. Her Fated One and a handful of humans under her care. I didn't feel like intruding, so I kept on my way."

The third tapestry is far more abstract than the others, the pat-terns simplistic and difficult to decipher. I gently dust it off as well and stare at the images long and hard, doing my best to discern the story it is trying to convey. There are delicate flowers woven into the border, billowing clouds of blue and white at the very top, and what appears to be the figure of a man in the middle, staring longingly not at the skies above, but at the vibrant world below.

"One of the Albeion monks' most famous teachings," I realize. "It's said that at the Steps of Heaven, the soul is given a choice. They may either ascend as they are or choose to return to the mortal realm—reborn—in the hopes of reaching greater achievements for a higher seat in Heaven."

The final tapestry on the wall intrigues me most. Stitched into the fabric in winding patterns are three dragons; one red, one green, and one blue. For some reason, it calls to me, tugging at something deep within my soul. My gaze lingers on the little blue dragon, a terrible familiarity stewing in the pit of my stomach. The little prince from my dreams . . .

An inexplicable grief consumes me.

Who is he? Why does he haunt me so?

Behind me, I hear Jyn shifting. "Sai. Come and rest." There's an edge to her tone.

I'm too entranced by the arras to heed her. My attention turns next to the green dragon, her form looping and winding throughout the entire piece. The more I study the tapestry, the more I begin to realize that it's *her* story. At the very top, she is linked to her Fated One with a bright red thread.

"*Sai.*"

When I get to the scenes in the middle of the tapestry, I notice that the blue dragon is nowhere to be found. Gone. Erased from the story. The red dragon lies in a broken heap, speared through with dozens of arrows. Thereafter, the green dragon is in isolation, her red thread nothing more than a black loop around her claw. The colors here are darker, foreboding. She remains there, weathering the seasons and the passage of time alone.

Until, at the very bottom, a new red thread is attached to her claw and sweeps off to the side of the tapestry. The story is not yet concluded, the bottom threads not yet tied off. It appears that the master weaver never got around to finishing his project.

Jyn hobbles over to join me, and she gazes up at the tapestry for all of two seconds before reaching up and ripping it off the wall. She grips it tight in one hand, running her fingertips over the blue dragon's design. Her eyes become glassy with the threat of tears, but none fall, instead balancing on angry red rims.

Our connection screams in agony and sorrow, filling my nose with the scent of ash and coating my tongue with bile. My skin is suddenly alight, a searing heat shredding its way through me.

"Jyn . . ."

She lets go. The fabric pools onto the cold floor, a plume of thick dust billowing into the air.

"I said *rest*," she commands, turning away.

I glance down at the forgotten tapestry, my thoughts a quiet storm as I attempt to puzzle together what it means. I hate to see Jyn upset, and it's only made worse now that our connection reinforces my empathy.

She doesn't speak another word to me the rest of the night.

22

I'm *starving by the time* I wake the next morning. At least, I *assume* it's the next morning. Without sunlight, it's impossible to keep track of time. Jyn is already up and about, her ankle and minor cuts miraculously healed. I, too, feel born anew. Wordlessly, we start down the never-ending stairs.

It's difficult for me not to lament all the scrolls and books that pass us by. What untold stories remain hidden here? They call to me, and yet my cramping stomach calls louder still. If Jyn and I don't escape this place quickly, I fear starvation may well be on the horizon. That, or cannibalism—though my preference is obviously the former.

Jyn takes the lead, remaining two paces ahead of me at all times. I would not describe her mood as foul, merely distant. Her defenses are impenetrable, a stone-cold wall. All my attempts to reach out over our connection are met with a stifling silence. Have I angered her in some way?

I'm about to ask when she stops abruptly.

"Do you hear that?" she asks, straining her neck to listen. "It sounds like—"

"—water," I finish for her. The undeniable rush and hiss fills my ears. It's close. "An underground river, perhaps?"

"Which means there might be a way out," she says. "Come."

We have only a few more flights of stairs to climb down. By the time we reach the ground floor, my knees are wobbling. When I look up, I can barely make out the top level of the library, the upper floors almost completely consumed by darkness.

The main entryway to the library has collapsed in on itself, the wooden beams having rotted away centuries ago. Coarse sand covers the lobby floor, and shredded remnants of old talismans are scattered about the waste. I pick one up and study the red markings on the thin strips of yellow parchment. Now that I look around, I see that the whole bottom floor is covered in them.

"This was how the monks harnessed enough magic to sink the place," I say. "They must have been quite desperate to turn to shamanistic practices."

She reaches out and takes the talisman from me, her expression hard. "They were." Her tongue flicks out from the corner of her mouth before running along her bottom lip. "I smell fresh water. Moving fast." She pushes on without me, squeezing past two large boulders blocking the exit.

"I don't think I can fit through there."

She sighs, her eyes flicking between me and the gap. I'm nowhere near as slender as she is, but I've come too far to be trapped for good. She crooks a finger, beckoning me over.

"Come on," she says, and pushes one of the heavy rocks out of the way easily with one hand. I marvel at her inhuman strength. The tips of my ears heat up. I'm only slightly ashamed to admit that this arouses me. Anyone who doesn't admire a strong woman is, in my humble opinion, a fool.

"Hurry up!" she snaps.

"Oh, right."

I slip on through, joining Jyn on the other side. She carefully replaces the boulder in its original position, mindful not to disturb the rest of the structure. We now find ourselves in a large, open cavern, a tranquil underground pool before our feet. The water glows, bioluminescent. It flows so clearly that I can see straight through to the bottom. Unfortunately, there doesn't appear to be an exit. Another dead end.

"Should we try elsewhere?" I ask.

Jyn shakes her head, holding up the scrap of talisman she took from me earlier. She walks to the water's edge and sets the paper down on the surface of the pool, giving it a light push so that it floats to the center. I watch quietly as the paper moves, carried by an invisible current. It goes in circles until it's finally dragged under and pulled through a crevasse in the cavern wall.

"That's our way out," Jyn explains, already slipping into the water.

"W-wait!"

She sighs, now thigh-deep. The glow of the water makes her look otherworldly, caught between twilight and this mortal plane. "What now?"

I exhale shakily. "I don't know how to swim."

"Another of your jests? Now isn't the time, Sai."

"I'm serious, my lady. I . . . I'm terribly afraid of the water."

"Why?"

My cheeks heat with embarrassment. "When I was a little, I was playing too close to the river. I couldn't have been more than five. My mother had warned me to be more careful, but I didn't listen. I slipped in. Nearly drowned. Ever since, I've tried my best to avoid deep water."

Jyn doesn't laugh at my inability to swim, nor does she grow frustrated and angry. Instead, her expression is marred with something that almost looks like . . . *guilt*, though that makes no sense—I must be misreading things. After a moment, she simply nods and holds out her hand to me. The gray thread of fate between us goes taut, its middle gleaming with far more intensity than I've ever seen before.

"I understand," she whispers. "But this is the only way out, Sai."

"We have no way of knowing how long this underground river is. What if we don't find air in time? What if the river only runs deeper underground?" My heart thuds frantically at the thought, my lungs preemptively beginning to burn. I would absolutely prefer to die of starvation than suffer a watery death. My palms are clammy, my skin covered in goose bumps. "Please, Jyn, is there no other way?"

"There isn't," she says firmly, but not unkindly. "Do you trust me?" she asks.

I swallow. *Do* I trust her? Though she may be my Fated One, she has done nothing but keep secrets from me. Jyn refuses to let me in, has told me so little of her past. Every time I attempt to bridge the gap between us, she pushes me away. The little progress I have made to get to know her hardly seems like progress at all.

My stomach churns. I know she's right. This may be our best chance of escaping this forsaken place. I can't count the number of times death has nearly claimed me this past week. At this point, I see no harm in tempting him again. Slowly, I reach out and take Jyn's hand.

The water is distressingly cold, though that makes sense. The water runs deep underground, where the sun cannot bless it with warmth. Nevertheless, the sudden drop in temperature makes me shiver.

"Hold on to me," Jyn says, placing my hands on her shoulders. "And whatever happens, do *not* let go. Do you understand?"

I nod before I have the chance to fully process her words. Within a matter of seconds, Jyn begins to shift. She's no longer a

woman, but my serpentine dragon, her long, winding body stretching out beneath me. I grasp onto her soft mane, careful not to pull
too hard. She twists her long neck to look back at me, her elegant
features a sight to behold. I love that the shade of her eyes is the
same as that of her scales; the strength in her graceful movements;
the power radiating off her from fangs to tail. Our gaze connects,
and I can almost read her thoughts.

Prepare yourself. You can do this.

I take a deep breath, then another. I hold my third deep inhale,
my chest full to bursting with as much air as I can carry.

We dive below the water's surface.

She moves quickly, faster and more lithely than in her human
form. Her magic buzzes over our bond, setting off an almost electric crackle across my skin. I hold on for dear life as she slams her
body through the crevasse and breaks into the strong current of
the underground river. It hits us unrepentantly, the sudden force
of water sweeping past my body and nearly causing me to lose my
grip.

It's not a straight path, but a river with sharp bends and sudden
dips. As fast as she may be, she struggles to keep us steady. The waters are rough and unforgiving, hurling us into the cave walls and
dragging us along without remorse.

My lungs are searing hot.

I'm running out of air.

But I keep holding on, because this is the moment I realize I
do trust Jyn. She will see us out of this. I cling tightly to this hope.

And then I see it. A distant light.

Jyn flicks her tail, surges forward with twice the effort.

We're almost there now. We have almost made it—

The mouth of the river spits us out roughly, throwing us into a
marshy oasis overgrown with weeds and teeming with biting bugs.
I land on my side in the mud, hacking up mouthfuls of water as I

draw in a fierce breath. The afternoon sun beats down on me. I didn't think I would be so happy to once again know its unforgiving rays.

Jyn transforms back into a human and crawls up the riverbank. She breathes heavily and rushes over to check on me. "Are you all right?" she pants.

"Yes. Are you?"

Much to my relief, she nods. Without thinking, I wrap my arms around her in a tight hug. There's a newfound ease here, the harshest of our recent challenges now over. It's a miracle that we're still alive, one I will not take for granted. I breathe her in. A jolt of excitement lances through me when I feel her, slowly but surely, embrace me back.

"Jyn . . ."

I stare deep into her eyes. This time, she doesn't move away, as she normally would. Instead, she closes the gap between us and tenderly presses her lips to mine. It's chaste and sweet, and in that moment, the rest of the world seems to disappear. It's only once she pulls away that I see her face and note her bashful expression. Something tells me that this is the first kiss she's had in centuries, maybe even millennia.

"Sorry," she murmurs, a blush washing over her cheeks as she casts her eyes away. "I shouldn't—"

"Jyn."

"What?"

I lean in and kiss her again, thirsting for the sweetness of her lips and intoxicated by the soft moan that escapes her. I cup her cheeks in my palms as she grips my tunic tightly.

This feels so *right*. How have I managed to survive this long without her? Up until this moment, I'm not sure it can be said that I've ever truly lived. Every single one of my unanswered questions and doubts is erased with her kiss.

Why can I not shake this feeling that we have kissed countless times before?

Something is unlocked in the back of my mind as we embrace again, wrapped up in each other's need with a growing intensity. Jagged pieces come together, memories that aren't my own.

Sharp teeth and red scales that flare up in moments of anger. Three dragons. The story on the tapestry. Our red thread of fate. This inexplicable feeling of having known Jyn forever and always.

"Jyn?" I murmur, my forehead against hers.

"Yes?"

I pause. "In the old tale, there are three dragons: a red dragon, king of the skies; a green dragon, queen of the bamboo forests; and a blue dragon, prince of the sparkling seas."

Jyn starts to pull away. "I told you, I don't like this story."

"You are the green dragon of legend," I say slowly, watching her face for the barest hint of a reaction. My arms have gone slack around her waist. "And the blue dragon I keep seeing in my visions . . . He was your son?"

Her jaw grows stiff. "You've been having visions?"

I suck in a sharp breath. I might well be wrong, but if I'm correct . . .

Does she know who I am?

"The red dragon," I whisper. "Are he and I one and the same?"

A darkness crosses her features, her eyes wide in conflicting horror and remorse. She opens her mouth to say something, only to shut it again. Jyn tries to get up and leave, but I take her hands and press them firmly to my chest. I let her feel my heart pulse against her palm, let her into my mind without resistance.

"Please, Jyn. Tell me the truth."

"Sai, I—"

"Oh? What do we have here?" a stranger's voice cuts in.

Jyn and I both look up to find a young man and woman walking through the unkempt grass of the oasis. They're dressed in flowing white robes with charming light blue embroidery patterning around the hems. Strapped to the woman's back is a young babe, fast asleep. The man has a large basket of fresh fruit in his arms. The couple is connected by a healthy red thread.

I'll be the first to admit that it's strange to meet such friendly, *normal* people after so long away from civilization. They immediately strike me as trustworthy, not a hint of magic or anything suspicious about them. I'm especially glad to see they all have their noses and don't appear to hunger for human flesh.

"Are you lost?" the woman asks kindly.

I rise, then help Jyn to her feet. "Yes, we've been lost for quite some time. We're trying to get to the Moonstar Isles."

The man beams. "We can take you, if you'd like. We happen to live there. It's a short trip across the channel by boat, but we should arrive by early evening."

Jyn and I exchange a look. All it takes is a quick glance around to realize that we're only a few li from the seaside. We have managed to make our way across the Western Wastelands—or rather, underneath them—in one piece. Barely.

"That would be wonderful," I say with a relieved exhale.

"We've anchored our boat just over yonder," he replies. "Would either of you like something to eat? You look like you could use some food. We have plenty to spare, and even more back at the village. I'm sure the elder will be happy to feed you."

Jyn sighs. "Thank you very much."

"My name is Chyou, by the way," the woman says. "And this is my husband, Ming, and our daughter, Jia."

"Sai," I introduce myself. "And this is Jyn, my—"

"Travel companion," she says hurriedly.

I force myself to stand straighter and ignore the pang of hurt in my chest. "Right. My travel companion."

We follow Chyou and Ming toward a little wooden boat tied to a rickety old dock. The sands of the desert blend seamlessly with the sands of the beach, the divide practically indistinguishable between them.

The sea is calm, but my mind is a storm.

When we get to the Moonstar Isles, I will fight for an answer from Jyn. I must finally know the secrets she has been keeping, for my heart can't bear this much longer.

Until then, I will focus on not falling out of the boat. I've had quite enough of the water.

23

The stranger returns some years later, dressed in fine silks and a silver crown. The blue dragon is ecstatic to see his Fated One after so long apart, and greets him with a tender embrace. The prince studies the man's matured features, noting with quiet dismay the faint wrinkles at the corners of his eyes and the whispers of gray in his beard.

"They have made me their king," the stranger informs the prince, "for my good services rendered. Thousands praise my name, and it is all thanks to you."

The prince is overjoyed and in awe of his Fated One's tender heart, using his gifts for the people. The stranger asks the blue dragon to return with him. "Think of all the people we might help together!"

But his parents warn against such an idea. The red and green dragons know of the dangers that lurk in the lands out west, riddled with disease and vicious creatures and men with greedy hearts. They urge him to stay home where it is safe, where they may remain a family.

The blue dragon does not listen, however, yearning for adventure and eager to help those in need. Together, the prince and his Fated One set off.

Never to return.

Part 3

The
Doomed
Lovers

24

Large tents of pearlescent canvas are pitched in clusters, fanning out in a circle from what appears to be the village center. There are people everywhere, dressed in lightly colored linens with berry adornments in their short black hair. They appear unaccustomed to having visitors, though they don't seem unfriendly, just curious.

The Moonstar Isles is an idyllic place. Serene. Far more stunning in person than any of the tales told by the merchants back home. It's a chain of small islands, every single one connected to those adjacent by expertly crafted suspension bridges made of bamboo planks.

"That little island there," Ming says as he rows, "that's where the village is. One island over is where we raise the chickens and sheep. And the one just beside is where we do all our farming. The soil's rich and fertile for it."

"And the islands beyond that?" I ask.

"We let them grow wild," Chyou explains. "This is as much our home as it is that of the plants and animals. We only use what we need here."

Paper lanterns float on the calm waters between each island, drifting about lazily while the lightning bugs hover amid the long cattails, mimicking the twinkling stars above. Festive music fills the air, the beat of drums and the enchanting harmonies of sea shanties lifting my mood. This here is a land of plenty, untouched by the emperor's devastating war.

"Village elder!" Ming booms as we step into the village center together. "We've made some new friends!"

A man steps forward with a hearty chuckle. He's an older gentleman with a long white beard and bushy brows, his hair pulled back into a neat bun. He's dressed in far more intricate robes than the others, light blue flowers embroidered into the white planes of his silk. The heavy-looking necklace draped over his neck is made up of white jade beads, with a carved pendant swinging at the base just above his navel.

"Welcome, dear travelers," he says, his voice low and warm. "My! Yet another set of bowls to put out for dinner tonight. I can't remember the last time we had so many visitors!"

"Are we not the first?" I ask.

"A young woman from the Southern Kingdom arrived not three days ago," he explains. "She has not given us the courtesy of her name—she's rather strange—so we villagers have been referring to her as the hunt—"

"Hey, Leaf Water!" Feng shouts. She stomps over, her hair wild and lip curled in a triumphant sneer. "I *knew* I'd find ye here."

Despite the tightness of my painfully dry skin, I manage to put on a weak smile. "Oh . . . what a pleasure, Feng. I'm so glad to see you again."

"Bet yer ass yer glad to see me! I've been looking for ye everywhere."

"Were you worried about me, dear huntress?"

"Yer dumb ass was hauled off by my dragon," she says under her breath through clenched teeth. "Of course I was worried."

"But how did you know to look for me here?"

"Blasted creature set off west. Not even a dragon can last in the Wastelands. I found this oasis, ye see, but it looked abandoned. And I saw signs of some sort of struggle. Lots of blood an' all that, along with a few torn scales. I figured the dragon must've gotten hurt and kept on going west. The next best place would be the Moonstar Isles. Made a straight shot fer it on horseback. Had plenty of water t' keep us both goin' day an' night. Probably how I beat ye here."

"How very impressive," I murmur dryly.

"Who's *she*?" Feng snaps.

"Oh, uh . . ." I turn to give Jyn the most discreet of glances. My guts tie themselves up into knots. What will happen if Feng learns the truth? Can she handle such a secret?

My instincts tell me no.

Jyn cautiously grips the back of my tunic. I can feel her wariness tugging at our connection. It's for this reason that I say nothing about the matter and keep my mouth shut.

The kind village elder looks among the three of us, his bushy white brows raised in surprise. "Ah, you know each other, do you? How fortuitous to be among friends."

"Fortuitous indeed," I say dryly.

"How long do you and your wife intend to stay?"

Jyn's cheeks turn bright crimson. "We are not—"

"She's not my wife," I say around the lump in my throat.

"Ah, well, if that's the case, I will see to it that you are given two of our spare tents rather than one. Chyou, my dear, would you show our guests the way?"

Chyou carefully hands her baby girl to her husband. "It would be my pleasure."

"Stay as long as you like, dear friends," the village elder says. "We have been blessed with a bountiful harvest and another successful hunt. There's more than enough to go around. Tonight, we shall have a feast in your honor. I look forward to hearing the tales of your travels."

Jyn is quick to follow Chyou, stiff and uncomfortable. "Thank you for your kindness, sir."

Chyou guides us through the maze of tents until we reach our own on the outskirts of the village. The edge of the bamboo forest sits directly behind them. Chyou pulls one of the flaps open. The inside of the tent is surprisingly spacious, filled with soft cushions and knitted blankets.

"This one's for you, Sai," she says cheerfully. "And this one over here is for you, *jiějie*." *Big sister*. "The village feast will be soon, but there should be some fresh fruit waiting for you inside. Let us know if there's anything you need."

I bow my head. "Your hospitality is much appreciated."

Chyou giggles. "No need for such formalities. Rest. I'll retrieve you when it's time to eat."

The woman skips off, leaving me and Jyn alone together for the first time since our escape from the Lost Library. We stare at each other, the tension thick. The question I asked her by the oasis is an ax lingering over our heads, waiting to fall, though her silence has said plenty. I may not have the whole truth, the finer details missing, but its outline is undeniable.

All I need is for Jyn to confirm or deny.

She does neither.

"I'll be in my tent," she mumbles, turning away.

My forehead throbs, annoyance digging a hole into it. "You asked me to trust you," I say before she can leave. "And I do, Jyn. Whatever you have to tell me, I promise I won't take it poorly, but I *need* answers."

Jyn pauses midstride. "No good will come from telling you the truth."

"How do you know that?"

"You won't be able to handle it."

"How can you possibly know what I can and can't handle?"

"We're not having this conversation right now, Sai."

"Then when?" I snap. "*When*, Jyn? Because at the rate things are going, I may well be on my deathbed before you tell me what all this is about!"

Jyn bristles. "I'm trying to *protect* you!"

I set my jaw. I'm tired of pretending this doesn't hurt. "Why do you keep pushing me away?" I ask, my voice so thin it feels like it might break. "Have I done something to upset you?"

"Hey, Leaf Water!"

A heavy sigh escapes me. Gods have mercy on my weary soul.

Feng stomps over, her nostrils flared. "Don't think ye can get away from me that easily. I've got a bone to pick with ye."

"Can it wait until after I—" I glance to my left. Jyn has already disappeared into her tent. I wish I could say I was surprised.

Feng leans forward, jabbing a finger against my chest. "What happened after the dragon carried ye off? Where'd it go? How'd ye escape? Where'd ye last see it?"

"You know, it's the damnedest thing," I say with a forced laugh. "I can't remember what happened."

"Ye really expect me t' believe that?"

"I was half-dead when she rescued me. You'll have to forgive my poor memory."

"She?" Feng needles, raising an eyebrow.

"It," I correct myself, gritting my teeth.

"So it flew off and didn't eat ye?"

"Perhaps it wasn't hungry."

"And who's she?" Feng asks, glancing askance at Jyn's tent. "Met her during yer miraculous escape, did ye?"

"I stumbled upon her home in search of assistance, that's all."

Feng frowns. "Then how'd she end up comin' all this way with ye?"

"She wished to travel," I say, vexation coursing through my blood. "And we happened to be headed the same way. I didn't realize it was frowned upon to form a traveling party."

"But what about—"

"*Enough*," I snap. I can't help it. Feng is testing my patience, and I'm in a foul mood to begin with. I will myself to be calm. "Please, I need a moment's respite before you continue your interrogation, though there isn't much else I can tell you. The creature is *gone*, Feng. Leave it at that."

Her face falls, and it catches me by surprise. I know how badly she wanted the prestige that came with hunting the last dragon, but her reaction to a missed opportunity for glory seems stronger than it should be.

Curious, I step forward and lower my voice. "Why do you want this dragon so badly?"

She snorts, folding her arms over her chest. "Because the blasted thing killed my parents ten years ago."

Her admission floors me, her words ringing in my ears. Jyn killed Feng's parents? Then this was never just about money or renown, but *revenge*. It's no wonder she's so persistent.

"How did it happen?" I ask.

Feng's jaw tenses. "They went off huntin'. I was sick, so they left me in my grandmother's care. Couldn't have been older than six and ten. They were gone fer days, and when my father came back . . . it was with my mother in his arms. Chewed t' bits. They stumbled upon a dragon, he said. As green as emeralds. It tore 'im up good, too. He died from his injuries a week later."

"So you went after it," I say.

"And wound up bein' banished by my own village fer it," she replies with a huff. "They kept spoutin' nonsense about lettin' it go. How it wasn't worth it. How I'd displease the Gods."

I imagine Jyn in her mighty dragon form and how she must have curled in on herself to hide in the thickest parts of the jungle. She wouldn't have attacked without good reason. In the brief time I've gotten to know her, Jyn hasn't been the one to seek trouble. It comes searching for *her*.

"It could have been an accident," I say. "They might have spooked the poor creature."

Feng hits me with a hard glare. "It's too dangerous to be left alive. As long as it breathes, others could get hurt. Nearly ten years I've been on the lookout fer this thing. I'm gonna be the one t' make sure it doesn't get the chance t' harm anyone else."

I want to argue further, but the huntress grumbles something under her breath as she stomps away. Her resolve is ironclad, her willingness to listen going only so far as information that will serve her cause. I doubt I'll be able to talk sense into her, for I, too, understand the lengths one is willing to go to for a most beloved parent. I've already crossed two kingdoms and a Godsforsaken wasteland just to get back to my mother in one piece with aid for her illness, so Feng's obsession is the furthest thing from laughable to me.

I close my eyes and take a deep, refreshing lungful of the sea breeze. At long last, peace and quiet. At least I'm finally rid of the huntress—for now.

My first instinct is to check on Jyn, but just as I wish to avoid Feng, I can tell that Jyn wishes to avoid *me*. Her guard is up and will only be strengthened should I continue to press her. We are both weary from our journey, in desperate need of water, food, and sleep. I'll be sure to press for answers later, but for now, I yearn for nothing except a long nap and the sound of the ocean waves crashing upon the distant shore.

My first and only thought is to jump directly onto the nearest pile of cushions in my designated tent. Seconds later, I fall fast asleep.

25

I *awake sometime after sunset.* ***The*** inside of the tent is comfortably warm thanks to the two iron censers placed on either side of me, lumps of charcoal burning slowly within. Blinking away the sleep from my eyes, I allow myself the time to take in my surroundings.

Resting beside me on a low writing table is a set of fresh clothes and a hefty winter overcoat. I have been mostly stripped of my garments, or what little remains of them, having been torn to shreds by the crow attack. I move slowly, stretching my arms and flexing my toes. My muscles are sore, but I'm otherwise rejuvenated. Jyn is nowhere to be found, though I suspect the trace of dried blood I taste at the corner of my lip has something to do with my quick recovery. She must have snuck into my tent while I slept to tend to me.

I eventually rise and get dressed. When I step outside, I'm greeted by the distant horizon awash with crimson and gold. The village is alive with activity, the sound of distant chatter and the crackle of a large fire reaching my ears. The scents of roasting meats and lavish spices waft in on the wind's breath, and my stomach grumbles loudly for a taste of whatever meal is being shared.

Everyone's gathered around a great bonfire, the roaring flames casting dancing shadows against the canvas of nearby tents. Several large fallen logs have been set around the fire, offering plenty of space for people to gather, sit, and eat. Large bowls of sweet fruits, garlic-roasted vegetables, and steaming heaps of rice are passed around, along with gourds full of delicious rice wine and pots of fragrant tea. There's a hearty sense of community here. They are few in number, but a mighty and most generous people.

"Ah, our other guest of honor!" the village elder exclaims with a deep laugh, his arms open wide in greeting. He claps me on the shoulder, gesturing to the joyous gathering on display.

"Where's Jyn?" I ask, the first and only thought on my mind.

"She has a spot beside me. Come, dear friend. You must be famished."

That, I can't deny.

I find Jyn surrounded by a group of young girls, all of them giggling as they weave flowers into her long hair. They've brought along with them small grass-woven baskets full of delicate winter flowers, likely picked from the area surrounding the camp, boasting vibrant red, elegant white, and cheerful yellow petals. I can sense Jyn's discomfort, and yet she makes no move to shoo them away. She gives me an almost pleading look as I approach.

"Make them stop," she whispers.

I pluck a small white flower from one of the girls' baskets as I sit down and tuck it behind her ear. "Now, why would I do that?"

She gives me a withering look, and yet there is no denying the warm glint hiding just behind her eyes or the light dusting of pink that spreads across her cheeks. If only I could bask in her loveliness forever, that might give my soul some semblance of satisfaction.

And yet the more I spend time admiring her, the more I understand that her beauty is a haunted one. Every time I look upon her face, I see a double-edged sword of love and loss. I peer at her through a thousand different eyes, unable to explain how I know there's a faded freckle at the corner of her chin and a small, barely noticeable scar above her left temple. Minute details, hidden from most—but not from me.

Because I *know* her, this soul keeping me at arm's length. I can see the shape of her, the outline of our intertwined fates, just out of reach. I just wish Jyn would help me fill in the blanks.

Out of the corner of my eye, I spot Feng. She's seated on the other side of the bonfire, glowering at me as she stuffs her mouth with spiced meat. Feng's far too sharp, too inquisitive.

I try to focus on the food, eating little bits at a time. Pieces of fruit, a handful of berries, a bowl of hearty stew. It's incredibly delicious—but my stomach churns all the same. While I'm grateful for this much-needed meal, it's difficult to enjoy it with Feng studying us so carefully. She's a hawk determining the best time to strike at two skittish rabbits.

Too anxious to sit still, I stand and offer Jyn my hand. Several couples have already gotten up to dance to the beat of the drums, linking arms so that they circle the bonfire as one big group.

"Shall we?" I ask Jyn with an amused grin.

She frowns. "I don't dance."

"Because you don't know the steps, or because you don't like it?"

"Yes."

I laugh and drag her toward the line, easily slipping into place with the other dancers. Jyn tries to weasel her way out, but then the circle starts to rotate around the fire as the drums pick up speed. There's laughter, hooting and hollering. It's hard not to stumble over my own feet, but that's the point of the dance—to keep up with the rhythm or fall into a heap.

Jyn looks like she would prefer to be anywhere but here, scowling as she watches her steps. Who knew a dragon could be so shy? As the dance grows faster and faster, every pass around the bonfire more exhilarating than the last, something amazing happens.

She *smiles*.

It's unlike anything I have ever seen before: a real, wide, joyous, carefree smile that makes her eyes glimmer like the stars. The first, I hope, of a countless many. Her whole face lights up, illuminated not only by the light of the crackling fire, but by a bliss that hums over our bond like morning sunlight. The lightest of laughs rises from her chest as we both lose our balance, thrown from the dance circle onto the soft grass below.

I catch her, Jyn's body pressed against mine. We're both breathless, staring at each other in an amused haze of warmth. Her hair is a sweeping mess, her cheeks are flushed, a few flowers are on the cusp of falling from her inky locks. I don't miss the way her eyes flit down to my lips, lingering for a moment too long—not that I mind.

"See?" I say, just as fascinated by the shape of her mouth and intoxicated by her scent of jasmine. "Not so bad, right?"

"No," she admits quietly, looking over at the whirling, dancing crowd, backlit by the bonfire. "I suppose not."

I can't bring myself to look away. I don't want to. I'd gladly admire Jyn until the end of time. An intense craving floods my veins, a little voice in the back of my head begging me to kiss her again. When I place my hand on the curve of her hip, she doesn't move away. Instead, she melts into my touch, her lips slightly parted.

"Sai . . . ," she whispers.

My hand flies up to comb through her hair, her silky locks slipping through my fingers. In that single moment, everything is right with the world. I don't want it to end, but—

"Well done, well done!" the village elder says with a boisterous laugh, clapping for the two remaining dancers, Chyou and Ming. The happy couple embraces under the starlight, giddy as can be.

"And now, for the main event!" he continues, gesturing toward me and Jyn as we retake our seats. "To honor our distinguished guests and the Gods above who bless us with this abundance, please enjoy the show."

At first, I don't understand his meaning. In an evening full of food and dance, what other festivities could we possibly look forward to?

The sudden whistle and then crack of a firework overhead is answer enough. Colorful sparks fizzle into the air in a lively display of bright reds, greens, and yellows. Fireworks have been a rarity ever since the emperor's declaration of war, their ingredients better used for cannons than for spectacle.

I was quite fond of them as a boy, running excitedly through the markets as year-end celebrations took place. I stare up at the skies now, entranced by their luminance, rivaling even the moon and stars.

Beside me, Jyn jolts at the sound of the next firework. She does so each time another is lit, flinching with the noise. Skittish. On the verge of running away.

"What's the matter, my lady?" I ask her, concerned.

She shakes her head, casting her eyes down. "It's nothing," she murmurs, though she flinches again.

"We can leave, if you'd like."

"No, it would be rude."

"The noise . . . It bothers you?"

Jyn chews on the inside of her cheek, squirming uncomfortably when yet another firework—louder and bigger than the previous ones—booms in the air above. "Cannons," she mumbles, barely audible. "They remind me of the cannons he fired. . . ."

"Cannons?" I echo, frowning.

Her eyes glaze over, becoming distant. Her mind is trapped in a memory I'm not privy to. The only thing I can think to do is reach around to press my palms over her ears. I gently tilt her head up so that she can look at the colorful sparks without hearing them. The tension in her shoulders melts away, her eyes widening in awe and her mouth dropping open.

While she watches the lights, I, in turn, watch her.

Shadows dance across her face, the fleeting sparks reflected in her eyes. Her rare smile returns, this time sweeter than before. I can't explain the instinctive protectiveness stirring within me.

Cupping her face in my hands, I gently lean in. All the stress and tension I've been holding melt away when my lips find hers, a lock and its key. No words need be exchanged to understand that she is mine, and I am hers.

I will protect Jyn with every fragment of my soul, no matter what it costs me.

But I should know by now that my fortune is anything but plentiful.

Jyn breaks away and stands. "I . . . should get some sleep," she mumbles. Before I have a chance to protest, she leaves for her tent without another word.

26

It's a brisk winter morning, the air thin and the breeze light. We have spent the last two days recovering from our journey across the Western Wastelands, though I never truly settled in. I can sense Jyn's growing restlessness. I can feel her itching to leave this place.

She has kept her distance ever since our kiss came to an abrupt and awkward halt.

"Oh, dear," Chyou murmurs, cradling her baby close to her breast. "Why won't she stop crying?"

We're gathered around the small fire in front of Chyou and Ming's family tent, an iron pot of bone broth and root vegetables simmering over the low flames. Little Jia has been sobbing all morning despite her mother's best efforts. No amount of feeding, burping, changing, sleeping, or playing stops the poor child's piercing screams. At the very least, it's nice to know that she is blessed with strong lungs.

"Perhaps I can try holding her for a while?" I offer. "Please, help yourself to something to eat. I can keep watch. Just until Ming gets back from tending to the chickens."

Chyou smiles appreciatively, the dark circles beneath her eyes unmistakable. "Thank you, Sai."

I hold the baby to my chest with the utmost care. My experience with children is minimal, though I like them well enough. A-Ma always used to call them little bundles of endless potential. Who knows what great feats they may accomplish one day? What wonderful people they might become?

Chyou stands and stretches, then helps herself to a bowl of soup. "I can't help but notice that your darling is not here. Did something happen?"

"My darling?" I echo. "Oh, you mean Jyn. You have it wrong, I'm afraid. We're only—"

"Travel companions?" she teases, her eyebrows raised. Chyou sits back down beside me and takes a sip of her stew. "Please, Sai. I sincerely doubt that 'travel companions' act as passionately as we saw the two of you doing last night."

My ears burn, either from the cold or my rising embarrassment. I keep my eyes on little Jia, who has fallen quiet for a moment, perhaps to catch her breath. She squirms and wriggles in her blanket, one arm outstretched. Her little fingers flex up toward the sky as though to grab onto it, and her cries fade into discontented whimpers. Anything could set her off again.

"Things are . . . complicated," I admit.

"Do you have feelings for her?"

I take a deep breath. "Yes, but—"

"But what? Love is never that complicated, *dìdi.*" *Little brother.*

"'Love' is putting it very strongly. We only just met."

"Really? You two look as though you've known each other for ages."

"Well, it certainly feels that way."

"Do you know if she feels the same?" Chyou asks bluntly. I admire her candor. It makes it surprisingly easy to say what's on my mind.

"I can't be sure," I confess. "But regardless, I won't force her to reciprocate. That wouldn't be right of me, nor fair to Jyn. I suspect . . ." I trail off.

"What is it?" she urges.

I'm silent for a moment, chewing on the inside of my cheek as I think. "She's been through something harrowing. I don't know what, and I doubt she'll ever tell me, but I do know she carries the burden of it entirely on her own. I don't wish to trouble her with my feelings."

Chyou gives me a sympathetic look. "May I offer a word of advice?"

"Of course."

"I think you should be up-front with her. There's no time like the present."

My stomach flips. "But what if—" I sigh. "What if she doesn't feel the same way?"

"Then at least you'll know. You'll both be able to move on, though I very much doubt it will come to that."

"What makes you say that?"

Chyou grins at me. "Do you not see the way she looks at you?"

"The way she—?"

Her eyes flit up to look across the way. I follow her line of sight, curious. Past the tents and the movement of the other villagers, I spot Jyn at the base of a steep hill, surrounded by a group of young girls, the same ones from the banquet. They've taken a liking to her. They run around her in circles, giggling as they play. Jyn sits on the grass, legs tucked to her chest while her chin rests on her knees, arms wrapped around just so. As much as she feigns irritation, I can feel her contentment softly humming over our bond. Even at a distance, I can sense her quiet amusement.

Something tugs at my heart. Jyn looks surprisingly comfortable and right surrounded by these little ones. Motherly. There's an ease to her now that I haven't witnessed before, a sweetness to her small grin as they hand her bouquets of fallen leaves tied together with long blades of grass. Jyn humors them, holding on to these little trinkets protectively as the girls babble on

For just a moment, our eyes lock. Is she looking at me, or the newborn in my arms? I can't be sure. But there's a fondness in her gaze, something patient and tender. Then she realizes she's staring and looks away.

Only to shift her eyes back to me when she thinks I'm not looking.

My heart skips a beat when Jyn stands up to come this way. The little village girls chase after her, one of them going so far as to hold her hand as they traverse the frozen grounds. She trips, but Jyn expertly holds her arm up to keep the girl from falling flat.

Chyou smiles wide upon her arrival. "Ah, good timing. Would you care for some bone broth, Jyn?"

"No, thank you. Perhaps later." Jyn glances at baby Jia, who has begun to stir again. "Still upset, I see."

Chyou lets out a breathy laugh. "Unfortunately so. I fear the rest of the village will cast us out at this rate. We've been trying to get her used to solid foods, though as you can see . . ." Chyou gestures toward her red-faced daughter.

"Have you any honey and goat's milk?" Jyn inquires.

"I believe we have a little of each in the stores, yes."

"If you could please fetch both, as well as a clean towel."

Chyou tilts her head to the side, considering. "Very well. I shall return."

Jyn takes her place beside me, kneeling gracefully on the grass. She extends her hands out for the baby. "May I?"

I nod, carefully transferring Jia from my arms to hers. It is a heartwarming, natural gesture.

"How have you been?" I ask, my throat uncomfortably dry. "I've not seen much of you lately."

Jyn rocks the child slowly in her arms. "I've been . . . thinking. About your question."

My heart leaps up and lodges in my throat. It takes all my will-power to keep my voice even as I say, "Oh?"

"I've decided to tell you the truth, Sai, but . . ."

"What is it?"

"You must promise that you'll listen fully and not act rashly."

I lean a little closer, suppressing the excitement vibrating in every fiber of my being. "I swear it, Jyn."

She nods, though apprehensively. "I'll tell you when we're alone. This isn't the place."

I, for once, agree wholeheartedly. The huntress has been lurking about the village. I may not have seen her these last few days, but I know she's keeping watch somewhere—best if we don't discuss such things out in the open.

Chyou returns with the requested items, the goat's milk sloshing about inside its cup. "What should I do next?" she asks.

"Mix the honey in with the milk, then soak the rag in the mixture," Jyn instructs. She speaks with confidence and ease, as if she has done this a thousand times before. Once Chyou finishes the task, Jyn takes the cloth and brings the corner of the rag to the baby's lips.

Miracle of miracles, the child latches on at once and begins to drink, too distracted by the sweet concoction to keep up her noise. Around us, the entire village seems to breathe a collective sigh of relief.

"Oh, thank the Gods!" Chyou gasps.

"I can finally hear my thoughts again," I jest.

Jyn rolls her eyes. "This should tide her over for now, but don't give it to her regularly. It should be reserved for the most difficult of fits."

Chyou nods gratefully as she takes her daughter back. "How did you know this? Do you have children of your own?"

Jyn manages a nod, though her eyes are empty and tired. "Just one. He has . . . long since left me."

The weight of those simple words crushes my chest, and I swear I feel my heart fracture in time with hers. I can't just sit here any longer.

"Jyn and I were thinking of going for a walk," I tell Chyou. "Will you be all right by yourself?"

Chyou waves me off with a grin. "Of course. Ming should be back soon. You two have done more than enough."

I offer Jyn my hand. She takes it without question.

Together, we make our way back to our tents. There are so many questions brewing within me. I have no doubt that Jyn can feel my anticipation, because I sense a slight tug on our thread, almost as if she is trying to reel me in.

"Leaf Water!" Feng barks, marching over with a determined look in her eye. "I need to talk to ye."

Gods, give me patience.

Jyn tosses me a wary look over her shoulder. I only nod in response. She goes on ahead while I remain behind. The more distance I can put between my dragon and Feng, the better.

"Still here, I see," I say, crossing my arms over my chest. "I thought for sure you would have returned to the Southern Kingdom by now."

She reflects my stance, crossing her arms—which I daresay are far more muscular than mine—and snorts. "Ye haven't answered my questions."

"I already told you, I remember nothing."

"And why don't I believe ye?"

"Because—no offense—you have a very distrusting nature."

"It had ye in its *claws*," Feng presses on. "Why didn't it eat ye?"

I shrug. "Perhaps I smelled too ghastly."

She squints at me, scrutinizing every inch of my face. "What aren't ye telling me, Leaf Water?"

Unease bubbles right beneath my skin, my hands suddenly clammy and stiff. She's a determined one, I'll give her that, but Feng will have to work a hundred times harder to pry the truth from me. I can't and *won't* expose Jyn. Even if I tell her the truth, that me and Jyn are a fated pair, I doubt Feng can be swayed to give up her hunt.

"Ye were on the brink of death when it carried ye away," she says firmly. "An easy meal."

I grind my teeth so hard, my molars squeak against one another inside my skull. "It sounds as though you *wanted* to see me eaten, huntress."

"Not that. It's just the more plausible answer."

"It must have dropped me. I have nothing more to say on the matter."

"How'd ye survive such a fall?" Feng leans in close, her brows knitted into a deep frown. "Those soldiers beat ye to a pulp. I heard yer bones break."

I sneer, an overwhelming heat rising into my chest. "Close enough to hear, and yet you did nothing to stop them?"

"I couldn't give away my position."

"I needed your help."

"Not my fault ye ran in headfirst."

"It was the right thing to do."

"And it almost got ye killed." I've barely taken a step toward Jyn when Feng scoffs. "Hey, where do ye think yer goin'? I've still got questions, Leaf Water."

"We're done here," I growl, turning away.

"Ye slayed it, am I right? Ye killed the beast and hid it somewhere so that ye could claim fame and fortune for yerself!" She grabs me roughly by the shoulder. "If ye won't tell me, I'll ask yer woman—"

Anger flares up from my core. It's sudden and blinding. It's not in my nature to snap, and yet I can't control myself when I whip around and grab Feng by the throat. I pin her against the post of a nearby tent, snarling in her ear with a fury I have never experienced before.

"Leave us alone!" I seethe. My blood is on fire, my heart a war drum. "I've already told you, I don't know where the dragon is. Now, cease this incessant barking and return to the mountains whence you came."

Feng gawks, startled by my about-face. She gasps against my hold, clawing at my wrists. "Yer eyes," she rasps, her own wide with alarm. "They're *red*."

27

I pull back, genuinely confused and appalled by my own behavior. This isn't me. I would never harm a fly, let alone another person—crazed, flesh-eating cannibal aside. I don't understand what's happening. It's true that Feng is an annoyance, but not so much that I would think to harm her for it.

I stumble back, my hands trembling uncontrollably. I can't catch my breath. Everything is too hot, my skin too tight. The scents of the village grow overpowering, burning in the inside of my nose. When I run my tongue along my top teeth, I am alarmed to find that they are . . . *sharp*.

"Sai!"

Jyn's voice cuts through the air. She runs and throws her arms around me before I have the chance to look at her.

"What's wrong with 'im?" Feng wheezes, recovering her air.

"Sai," Jyn whispers against my ear, holding me close. With one hand in my hair, she presses my face down to the crook of her neck. "*Breathe*, Sai. Calm down, right now."

By some miracle, I do manage to draw breath, drinking in the scent of her jasmine-scented skin. Her voice is a balm over my nerves, her touch warm and soothing. It takes a few moments before I am finally able to clear the haze from my mind.

"*Jiějie?*" one of the nearby village girls says, timidly approaching us. "What's the matter with *gēge*?"

"He's not feeling well," Jyn replies quickly, ushering me back toward our tents. "Run along to your parents now."

"But—"

"*Now*, little one."

"Wait a fuckin' second—" Feng starts after us. "The fuck's the matter with 'im?"

"A fever," Jyn says, and rather convincingly at that. "Step away, lest you catch it."

"That's no fever. What's—"

"*Move,*" she says urgently against my ear.

Jyn ushers me away, but I can feel the daggers she glares in Feng's direction. We don't stop until we find ourselves in the confines of her tent, the entrance to which Jyn immediately ties shut.

"Sit," she commands.

I do no such thing, too frazzled to listen. Instead, I scramble over to the porcelain washbasin tucked away in the corner and brace my hands on either side of the bowl. I stare at my reflection, the details of my face rippling with the water, but there's no denying it. I'm aghast to find my dark brown eyes are now a near-glowing crimson.

Panic tears through me.

"What is this?" I ask. "What's happening?"

Jyn takes my hand and pulls me to her nest of pillows. She has them piled up high, creating a fort of sorts out of the soft silks and blankets. "I'm not sure," she admits. "It's never come back before."

"*What* has never come back?"

Before she answers, Jyn pauses and sniffs at the air, her tongue flicking out to the corner of her mouth. Satisfied that no one is too close by, she whispers, "Your magic."

My mind swirls. The revelation comes as both a shock, and not a shock at all. I think back to our encounter with Emperor Róng's crows out in the Western Wastelands. I remember not being entirely myself, overpowered by a feral instinct to devour and protect. I think long and hard about the encounter with our unfortunate friend underground—how I lost control, consumed by rage and bloodlust. Is this the magic Jyn is referring to, or perhaps side effects of it?

I think back even further, drawing upon a memory that feels more like a dream. I was a boy, playing by the water despite my mother's warnings. One moment, I was safely on the riverbank. The next, my head was beneath the water's surface. Did I slip in? I can't remember precisely how it happened.

I shake my head, clearing my thoughts. "You're not making sense. I'm not capable of magic. I can see threads, but that's it."

"That's the Sight. In every life that you have returned, that is the only power you have ever retained. But your ability to transform . . . I thought you'd long since lost it."

"Transform," I echo. "You mean . . . into a *dragon*?" I stare at her in disbelief for several seconds before remembering how to speak again. "So I *am* the red dragon of old, and those visions were no coincidence. But how—how is this possible?"

Jyn looks me firmly in the eye. "The third tapestry in the Lost Library. What story did it tell?"

"The monks' tale of reincarnation," I say, my face surely betraying my bewilderment. "But that . . . It's impossible."

"It's fact, Sai. The legends are true. You can see red threads of fate, you've come face-to-face with a fei beast, your Fated One is the last dragon in all the lands, yet you believe the concept of rebirth is impossible?"

"Forgive me, mooncake," I mumble weakly. My attempt at a joke to ease my own trepidation falls flat. "This isn't exactly easy for me to process."

Jyn sighs. "Please never call me that again." She throws a cautious glance over her shoulder, no doubt keeping an eye out for Feng-shaped silhouettes keen on eavesdropping on our conversation. The last thing we want is for Feng to overhear this conversation. When she looks back at me, I can sense that something has changed—a part of her wall has crumbled away.

"These visions I keep having," I say. "They're my own memories from a previous life?"

"One of many, yes."

I frown. "You mean to say this isn't the first time I've been reborn? Should I guess how many?"

"No."

"Is it my third time?"

"Sai—"

"My tenth?"

Jyn mutters impatiently, "Not your tenth."

"Well, then? How many lives have I lived through? I can keep guessing, should it please you."

The silence that follows is deafening. A sob bubbles past her lips, her pain overwhelming our bond. She begins to cry in earnest, her shoulders trembling as she struggles to swallow the sound.

I reach out gingerly, afraid she might crumble beneath my touch. I want to bring her comfort, do whatever it takes to soothe her mind. But when she allows me to caress her cheek, to comb my fingers through her long hair, I can't help but wonder . . .

"Why is it gray?" I ask.

Jyn cries a little harder, her body shaking against mine. "I made a mistake."

"What do you mean?"

"It was a mistake. A *mistake*. You have to understand, I—"

She breaks down completely into tears, no longer able to speak.

I wrap Jyn up in my arms, allowing her to press her face against the crook of my neck. "It's okay, Jyn. Thank you for telling me." It's more than enough for now—I had almost forgotten this is just as difficult for her to navigate.

We remain there for a while longer, with only the sounds of the distant sea waves, the sounds of the villagers going about their usual business, Jyn's quiet sniffles, and the rapid beat of my heart. An eventual calm blankets us, insulating us both from the world and its madness. I have my Fated One and she has me, and in this moment, that's all we need. We hold each other tight—maybe too tight, as though a force threatens to tear us apart without notice.

I breathe her in while I allow her words to sink in.

Dragons. Reincarnation. Our fated souls, finding each other once again.

It's overwhelming, to say the least.

Overwhelming and utterly miraculous.

I expected to run the family teahouse my whole life, perhaps match a few interesting couples in town, but now I'm farther than I have ever been from home, learning I am part of a legacy that may have shaped all of humanity.

I am the red dragon of old, the one from all the stories of my childhood. I was once king of the skies! What other memories of mine are locked away? Why is it that I can only recall fragments, and so few? My mind reels, the sheer magnitude of it leaving my body numb. It would be easy to panic in this moment, to deny everything outright. But I know deep within that Jyn has spoken the truth.

Besides, I promised not to take it poorly.

Every answer has begotten so many more questions. But with time, I'm sure all of them will be addressed.

Eventually, Jyn's soft sobs taper off. She wipes at her eyes before turning her attention to me. "How are you feeling? Don't let the huntress get under your skin."

"You're right," I admit, my hands still trembling lightly from the shock of how I behaved. "It was an ugly feeling, Jyn. Terrifying. I couldn't stop myself. What if . . . what if I transformed right there and then? I could've killed Feng. Gods, I could've hurt the children."

Jyn cups my face and holds my gaze, her emerald-green eyes both tender and determined. "Calm yourself, Sai. Nothing will happen, as long as you maintain control. Deep breaths, my lo—" She stops herself, but leans forward to tap her forehead to mine. "Deep breaths. All is well."

"The huntress," I murmur. "She saw my eyes."

"I told her you were ill."

"There's no way she'll believe that."

"She'll have to."

"Or what?"

"I'll eat her alive," she says, deadpan.

I give her a pointed look. "Do you find that funny?"

She shrugs. "Just trying to lighten the mood."

At the very least, I can appreciate her attempt, given how little Jyn jests. She holds me until my breaths come easier, my heart returning to a steady cadence. Her cool fingers graze my cheek, the tip of her nose bumps lightly against mine. My soul finds ease in the tickle of her breath against my lips and the heat of her skin.

"There we go," she whispers, looking into my eyes to inspect them. "Back to normal."

"Thank you," I whisper back.

"We have to be more careful from here on out."

"You mean I need to temper my temper?"

Jyn huffs in a pretend pout. "Yes, as best you can."

"Then you'd best stay near, my lady."

"I'll stay with you," she promises.

"Feng has been nothing but suspicious since our arrival."

"Then we'll do what we must to avoid her."

"That won't work forever."

"We could tie her up," Jyn suggests. "Bind and gag her? Allow the villagers to find her a few days from now, when we're already gone."

I grimace, not knowing if she's serious. I couldn't bring myself to do that, even to Feng—she's a friend, albeit one with horribly misguided intentions. "I doubt she'll make her move while there are so many witnesses present. But she's keen on slaying you herself."

"But why? I've never wronged her."

I take a deep breath. "She claims you killed her parents."

Jyn stiffens. "I did *what*?"

"Ten years ago," I explain. "She said her parents were hunting. They apparently crossed your path, and . . . well."

Her eyes grow distant as she loses herself in thought. "Ten years, you say?"

"Do you remember something?"

She nods slowly. "Yes. Distinctly, in fact."

"What happened?"

She frowns as she searches her mind for the exact details. "A pair of hunters stumbled across my home in the jungle. It's why I moved out to the Wastelands after. To avoid any more run-ins with humans. There was a pack of fei attacking them. It tore them to bits. I tried to scare the beasts away, but they must have mistaken my own actions as hostile or even thought I was in league with the fei somehow. I didn't harm anyone. I swear it."

I hear the truth in her voice, nothing but honesty in her words. Jyn may be prickly at times, but she certainly doesn't strike me as a senseless killer. Time and time again, she's come to my rescue. And she is certainly no friend to the fei.

"We should tell her," I reason. "Feng should know what really happened."

"But is she levelheaded enough to listen?" Jyn sighs, her exhaustion heavy over our bond. "Mortal hearts are so unpredictable."

I reach out and wrap Jyn in my arms. "For now, will you just ... lie with me?"

She nods with the sweetest of smiles. "As you wish."

A delightful warmth floods my body, a thrill jolting through my veins. In this life, I've known her only a couple of weeks, yet a love from past lifetimes surges forth.

It's enthralling. Pure bliss.

I comb my fingers through her hair, my lips only a whisper away from hers. Her cheeks are flushed, her pupils blown wide within sparkling green. She clings to me as if I'm a lifeline in stormy seas.

"Sai," she whispers, the expression on her face almost resembling agony. *"Please."*

I lean in and kiss my Fated One like my life depends on it.

In some ways, I feel as though it does.

28

have never known a craving like this before.

Every single one of my senses is attuned to Jyn.

They overwhelm me: the smell of her hair, the impossible soft-ness of her ivory skin, the taste of her lips, the sound of her languid moans, the sight of my want reflected in her own glowing gaze.

I slowly peel away the layers of her robes, memorizing every dip and curve. As I undress her, I can't help but wonder in how many of my past lives I have had the privilege of knowing this feeling. Being able to admire her for the first time, possibly the first of many—I'm convinced there is no better blessing.

She kisses with a hunger that I match, savoring the taste of her. Jyn is far rougher than I am when it comes to disrobing, practically tearing away my clothes. I have no complaints, reveling in her ea-gerness. I lay her down on her jumble of pillows, lifting away the last of her silks—

And pause.

Her body is covered in scars. The majority of them are an angry red, deep and jagged across her tender flesh. Her arms, her chest, her ribs, her belly, her thighs—marred by unspeakable violence. I can't recall seeing such terrible marks on her when she was a dragon, though I suppose I was too mesmerized by her to have noticed. Now, I can't look away.

Especially the jagged scars upon her wrists. Row upon row upon row of puckered flesh, usually hidden beneath the cover of her long sleeves.

I carefully trace the tips of my fingers over the scars, struggling to keep my sorrow off my face. "Who did this to you?"

Jyn tries to squirm away, but I hold on to her tighter. Her cheeks flush as she casts her eyes down in shame to avoid mine. She doesn't answer me for a long while. And when she does, it's barely a whisper, the sound of her voice almost lost to the soft winds just outside our tent.

"I did."

My stomach churns. "What?"

Her eyes won't meet mine. "Don't think less of me, Sai."

"I would never. I only want to understand why."

"It was . . . lonely, these seven thousand years." Her emerald eyes go dark and distant as her lower lip trembles. "There were times where I thought perhaps it might be . . . easier. To end it. To finally be at peace."

Her confession stops me from breathing. I'm heartbroken, horrified that she almost erased her light from this world, yet grateful it never came to pass. With all those years spent alone, how could I blame her?

"Yet you remain," I say.

"Because I'm a coward. I was too afraid to reincarnate."

"Why?"

"I was scared of forgetting you," she confesses. "You know what it's like, seeing bits and pieces, but never understanding the whole. If I forgot who you were to me, there'd be a chance I would never find you again. I couldn't bear the thought."

I take both her hands, lacing her fingers gingerly between mine. "You're no coward. You are the bravest soul I have ever met. I can't imagine the things you've endured."

My jaw tightens as I notice a different scar, tracing its shape. This one runs deeper than the rest, cutting all the way across the width of her torso. "Were all of these really by your own hand?"

"Not all. Some were his doing. I narrowly escaped before deciding to go into hiding for good centuries ago."

Jyn wraps her arms around my neck as our bodies press together. Her bare skin against mine is heaven incarnate, fulfilling a need I didn't realize I had. "Please," she rasps. "Whatever happens, Sai, stay away from Róng. That man is—" Her voice breaks, a sob rising instead. "I can't lose you again."

"I promise you, that won't happen."

"But Sai . . . it *will*."

I frown. "What do you mean?"

"You'll grow old again," she says. "I'll only be able to watch you grow old and gray. You'll pass on, and I'll be alone again."

I breathe her in, holding her with more care than I would the finest silks of all the lands. I don't know what to say—if there's anything *to* say. I wouldn't want to watch my Fated One fade and leave me again, either.

Her tears betray her, streaking down her cheeks as I kiss her. "Sai—"

"This time will be different," I say slowly, softly stroking her thighs.

"How can you possibly know that?"

I hold her gaze, steadfast. It would be foolish of me to make grand, sweeping promises after everything Jyn has been through. I can't wipe away the misery of seven thousand lonely years, but I have never been one to give up hope. There's no telling what the future has in store for us, but I am as determined as I'll ever be to keep Jyn safe. I may not be able to move Heaven and Earth, but that won't stop me from trying where my Fated One is concerned.

In the same way I can sense her over our thread, I allow her to feel my conviction. I don't need words, I realize, when she can know my entire mind. How do I know that this time will be different? Because we are here together against all odds. Fate has helped us find one another. In this lifetime, maybe we stand a fighting chance.

Jyn relaxes beneath me, her nerves soothed. She brushes her fingers across my cheek with a placated sigh. She knows, just as I know: I will never leave her again.

"May I, my heart?"

Jyn murmurs against my lips, "Yes."

We move as one, our bodies intertwined in sweet bliss. Her pleasure sings over our bond with every soft caress and roll of our hips. Each desperate kiss is amplified tenfold by our connection. We fit perfectly, made for each other in every way. Two halves of one fated whole.

The heat that has been pooling in the pit of my stomach grows—a tight coil, hotter and brighter with every touch. Jyn's contented sighs soak into the tent's canvas, the sound of her moans for my ears alone. She drags her fingers down my back, her hips bucking eagerly against mine.

"You don't need to be so gentle," she says with a light laugh as I wipe the tears at the edges of her eyes. The sound is so innocent and giddy that my heart almost stops. Gods, what I wouldn't give to make her laugh like this every day.

"I don't want to hurt you, my lady."

"You could never hurt me this way," she murmurs against the corner of my mouth. "Not in this life, the ones before, or the ones to come."

I pause. "Jyn . . ."

My eyes fall to our thread of fate. Its middle is a stunning crimson, but it remains gray and frayed near the ends where it wraps around our fingers. Our bond has repaired itself almost completely, and yet it remains incomplete.

It was a mistake.

What did she mean by that? What other secrets has she kept to herself, and more importantly, why?

"I've waited so long for you to come back, to return to your true self," she whispers against my ear, her fingers tightly grasping the roots of my hair. My attention snaps back to the present and I forget my concerns in an instant. "Take me, Your Majesty."

Our lips crash together in a frenzy, our movements transforming from sweet and gentle to rough and wild. I've never felt this sudden hunger before, this animal instinct to devour and claim. Perhaps it's the result of many missed lifetimes. I decide not to question it, instead seeking out her pleasure with every wanton thrust.

She's divinity incarnate, her beauty unmatched. Together we are union and sweat and ecstasy. When we finally find the edges of our sanity again, we fall together, still locked in a tight embrace. We kiss lazily through the warm haze, breathing as one, staring deeply into each other's eyes.

Quiet finds us, though it's not an uncomfortable silence. There's peace to be found when all there is to listen to is our own beating hearts, the distant whistle of the breeze, and the quiet calls of songbirds outside. Even the activity around the village is nothing but a dull, soothing murmur.

I wrap her up in the softest collection of blankets, brushing my fingers through her hair. I admire the warm color of her cheeks and the way her eyes flutter closed. I dare not disturb her when she falls asleep in my arms, more than happy to take in the subtle rise and fall of her chest.

I don't find rest as easily as she does, so after I'm sure Jyn is fast asleep, I carefully slip away and get dressed. Perhaps I can venture to the village center and barter for something to eat. I'm sure she'll be famished by the time she wakes.

I take my time, enjoying the opportunity to stretch my legs. It seems that we've spent the better part of midday in our tent. People are out and about this afternoon, gathering firewood from the bamboo forest and fresh water from the nearby stream. Everyone has a part to play here, the women and men taking up work in equal measure. As I pass through, I notice that it's not at all uncommon to find village men tending to their children as women sharpen their tools.

"Sai, my friend, might I have a word?"

I look up to find the village elder quickly approaching. "Of course. Good day to you, sir."

"I wish it were," he says, worry weighing down his wrinkled features.

"Is something the matter?"

"Have you seen Mei? She's roughly this tall," he asks, gesturing to just above his knee. "She's one of our youngest. I believe your lady was playing with her and a group of other girls earlier today. She's gone missing, you see, and it will soon be nightfall."

I frown. That's concerning indeed. "I haven't seen her, but I can ask Jyn."

"Ask me what?"

I turn to find Jyn walking toward me, rubbing her weary eyes with the backs of her hands. She's fully dressed, though her hair is an endearing mess.

"What are you doing up, my sunshine?"

"You weren't there when I woke up," she mumbles, quiet enough for only me to hear. She combs her fingers through her locks and smooths out her robes. "I was worried."

"I left to find you something to eat."

Jyn gives me a small, almost bashful smile. "How thoughtful." She turns to the village elder. "What were you saying earlier?"

"A child has gone missing," the village elder explains. "Mei. We must find her before dark. A few of us are gathering to search the forest."

I lean in to whisper in her ear. "Do you think you can track her scent?"

Jyn nods. "We'll find her."

The village elder sighs in partial relief. "Thank you both. Quickly, we must make haste. The surrounding forests are relatively safe, but Mei is far too small to be out alone."

"Then I'd better join you," Feng interjects, stepping forward. Her bow and a quiver of arrows are already thrown over her shoulder.

The muscles in my neck and back strain, and my nostrils flare out of reflex alone. How long was she standing there? Why will this huntress not leave us be?

"Let's go, Leaf Water," she says, taking the lead. "Try not t' get yerself eaten."

My first instinct is to suggest that she stay behind. I'm not pleased by the thought of having her so close to Jyn, but then I think better of it. The huntress is a far better tracker than most. If anyone can find the missing child, it's her.

Beside me, Jyn presses her hand to the middle of my shoulder blades. My muscles release at her touch. I didn't realize how tense I'd become.

"Come along," Jyn says. "The sooner we find the girl, the better."

I take a deep breath, more than a little aware of how the huntress eyes the two of us suspiciously over her shoulder. Her demeanor is cold and untrusting, her unusually alert posture betraying her paranoia. We will have to be exceedingly cautious around her; there's no telling what she'll do once she gets us alone in the forest.

Reaching down, I take Jyn's hand and give her fingers a light squeeze.

Stay close to me, my heart.

29

Bamboo forests *are few and* far between where I'm from, cleared out centuries ago to make room for sprawling rice paddies and fields of wheat. The bamboo here is excessively dense, sprouting up out of the cold ground every few feet. It's difficult to navigate through, which I'll admit does not aid our search. Thankfully, we have Jyn's keen sense of smell working to our advantage.

She's discreet, flicking her tongue out to taste the air only every few minutes. She sniffs silently, too, facing away from the huntress when she does so.

"This way," Jyn says, tugging me . . . north? I dare not let go of her hand, afraid that the search party will have to look for not one, but two lost souls.

The huntress follows. Our own personal specter.

It's unnerving. She hasn't spoken a word since stepping into the forest with us, always making sure to stay a few arm's lengths behind us. I'm beginning to doubt that she has any interest in finding the missing child, given how intent she seems on catching me and Jyn off guard.

"Anything?" one of the villagers calls to the group, which has now fanned out to cover more ground.

"Nothing yet!" I shout back.

All around us, the light of day slowly fades, bringing with it a chill that seems to seep into my very marrow. It's not long before I can see my exhales rise in silver clouds, my teeth chattering despite all the layers I'm dressed in. I can only hope we find the child before the cold does.

"This is takin' forever," the huntress utters as she nocks an arrow to her bowstring.

"There's no need for such a weapon," I point out, exasperation leaking into my tone.

"Ye can never be too careful," she says, with a pointed look in Jyn's direction. "Ye never know what beasts lurk in the shadows."

Irritation flickers at the nape of my neck as a protective instinct stirs within. It's only when I feel Jyn's hand graze my own that I remember myself. Now isn't the time to lose control. I must play no part in confirming the huntress's suspicions.

"Let's try this way," Jyn says, marching off at a brisk pace.

An eerie stillness has fallen over this section of the bamboo forest. There's not a hint of light nor sound, including the gentle rustle of the breeze. We have traveled so far that we are completely removed from the village. The ground is soft beneath our feet, this landscape untouched by human presence.

"Are you sure we're headed in the right direction?" I ask, knowing full well that I'm already terribly turned around.

"I don't understand," Jyn says. "Her scent is so strong here, and yet—"

The sharp cry of a child pierces my ears, the sound so sudden and shrill that it sends a chill down my spine. The little girl cries and sniffles, hidden somewhere near.

"Mei?" I call out. "We're here for you, little one. Let's take you home."

I step forward only for the huntress to yank me back by the arm.

"Wait," she hisses, drawing her bowstring.

"What are you doing?" I snap.

"No, she's right," Jyn says hastily, her eyes wide with concern. "Something's wrong."

"What do you me—"

Before I can finish the thought, a gargantuan mass charges forth out of nowhere. I have never seen a more grotesque creature, which is truly a wonder, considering I have recently come face-to-face with a fei and a murder of three-legged crows.

It has the face of a person, but the body of a feral ox, with the slimy tongue of a snake reaching out to us in a winding curl. Its human visage is covered in all manner of warts, its skin wrinkled and rippled and pulled back awkwardly as if it's a mere mask of flesh. When its mouth falls open, the sound it makes mimics that of a crying girl.

That was no child we heard.

The beast has lured us into a trap.

"Move!" the huntress shouts, shoving me out of the way as she lets her first arrow fly.

It screams through the air but misses its mark. Incensed, the beast snorts from its bulbous, misshapen nose, charging with murder in its eyes. It comes straight for me, its hooves digging up the earth as it runs. I turn on my heel and sprint away, leading it as far from Jyn as I'm able.

"What is this thing?" I shout over my shoulder, grabbing onto a bamboo pole and using my momentum to slingshot myself into a different direction.

"A yayu," I hear Jyn breathe as she chases after us. "I thought they were extinct."

"Clearly not!" Feng roars, nocking another arrow before letting it fly. This one nearly nicks me, the fletches sluicing past my cheek. Were I not so preoccupied with running for my life, I would be concerned that she was aiming at me on purpose.

No matter how hard I dash, the yayu remains well within sight, driving me deeper and deeper into the forest. My lungs burn, my legs cramp. How much longer can I keep this up? Will the huntress be able to kill this foul creature before it devours me whole? I realize exactly how much trouble I'm in when the fog rolls in, thick and gray and severely limiting my vision. I can no longer see Jyn or the huntress behind me.

I run and run and run—

And very nearly tumble over the edge of a sharp cliff. I flail my arms to keep balance, thankfully falling backward onto solid ground. My heart leaps out of my chest when I make the mistake of peering over the ledge. The drop is so long that I can't see the bottom, the endless pit dark and unwelcoming.

I turn slowly. The yayu stares me down, stamping its front hoof as it prepares to charge. There's no escape for me. This time, I'm on my own.

With an ear-shattering shriek that curdles my blood, the yayu runs forward at full speed. I brace myself, waiting until the very last moment before leaping out of the way. I manage to dodge, but not before its tail winds back and whips me across the stomach. The impact throws me off-kilter. To my great dismay, I tumble over the edge of the cliff.

I scream.

Or at least, I attempt to.

My voice is caught in the back of my mouth. The sensation of the fall ties my gut into impossible knots. I plummet—down, down, down—with no end in sight. The air claws at my skin, through my hair, down my lungs. I am weightless, adrift and untethered. It occurs to me, many seconds in, how much falling feels like flying. Were it not for the morbid fact that I will soon meet my painful end—bones crushed, skull caved in, flesh splashed across the earth in a wet heap—I might have enjoyed the sensation a while longer.

As the earth draws closer and closer, a great regret lances me through the heart.

I do not want to die.

Not again.

As I stare death in the face, something miraculous happens. My life flashes before my eyes. Not just this life, but all the previous ones. They hit me all at once and with great force.

As the ground comes up to meet me, I relive every single one.

30

The first time he is reborn, the red dragon returns in the form of a pauper's son. He mistakes the memories of his past life for nothing more than the most vivid of dreams. The boy is fascinated by the red thread tied around his finger, though his parents do not seem to know it is there. He grows to the tender age of four before a pox sweeps through the village.

It takes his mother first, then his father. He cries until his eyes run dry, his stomach cramping with hunger. A strange woman finds him a few days later, her brilliant green eyes the most beautiful thing he has ever seen.

It is too late, however. His light flickers out only a minute later. He dies in her arms.

The second time he is reborn, he grows into a beautiful bird of paradise with colorful feathers that could rival the rarest of gems. He enjoys soaring through the skies. It feels familiar to him, being so high up above. It reminds him of a past life that he scarcely remembers.

But humans are incapable of letting beautiful things be.

Enamored by his sweet morning songs and dazzled by his brilliant plumage, a hunter snatches the bird from his nest in the dead of night. Trapped in a golden cage, the bird can no longer spread his wings. Resigned to his newfound confinement, he ceases his songs and his feathers slowly dull—only for him to die in captivity a week later.

Alone.

———

The twentieth time he is reborn, he returns to the mortal realm in the form of a fei beast. He lives alone in the sticky humidity of the southern jungles, clinging to the shadows and dense underbrush. He is particularly afraid of the humans who live around the river bend. They have sharp sticks and move in packs, their faces painted with root dyes in patterns that make him dreadfully dizzy. He lives most of his life in fear, spending his days staring at the skies above, yearning for something he cannot name.

Miracle of miracles, he comes across a green dragon who is as lonely as he. There are no words for the bond that they share—he only knows that when he is with her, he feels whole and safe. They do not share the same language, and although their friendship is an unlikely one, it is perfect.

They spend their mornings swimming in the lagoon, and their afternoons lounging together in the warm sun. The dragon and the fei are always on the move, making sure to stay as far from the growing settlement of humans as possible. They can both smell people drawing near. The last thing they want is trouble.

One day, while crossing the riverbed, one of the fei's front hoofs gets stuck in the mud. He panics as he sinks, thrashing about to free himself—to no avail. Afraid that he might hurt himself, the dragon shifts into her smaller human form in the hopes that her nimble hands may serve to help him better.

This is a mistake.

Startled and afraid of the human's sudden presence, the fei howls frantically. Humans have only ever hurt him. They only ever yell and scream and give chase.

She pleads with him, her hands raised before her. "Be still, my love! I mean you no harm."

His simple mind cannot comprehend her words. He howls and snarls and kicks, afraid for his life and heartbroken at his great love's sudden disappearance.

Drawn to the commotion, a group of hunters emerge from the jungle with weapons at the ready. Humans see what they want to see—a woman desperately crying out as a monster prepares to attack.

They riddle him with arrows, piercing him through the eyes, the neck, the belly, and the heart. He dies slowly and painfully, all to the sound of the green-eyed woman's heart-wrenching wails.

With his last breath, he hopes that his dragon will be safe without him.

The fiftieth time he is reborn, he is a stillborn fox pup. His family moves on while his body remains behind to be reclaimed by the earth. His Fated One senses their bond forming for a moment, only to then feel it disintegrate, never to know what happened.

The hundredth time, the red dragon is reborn as a human girl. She is by far the fairest young maiden in the village. On the day of her birth, the village shaman sensed the magic running through her veins. It is an ancient thing—remnants of a history locked away beneath her pretty smile and light brown eyes. In the sunshine, her irises appear to have an almost crimson hue.

She marries the village elder's son. They have four beautiful children together. She is happy and lives to a ripe old age. The last thought she has before passing away peacefully in her sleep is to wonder why the soul on the other end of her red thread never came to find her.

31

Something catches me.

No, not something. Some*one*.

Jyn swoops in, her claws outstretched, and her serpentine body wraps around my own. I gasp, shaken and heartbroken from my memories. I cling to her back, careful not to pull on her mane. The sudden shift in momentum gives me whiplash, but then our rise into the skies proves as exhilarating as the fall.

As she brings me back up toward the ledge, I catch the glint of something metallic flying straight at us. An arrow. At the edge of the cliff, the huntress stands poised with her bow drawn. She leads her shot, her sights set on Jyn's curling form.

"No!" I shout.

It's too late.

The arrow pierces Jyn's chest, causing her to roar loudly in pain. There's nothing I can do except hold on, panic screaming over our thread. My dragon, my heart, begins to plummet.

Desperation cuts through me. There has to be *something* I can do.

I think back to my outburst back at the village, how my anger somehow ignited the first step of a greater transformation. I remember my red eyes and sharp teeth and unspeakable surge of strength. If the red dragon's magic flows through my veins, surely I can harness its power.

What a shame I have no idea how to control it. How am I to save my Fated One?

"Jyn!" I cry as I prepare to meet my demise for the second time this day. "Jyn, *please*, you have to—"

There isn't enough time to pull up, so she takes the brunt of the fall. The harsh thud as we slam into the cold, hard ground is enough to rattle my bones. I'm in excruciating pain and shock, but at least I'm *alive*.

Dust billows out from under us, coating my skin and stinging my eyes. Wherever we are, it's freezing and dark. There's barely any light down here at the bottom of what I can only assume is an empty ravine, long since dried up and abandoned by the living. Even the weeds, normally stalwart and steadfast against the harshest elements, have shriveled up and died here.

I clamber to my feet, ignoring the sharp twist of what feels like a broken ankle. By all accounts, I'm lucky.

My dragon, on the other hand, is alarmingly still.

A shaky breath escapes me as I reach out to her, gingerly pressing the tips of my fingers against her cold scales. "Jyn?" I call out weakly, my throat uncomfortably tight. *"Jyn."*

I glance down at our thread for reassurance—still there, but for how much longer?

With a pathetic limp, I hobble over to her head, stroking the debris from her eyes. Jyn stirs with a whimper and a groan, struggling to right herself. The shaft of the arrow juts out, a painful splinter, the tip lodged deep within her chest.

"Don't move, my lady. I will get . . ." My words die on my tongue as I look around. There's no help to be found. Swallowing hard, I cradle her head beneath her chin and tap my forehead to her snout. "Please, hang on just a while longer. I'll get us out of this."

A low, ominous growl reaches my ear.

I turn slowly, goose bumps sliding over my aching flesh. Now that the dust has settled, I finally realize that this ravine is far from abandoned. Peeking out at me from the inky dark is a pair of glowing red eyes and the glint of sharp fangs. One pair grows into two, two into four, four into eight. Before I know it, Jyn and I are staring down an entire horde of bloodthirsty beasts.

An entire family of yayu. It seems we've had the misfortune of plummeting directly into their lair. They bare their teeth, and thick strands of saliva drip from their yellowed fangs. Their nostrils flare as they crouch, ready to pounce. Jyn and I are outnumbered twenty to one. There is no escape. We either fight, or we die.

As they circle not just me but Jyn, I envision them tearing us limb from limb, feasting on our remnants. The thought of my Fated One perishing awakens something within me. So long as I draw breath, I will fight so that nothing can touch her. If these damned beasts want a taste of dragon's blood, they'll first have to go through me.

I take a deep breath.

And then I let it all out.

Every ounce of frustration, of rage, of madness within me is unleashed, drawing power from a deep, untapped well. My skin ignites with the heat of a thousand suns, my teeth grow sharp so suddenly that they cut into my own tongue, my nails become long and as sharp as ten savage blades. The roar that escapes me is not quite that of a dragon, but it can't be described as human, either. It's not a full transformation—I don't know if I'm even capable of that—but it's enough to unleash my wrath.

The yayu pounce with vicious snarls, but I'm ready. I know no fear, only unbridled hatred. Nobody will hurt my Fated One. *Nobody.*

It's a bloody affair.

They bite, they claw, and I do the same. I'm no longer myself, so moved by my anger that I'm blind to the rest of the world. I can't differentiate one foe from the next. They blur together, one massive threat that I alone must eliminate. I tear the beasts apart with my bare hands, gnashing my teeth, casting dirt into their eyes. One kill, ten kills—it makes no difference. The power I wield is dark and dangerous.

"Sai!" Jyn sobs my name. "Sai, *enough*!"

But I can't stop. My sanity slowly slips away. These movements, this heartbeat, this all-consuming craving for blood are not my own. I won't hold back. I refuse. I will destroy every last creature in my way if it means that I can keep my Fated One safe. Even if that means I must destroy myself.

Jyn shifts back into her human form and throws her arms around my neck. "They're dead," she rasps. "I'm safe. We're *fine*."

I throw Jyn off me without thinking, sending her crashing to the ground. It's only when I hear her cry out, my hand coming away red from her chest, that I manage to grasp hold of my senses. Clarity finally washes over me, followed by a gut-wrenching horror.

What have I done?

"I'm sorry," I say shakily, hurrying over to pick her up and cradle her in my arms. How did I lay a hand on her, when I was only here to protect her? "I'm so sorry, my heart. I didn't mean to—"

She grits her teeth as she inhales, clearly in agony. As lightly as I can manage, I move the top of her robes to inspect her injury. The huntress's arrow is embedded just below Jyn's collarbone. Red stains her skin, flowing freely.

"I have to pull it out," I tell her regretfully.

She shakes her head slightly, grimacing. "N-no, not here. There c-could be others."

I know she's right. More blood on top of this carnage will only attract more beasts. The best course of action is to find shelter before the night's cold overwhelms us.

"Hold on to me," I tell her, lifting her up into my arms.

Jyn groans against my chest, her head lolling to one side as sweat breaks out across her forehead. Her breathing is ragged, her complexion too pale. Jyn mentioned once that she heals quicker than most, but what happens if she bleeds out faster than even her magic can repair? I need to remove the arrow as soon as possible, but first I must find us someplace safe.

I venture deeper into the ravine, the air growing colder by the second. There's no sound down here, and barely any light. I can't tell if the pain I feel is my own, or if it is Jyn's that I'm sensing through our thread. Either way, the trek is excruciating.

I almost yell with joy when I find a deep alcove dug into the frigid cliff face. It will serve as a perfect resting point. After setting Jyn down on the ground, I quickly shrug off my winter coat and drape it over her shivering body. What we need now is a source of light.

There's plenty of tinder—twigs and dry grass and dead weeds— but the stones I use are too damp to spark a light. I grunt in frustration, so broken and beaten down that I find myself on the brink of tears.

"I wish we could breathe fire," I curse under my breath. "Gods, please just—"

A spark finally arcs, catching on the leaves. The tiniest of flames grows and grows. With a relieved sigh, I throw on a few more sticks. Before long, it's a strong campfire, casting shadows against the alcove and slowly warming the air around us.

"I did it!" I gasp.

"Huzzah," Jyn grumbles dryly. She can barely keep her eyes open.

I kneel at her side, carefully inspecting her wound. The whole area is red and swollen. Removing the arrowhead will be no simple task.

"Are you ready?" I ask.

"Are you sure we can't leave it in?"

"Be brave, my lady."

Her bottom lip trembles, fear etched into the weary features of her face. "All right," she murmurs. "You'll h-have to use the arrow to cauterize the wound."

I do my best to look brave. "I'll be as gentle as I can."

Jyn takes a deep breath, grinding her teeth as I grasp the shaft of the arrow. She swallows her screams as I dig the weapon out, her body trembling and seizing, her distress lashing out across our connection. It takes every ounce of concentration I have not to stop, not to break down from seeing her this way.

I eventually manage to free the arrowhead, and I waste no time in holding it out over the flame. The metal turns red with the heat, ready for the next phase. I give Jyn a hesitant glance, at which she only nods.

When I press the searing metal to her flesh, tears flow freely from her eyes, but she doesn't make a sound. My wretched work is over in a matter of seconds. I drop the arrow and pick her up, seating her across my lap so that I can hold her close. I rock her gently back and forth, pressing kisses against her temples, her cheeks, her hair. It's the only way I can think to apologize, because words are not enough.

It's a small comfort when her eyes flutter shut. As she dreams, I remain on guard, silently reeling at what has come to pass.

If I'm going to protect Jyn, I must become so much stronger.

No matter the cost.

32

*S*ai?"

The caress of cool fingers against my cheek pulls me from my light slumber. Soft morning light filters down into the ravine. I sit up immediately, heart racing as a sudden shot of adrenaline courses through me.

"How are you feeling?" I ask, reaching out to brush away a few strands of her loose hair.

"Better, thanks to you."

"I'm overjoyed to hear it, my sunshine."

"We should leave soon. The huntress may still be searching for us."

"But where will we go?"

Jyn shakes her head. "I'm not sure. Sometimes I fear there's no place left in the world for us to run."

"We'll think of something," I say with conviction. "As long as we're together, everything will be all right."

She nods slowly. "We should find someplace to wash off. Who knows what might be tracking our scent?"

"Is that your way of telling me I need a bath?"

Jyn pinches her nose. "No, of course not."

I laugh softly, relieved to see the warmth in her eyes once again as she kneels beside me. "Do you think there's enough magic in my blood to heal you?"

She shakes her head. "I'd rather not risk it. We're both too weak right now, and the amount we'd need to fully heal is not unsubstantial."

"Back at the oasis . . . How much did you give me?"

"I let blood for nearly an hour."

I grimace. Not only does the thought of draining myself of blood make me squeamish, but we don't have that kind of time. Such methods should remain a last resort.

Instead, I gently grasp her wrist and hold her heated gaze as I kiss her. Her thumb brushes gently over my mouth, her own lips parted slightly as she breathes in. I hum contentedly, tracing a line of kisses from the corner of her mouth, to her jaw, to the crook of her neck, relishing the way she shivers with delight.

"We must go," she says, though she doesn't sound so convinced. "Save your hunger for later."

"Oh, I will."

We both rise to our feet, doing a cautious scan of the area. It's true that we must make haste. If there's one thing we've learned these past couple of weeks, it's that staying in one place never bodes well for us.

"We'll have to fly our way out," Jyn says. "Hold on tight."

"But it will be easier to spot us that way."

"I'll be quick. Once we're out of this ravine, I'll transform back and we can continue on foot."

I nod slowly, contemplating our choices. It's certainly an easier option than climbing out of this blasted place.

"Don't worry," she says. "I won't drop you."

"That's the least of my worries."

In the blink of an eye, her form shifts. There will never be a moment when I am not in awe of her grace and beauty in dragon form. Her shimmering scales catch what little light there is, glowing like gems. Jyn digs her claws into the earth, gently lowering her head to bump my cheek with her snout, nudging me toward her back. I climb on and cling to her mane, sucking in a sharp breath when she stands to full height.

The ground suddenly disappears from beneath us as she launches herself into the air, the wind screaming past us as she soars upward. I press my body flat against hers, screwing my eyes closed as we take to the skies, amazed by her speed and fluidity. One moment, we were surrounded by the darkness of the pit, and the next—

The next, we touch the clouds.

A childish excitement shoots through me. I spent many a day as a young boy dreaming about what the world looked like from on high, whether the clouds felt as soft as they appeared. I'm filled with an inexplicable ease, marveling at the endless blue that is the sky. It's easy to forget about the rest of the world below us, everything—even our greatest problems—so distant and small that it's hard to care about anything except this moment.

I'm *flying*.

For the first time in seven thousand years, I'm finally able to look upon the kingdom that was once mine. From the top of the tallest mountain to the Heavens above, this was *home*. I'm loath to think about how the emperor took it all away from me.

Jyn begins her gradual descent, landing carefully in the middle of the bamboo forest that covers the majority of the Moonstar Isles. We find ourselves fortuitously next to a hot spring, steam rising into the air with a thick line of trees on all sides. She must have spotted it from above. It's the perfect hiding spot, tucked away from prying eyes.

My dragon goes to the water and steps in. The spring is just large enough to soak her long body. Jyn sinks below the water's surface, coming back up for air a few moments later in her human form. She grins at me, undressing under the cover of the steam and throwing her soaked clothes past the water's edge. I pick up her robes with a laugh, wring them out for her, and leave them to dry on a low branch.

"Laundry *and* a bath," I muse. "I admire your efficiency."

She swims toward the small waterfall adjacent to the spring, water trickling over a small overhang from deep within the earth. Jyn stays low to the water, her hair pooling over her shoulders.

"Are you coming or not?" she asks coyly, swimming out farther. "The water is shallow," she adds in soft reassurance.

The edges of my lips tug into a grin. How can I refuse her?

I strip out of my clothes and take the plunge, wading my way across the hot spring to join Jyn beneath the waterfall. My feet easily touch the bottom, so a fear of drowning doesn't seize me as it normally would. The steam soaks into my lungs, into my skin, but nothing is able to hold my attention quite like Jyn.

Droplets of moisture fall over her shoulders and down the plane of her back. Her cheeks and chest are flushed with the heat of the spring, bringing vibrant color to her ivory skin. Her lashes flutter as I draw in close, easily circling my arms around her waist. I am unsure who moves first, but in the end, it matters not. Our lips find each other, a perfect fit.

We are reduced to greedy hands, breathless kisses, and moans of desire. I don't know where she stops and I begin. She consumes my every thought. We move together with urgency, melding our souls into one. We have so much time to make up for, hundreds upon hundreds of lifetimes apart.

I silently pray to the Gods above that they will offer us this one reprieve.

Please, let me stay with her this time.

She licks a stripe up the side of my neck, sucking hard to make a mark on my skin. The ravenous look in her eye sends all other thoughts away. I grasp her hair by the roots to pull her head back and put my mouth to her throat, my teeth gently grazing over her tender flesh.

"Go on," she urges with a dark laugh. "Don't fight your instincts, Sai. Claim me, just like you used to."

I surge forward, biting just hard enough to break skin. I nick her lovely neck, and then the curve of her shoulder, and then her collarbone, suddenly overcome with the instinct to cover her with marks. *My* marks. The world needs to know that she is mine.

Her pleasure sings over our bond, satisfaction and euphoria mixing together into the most potent of concoctions. I hold her through the crest of it, not far behind her.

There's beauty in the aftermath, an intimacy in the long stretch of silence that follows. There's no need for words, for affirmations. The Gods promised us to one another, our union destined. I can't imagine bearing even a moment without her.

We stay in the water a while longer, bathing at a leisurely pace. We're both tired, deserving of a short break. She cups her hands together and pours water over my head with a light giggle, moving to massage my shoulders and arms while I steal kisses every chance I get. I allow myself the chance to savor the peace of the moment, because I know how fleeting it all is.

"We'll need to return to the village for supplies," I say. "I can go alone. I'll gather as much as I can, and then we'll make our way as far west as we are able."

"But what about the huntress? If you return to the village, won't she be lying in wait?"

"Perhaps, but she can do nothing to force answers out of me or stop me from leaving."

There's hesitation in her eyes, and I can't blame Jyn for her lack of confidence.

"I don't think it wise, Sai—"

"How about you keep watch?" I suggest. "Keep watch from the forest's edge while I return to the village. I'll just slip in and out with the supplies we need and thank them for their hospitality. Feng won't make a move with so many people around."

"What if she tells them?" Jyn asks. "About what we truly are. She *saw* me. What are the chances that they'll believe her?"

"I'm not sure," I admit. "All the more reason for me to be quick. Should anything happen, you can come in at a moment's notice."

Her anxiety plucks at our connection, but she says, "All right."

We step out of the hot spring and dry off, then quickly pull on our clothes. I braid her hair and give her a quick kiss before adding her silver hairpin. "We'd best get going, then."

33

We *remain on foot, knowing* that the huntress will be watching the skies. Jyn's keen sense of smell leads us on a path straight to the village. I keep an eye out for any movement in the underbrush, wary of what new creatures might be lurking there. At least I now know I possess the strength to rip them apart, though my lack of control is a cause for concern.

I'm unable to stop myself from reliving the moment I nearly lost my mind to that overwhelming power. If Jyn hadn't been there to calm me down, who knows the damage I might have wrought?

"Do you think I can do it?" I ask as we walk.

"Do what?"

"Fully transform."

Jyn glances at me as I offer my hand, helping her jump over a narrow stream. "You're well on your way there."

"Is it always such a process? You make it look easy to shift between forms."

"I've been doing it all my life, Sai, and you're relearning. With enough practice, it will come back to you."

I chew on the inside of my cheek. "What does it feel like? When you shift, I mean. The anger that leads to my transformation . . . it nearly tears me apart."

Jyn takes my hand, lacing her fingers between mine as we continue forward. "I don't feel anger, but sadness."

I pause midstride to look at her. "I don't like that at all. I'm sorry, my lady."

"It's just the way it is, I'm afraid. Evoking strong emotions makes it easier for us to wield our magic."

"But why?"

"I've never been sure. Perhaps because it comes from so deep within, emotion makes our ability to shift easier. It's easiest for us to channel our magic when we focus on one feeling."

"What of the prince?" I ask after a moment of contemplation. "The blue dragon. What did he rely on to shift?"

Jyn's eyes grow misty, though she forces a small smile. "Happiness," she whispers. "The emotion that helped him use his magic was pure joy."

My heart twists painfully in my chest.

"What was he like?" I ask gently.

"A rascal," she says, but with every ounce of love behind the word. "A-Qian was such a troublemaker. Just like you."

"A-Qian," I echo. His name fits in my mouth just as easily as Jyn's. It's familiar and sweet and fills my heart with a longing I didn't know I was capable of feeling. In this life, I can't boast of having any children, and yet there's no denying the paternal pride that comes forth when I think of the young blue dragon of old.

"He loved to swim," I remember aloud, pulling at the thread of a memory I didn't know I had. "And he was always asking to hear my stories."

Jyn beams. "Every day. And your jests, and your songs—though you never could carry a tune."

I chuckle. "You will be pleased to know that in this life, I have golden pipes. My doctor once told me so."

She laughs softly. "Maybe when we're someplace safe, you can serenade me."

"It would be my greatest pleasure."

Together we climb up a steep hill, the ground slippery with fallen leaves and overnight rain. The scents of cooked meat and roasted spices linger in the air. We're getting closer to the village.

"Has he ever come back?" I ask after a moment, the question popping into my head. "Our son. Has he reincarnated? It would be so lovely to find him again. Do you think—"

I stop short when I realize Jyn has halted in her tracks. She has grown deathly quiet, her face completely blank.

"My love?" I call out to her. "What's the matter?"

"He can't come back," she says, barely loud enough for me to hear her. "He can never come back."

I frown. "Why not?"

Jyn trudges forward, picking up speed in an attempt to outpace me and my questions. I rush after her, alarmed. I take her hand and pull her back toward me, wrapping my other arm around her waist.

"But the tapestry we found . . . The one about the Albeion monks' teaching of reincarnation. At the Steps of Heaven, your soul is given a choice to be reborn."

She grinds her teeth, her hands curled into fists against my chest. "Yes, that's how it's supposed to be."

"Did he choose to ascend?"

Jyn shakes her head, her shoulders trembling slightly. "He never got that far."

"Please, enough of these riddles. What happened to our son?"

Her lips become a thin line, her brow furrowing in distress. "In order to begin a new cycle, you must first possess a soul."

"And?" I urge, desperate for a proper answer.

"His was shattered and consumed," she says shakily. "Unable to move on."

A cold dread creeps down my spine.

"I don't understand. How is that possible? What happened?"

"A stranger arrived from the lands beyond the horizon."

34

The prince and his Fated One travel across the many lands and seas. They spend their years, their decades helping the people. Through famine, through disease, through war—the blue dragon does what he can, giving up more and more of himself with every passing moon.

His scales are sowed into the fields to ensure bountiful harvests. His teeth are built into effigies to ward off evil creatures that lurk in the forests. His hair is shorn down to his scalp, the strands of his mane ingested to stave off plague. It is not long before he is a shell of himself, a once-mighty divine beast now little more than skin and bones.

The stranger, meanwhile, reaps all the rewards and grows drunker on the feeling each day.

"They wish to make me their emperor," he tells the prince, addicted to his newfound glory and fame. "My beloved, please lend me your strength. When I take the Imperial throne, I will need you by my side."

"I have always been by your side," the prince says with a heavy heart. "But is this truly what you want?"

"Of course it is! Together, we shall rule for all eternity. Think of all that we could accomplish."

The blue dragon shakes his head, weary and worn down. He can smell the greed wafting off his Fated One's skin. Something's changed. Something terrible. "No," he says, "this is not you. This is not right. I wish to return home."

The emperor frowns. "You would abandon humanity and leave me alone, after all we've built together?"

"Please, say you'll return with me to the east."

"But why should we? We have everything we need here, my love."

"I long to see my family again."

"Why? To reunite with the mother and father who wished to keep you there?"

"They only wanted to protect me."

"By keeping you locked away," he says simply. "Here, we are free."

The blue dragon shakes his head, dismayed. He's suffocating. It is wrong to trap a dragon on land when he should be free to soar the skies. "I've had enough of this."

"You cannot leave me," the emperor says pointedly. "I forbid it."

Against his Fated One's wishes, the young prince walks away, desperate to return to his father and mother. How he has missed them. He should have listened to them—what a mistake it was to leave home.

The emperor's anger turns into a boiling-hot rage. "You will not leave me," he yells after the young prince, and gives chase.

The prince tries to shift into a dragon, tries to fly away, but his heart is so heavy and sad that he cannot harness his magic. It is not long before his Fated One has him captured.

"You will stay," the emperor seethes, "because you are mine."

The prince cries out, "Release me at once! There's no need for it to be this way."

"If you will not give me your power, then I will take it for myself."

Even the purest of love is not immune to poison. It can twist and mutate into something monstrous with enough obsession and control. Human hearts are far more susceptible to rot. And when love gives way to possession—it is no longer love at all.

The emperor draws his blade and carves out the young prince's heart. He devours it whole, consuming the blue dragon's magic and every fragment of his soul in a mere four bites. He is unfazed when their red thread of fate suddenly cuts clean through, their connection broken now, an ugly, unfeeling gray.

After all, who needs their Fated One when they can have wealth and power and immortality?

Where once he was regarded as a hero to his people, the emperor's reign begins to take a darker turn. Without his Fated One, he is erratic, teetering on the edge of madness. He tries and fails to fill the void where the blue dragon once stood, instead filling his life with riches and with those who will serve his every whim. The emperor craves total domination over his subjects, over his lands, and even the kingdoms just beyond his reach. . . .

But he realizes slowly, and all too late, that nothing will ever satisfy his now-fractured heart. He consumes everything in his path, the well-being of others be damned, all in the hopes that he will one day be free of the insidious, self-inflicted emptiness within.

Part 4

The
Emperor

35

I t isn't true," *Jyn says.* "They say red threads of fate can stretch and tangle, but never break—but that's not true."

I hold my breath. "What do you mean?"

"There's a way to sever the connection."

My heart lodges in my throat. I think back, remembering the emperor's severed gray thread. I didn't understand back then, but now I fear the worst.

"Tell me," I whisper, my voice raspy and foreign to my own ears.

"It's a deliberate choice," she explains, impossibly soft. "A permanent one."

I grasp Jyn by the shoulders, pressing my forehead to hers. "Please, just tell me."

She takes a deep breath, a long pause. "It happens when one half of a soul chooses to reject the other by their own hands. The level of malice it takes to carry out the task . . . It's enough to destroy any divine bond."

The words fall from my lips. "You mean *murder*."

"Yes. That monster murdered our son. His love of power was far more intoxicating than his love for his Fated One. A-Qian gave and gave and gave himself away to that beast, and it still wasn't enough to keep him satisfied."

I take a step back, aghast. "Then the emperor and the stranger . . ."

Tears stream down her reddened cheeks. "The soul resides in the heart. That demon carved it out from our son while he was still alive and swallowed every last bite. Even if A-Qian wished to return, his soul was fragmented, the pieces trapped within he who consumed him."

My stomach roils—I worry that I might be sick. "No."

Jyn runs her fingers through her hair, distress radiating off her in racking sobs. "His thirst for power couldn't be quenched. He could no longer use our son for his own gain, so he came for us. He arrived with an army of a thousand men near six millennia ago. They tore off your tail, ripped your tongue from your mouth. They pummeled us with cannon fire and speared you through the chest."

It feels as though I have swallowed a million tiny shards of glass. "What happened next? How did we escape?" I cup her face in my hands, everything in the current moment falling away. "I must know," I murmur. "Please, tell me."

The guilt that shadows her expression nearly rips me in two.

"I don't know how we managed it," she blurts out. "We fled to the mountains, but your injuries . . . You bled to death in my arms, Sai. I watched our connection turn black and crumble away as your body turned cold. And when I had to leave you behind, humans swarmed your body like ants. I had to watch as they took pieces of you, bit by bit, all for themselves."

My soul aches. I can't imagine living with this tragedy for as long as she has.

"But I came back, did I not?" I ask gently. "At the Steps of Heaven, I chose to come back. Every time."

Jyn nods, but she refuses to meet my eyes. "You did. The first time you were reborn, I discovered a new red thread wrapped around my finger. I knew it was you in an instant, so I set out to find you—but that was a mistake."

"Why?"

"Because we're cursed to relive an eternal tragedy."

"Wait a moment." I hold my hand up, showing her our gray, fraying thread. "How did this happen, then?"

Jyn is unable to look me in the eye.

"Jyn."

She shakes her head. "We should . . . we should keep going. The village is near."

"No," I say firmly, holding on to her hand as tight as I dare. "Why is our thread gray, Jyn? You've avoided my questions for weeks. Tell me *now*."

Her silence tells me everything, but I say it aloud anyway.

"You tried to kill me?"

The words come out tight and broken; I'm blinded by the tears welling in my eyes. This cannot be. None of it makes sense. The bitterness of betrayal weighs heavily on my tongue.

Our thread slowly begins to drain of its color, its crimson hue seeping away like blood in a stream. It unravels between us, the progress we've made eroding before our very eyes.

"*Why?*" I whisper, so quiet and pathetic that my own ears almost miss the question.

"Please, just—" She tries to push past me. I don't budge.

"Say something!" I roar, grasping her by the shoulders. "Tell me, Jyn. Why would you do it?"

"I lost my mind!" she yells, regret in her eyes. "You don't understand, Sai. You have known the pain of death, but I have known the pain of losing you hundreds of times over. How many times could you lose your lover without going mad?"

I pause. I don't know how I could've handled it even once. "How many times have I been reborn?"

"This is the *seven hundredth time*," she whispers. "I have counted every single time I've felt our connection rekindle. It finally broke me. Twenty years ago, I set out to find you. I was overcome with grief. You were a boy, no older than five. I found you playing by the river."

I rack my brain, trying and failing to recall our encounter. Perhaps I was too young to remember. I always thought my tumble into the water that day was an accident, but her confession shines a horrible new light on the reality.

Jyn's whole body shakes with her sobs. "I just wanted it to end. I knew you were going to meet another tragic demise anyway, so I thought—"

"You thought to murder me," I say in disbelief.

"It was *mercy*," she insists. "It was meant to be a mercy. I . . . I pushed you. Held you under the water."

I take a step away, disgusted and frightened. I remember what she told me when we were both trapped underground, the conversation we had mere moments after I killed that cannibal.

It was a mercy.

Do you really think his Fated One would want to see him like that?

"How could you?" I breathe heavily.

"I regretted it in an instant," she says, desperately grasping at my robes to keep me close. "I couldn't bear to watch you struggle. I pulled you out before it was too late, but the damage to our bond was done. It turned gray and the thread started to fall apart, but it didn't break because I . . . couldn't go through with it."

"You couldn't go through with *murdering me*?"

I take another step back, staring at her, aghast. I'm not sure how I'm even supposed to react to this. Lash out in anger? Break down in tears?

Instead, I am completely numb.

"Please, say something, Sai," Jyn whimpers.

"What is there to say?"

"I'm so sorry, my love. I am so sorry."

"I think . . . I think need some time alone."

Jyn tugs at the sleeve of my robes. "No, please—"

"Just stay here." I don't recognize my own voice. It's devoid of emotion, flat and cold. "I'll return to the village and grab supplies for our travels. Remain out of sight."

And with that, I stalk off. Shattered.

I march back to the village, stomping on twigs and whipping branches out of my way. A part of me wants to rip my own heart out to be free of this misery. I want to kick and scream and cry. How could my Fated One have even attempted such a terrible thing? Jyn says it would have been a mercy, but to whom?

And yet the more I think about it, the more I place myself in her shoes, the less I can bring myself to blame her. If our positions were reversed, could I stand to watch her die again and again over the course of millennia? My answer is quick and sure—absolutely not.

My love for this dragon transcends lifetimes, transcends our corporeal forms. I would choose her for all eternity over a seat in Heaven. If I had been in her shoes, I, too, would have lost my mind.

By the time evening falls, the first few tents of the village come into view. I've finally made it back. Taking a deep breath, I advance. There will be no time for conversation. I'm here to gather food and water for the road, no more.

But I make it no farther than five paces before I realize something is wrong. The village, usually alive with a cacophony of sound and activity, is eerily still. There are no children playing, no villagers out and about. It's as though the whole place has been abandoned. Alarmed, I make my way to the center in search of a fellow soul.

When I round the corner, my body seizes in shock. Huddled together in the village square are its residents, bound and gagged. They are surrounded by Imperial soldiers, swords to their throats.

Even the children have been taken hostage, unable to cling to their mothers now that their hands are tied behind their backs.

The sharp caw of a crow above sends a chill down my spine. I don't have to look to know it has red eyes and three legs. I know that he is here, as well. I can smell him on the wind's breath—the bastard whose greed led to so much tragedy.

"A pleasure to see you again," the emperor says, stepping out of a nearby tent. It's the biggest in the village, belonging to the village elder. The tent's flap pulls back far enough for me to glimpse the village elder's bloodied body just inside. His eyes are open, but they are lifeless.

"Let these people go," I demand.

"And why should I do such a thing?"

"They're innocent."

"And who are you to tell me what to do?" the emperor scoffs. "I should cut your tongue out for such insolence."

"Will you do it yourself this time, I wonder?"

I don't appreciate the smile and glint in his dark eyes as he asks, "You remember?"

"I do." I blink to clear the flashback of a soldier taking a blade to my mouth, to stop hearing my own screams. "You'll pay for everything you've done."

"Last I checked, I'm the one with the army."

Before I can get another word out, someone grabs me from behind and presses the sharp edge of a knife to my throat. It's no soldier, but a woman I know.

"Sorry 'bout this, Leaf Water," the huntress says against my ear. "Don't move, ye idiot. You'll bleed out faster than ye can blink."

"What are you doing?" I gasp, struggling to find my balance. Warm blood trickles down my throat, her blade breaking skin.

"Earnin' my keep, of course. I'm gonna be paid an emperor's ransom. Now, tell me where that bitch is hiding."

I can barely hear anything over the rush of blood past my ears. "You're making a mistake, Feng. Your hatred is misplaced. She wasn't the one who killed your parents."

"Shut up," Feng snaps.

"It's the truth. It was a pack of fei that did your parents in. She was trying to *save* them."

"I don't believe you."

Panic grips me. I can explain things to the huntress until my face turns blue, but it doesn't matter if she's unwilling to listen.

The emperor chuckles. "My dear boy, have you already forgotten? One word from me, and I will have this entire village executed. Surely that isn't what you want?"

It's hard to breathe, to think. I know by now how cruel the emperor is; this is no bluff. I can't watch these people die. There has to be a way out of this, but for the seven hundredth life of me, I cannot figure it out.

If I lie or say nothing, he will kill them. If I betray Jyn, I would rather kill myself. I'm petrified with indecision.

My answer is made for me, however, when the mighty roar of a dragon sounds overhead. I don't know whether to be relieved or frightened for Jyn. My dragon is here, and I'm not ready for the carnage that is sure to follow.

"From above!" one of the Imperial soldiers screams. "Draw your bows!"

"No!" I shout, swinging my elbow back to ram the huntress in the ribs. I grab her wrist and twist, forcefully snatching her blade to use as my own.

And then, all at once, havoc breaks out.

36

I *run to the villagers and* free the strongest of their men. I free Chyou and her child along with the rest of the women and children next, while the soldiers are preoccupied with Jyn above.

"Run!" I tell them. "As far and as fast as you can."

Bodies fall, the camp is overturned, and the scent of blood weighs on the air. I try to channel my magic, but I can't manage it. Instead of rage, I'm swimming in fear and helplessness; I cannot tap into the strength I once possessed. I have no choice but to fight blade to blade.

I lose track of how many soldiers I maim, the sensation of metal slipping through flesh happening again and again. Though the wet sound of skin and muscle and bone splitting open makes me sick, I attack anything and anyone that makes the mistake of charging at me.

The emperor is nowhere in sight. He's retreated for now—that coward.

Jyn roars as she dives down, scooping up soldiers in her sharp fangs and her claws. She drags them into the skies with her before tossing them to the unforgiving earth. They scream for their lives as the fall finishes the job for her.

The Imperial soldiers take their aim, letting their arrows loose. Thankfully, few hit their mark. Those that do ricochet off of Jyn's scales, the speed of her flight splintering arrows on contact. I come for them while they're distracted, stabbing and slicing through those who wish to harm her.

With a shriek, Feng tackles me to the ground. She sits on my chest, pinning me down, then draws her spare dagger from her sheath and winds back. The blade drives straight through my left shoulder, an excruciating fire radiating from the spot, leaving me without breath. Feng pulls the blade back, readying for another go. She's going to stab me to pieces.

"Nothin' personal, Leaf Water."

"Please," I beg. "Don't do this. The emperor is *using* you."

Much to my horrified amazement, the huntress pauses, her dagger flashing mere inches from cutting my eye in two. Her moment of hesitation is my advantage—and likely my only chance.

"You truly believe he'll make good on his promise?" I press on. "What reassurance do you have that he won't kill you the moment he has what he wants?"

"I—"

"*Please*, Feng. Don't allow your thirst for revenge cloud your judgment. He's bound to go back on whatever deal he's struck. He's taken a whole village hostage just to get what he wants. Imagine if these people were your own back home!"

"But ye lied to me," she hisses. "Over an' over again. About where the dragon was, about yer woman, about who ye are."

"Because she's my Fated One!" I exclaim. "I was trying to protect her. I still am. I beg of you, let me go before he hurts her. We both know the lengths we'll go to for the people we love."

The huntress sets her jaw, her gaze hard and scrutinizing. I can't tell whether I've gotten through to her. All I can do is pray.

If only I knew how to transform fully. I should be up there with

Jyn, defending her, and instead, she's fighting for the two of us. I shut my eyes tight and brace for the impact. Could this be it?

Just when I think I'm about to meet yet another tragic end, Feng throws her dagger overhead, the hilt tumbling through the air before puncturing a soldier through the side of the neck. He sputters, choking on the metal lodged in his throat. He fumbles helplessly, falls to his knees, and collapses flat on his face. The black loop around his finger tells me he's dead before he even hits the ground.

"Get up!" Feng yells at me, standing quickly while offering me her hand. She helps me to my feet.

"Thank you," I say, breathless. "You won't regret—"

"Less talk, more killin', moron!"

We remain outnumbered, but the fight feels less hopeless with an ally on our side. While Jyn soars above, swooping in with her claws extended to ram into large swathes of soldiers, Feng and I pick off Róng's soldiers one at a time. But it's quickly evident that I'm no fighter. Whatever blows I land are pure luck, and whatever strikes I take are unsurprising. It's frankly a miracle I'm still standing.

A soldier slices the side of my arm, and sticky blood trickles down my skin and drips off my fingers. Someone rushes me from behind with a war cry. I turn in time to see his raised sword, arcing down to sever my head from my shoulders, but Feng is able to come between us, ramming her dagger into his brain from just below the jaw. Jyn, too, shows no mercy, sinking her teeth into a soldier's flesh, the crunch of bones audible even over the clamor of battle.

When my dragon lands, it's with a harsh thud that shakes the ground. Arrows riddle her body, her exhaustion evident in the heavy hang of her head. I stagger toward her, half-dead but still putting myself between her and the approaching soldiers.

"You have to escape," I wheeze. "Leave this place."

Jyn snarls, as if in disagreement.

"I'll be back," I promise. "If he kills me, so be it. But you know I'll always come back for you. Please, you have to leave."

This time, she hisses.

"I'm not asking." Desperation shreds through my words. "You're the one he wants, Jyn. I can't let you fall into his hands. I'll hold him off for as long as I can."

"Get ready," Feng snaps at us. "The fight ain't over yet."

We are surrounded, Imperial soldiers cautiously closing in on us. My hands are shaking so hard that I can barely grasp my blade. I hold it up anyway, more than happy to strike down the next fool who dares make a move.

They rush at us.

We fight ferociously, moving together as one. Feng moves like smoke, impossible to catch until it's too late. Jyn picks off approaching soldiers one by one with her teeth, while I hack my way through anyone who gets too close. It's violent. I take on more damage than I deal, but I no longer care. One, three, five, the whole horde—Jyn and I will cut down each and every one of them.

Can we possibly make it out alive? I should know by now that luck is never on my side.

Something heavy and scalding hot hits us both. A net woven of metal, heated to a glowing orange. The Imperial soldiers have fired it from a cannon, the momentum knocking Jyn and me to the ground. Her concentration broken, Jyn shifts into her smaller human form. Her roar shifts into a woman's chilling scream.

The hot metal sears our skin, melts through our clothes. Trapped beneath its weight, we can only writhe in agony. The net crushes my strength to keep fighting, too heavy to lift, and my bones too brittle and broken.

The emperor steps out, finally showing his face now that our defeat seems certain. He crouches down and examines Jyn and me with a cold indifference.

"*Yuèmǔ*," he says flatly. "It is lovely to see my mother-in-law after so long."

Jyn roars, "Do not call me that, you *snake*!"

The emperor clicks his tongue. "Is this not nice? It has been several thousand years since we've had a family get-together. We should hold a feast in your honor."

"You have already devoured our son's soul!" I bellow. "What more could you possibly want from us?"

His eyes narrow. "What makes you think I would ever divulge my plans to you? I ought to execute you here and now."

Jyn shrieks. "If you harm him, I won't transform!"

The emperor pauses. "No?"

"That's what you want, is it not? To harvest us the way you did A-Qian?"

He goes stiff at the mention of our son's name, something shifting behind his eyes. The emperor seems to lose hold of his emotions for the first time, brow furrowing deeply as he clenches his teeth, sharpening the prominent line of his jaw. He tightens his hand into a fist, his severed gray thread still hanging freely from his little finger. He rises and gestures to a nearby soldier.

"Bind them," he orders. "And break their legs. We don't want our honored guests running off."

"What of the huntress?" one of his officers asks.

Emperor Róng regards Feng with general disinterest, like how one might notice a fly buzzing overhead, and motions for a sword. "I have no use for her," he says before driving the tip of the blade through Feng's back.

"Stop!" I bellow, but it's too late.

I see the light fade from her eyes, her pupils blowing wide without focus. It's a quick death, but horrifying all the same as I watch her thread fall away into nothing. Her Fated One, wherever they are, will not know her in this lifetime. Guilt racks my mind. We may not have seen eye to eye, but Feng didn't deserve this death, especially not at the whim of a monster. I silently thank her for sparing my life. Her death will not be in vain.

After they drag the metal net off us, they pin us down, kneeling between our shoulder blades and on the backs of our calves to keep us still. I reach for Jyn, only to have my arm twisted back painfully, my hands suddenly trapped by metal cuffs. The more I move, the more they tighten, sensitive springs within the contraption twisting the cuffs that much more.

"Where are you taking us?" I ask.

The emperor smiles again, though there is no warmth to be found. He has the eyes of a snake, black and cold and unfeeling. "My Winter Palace. I rather think you will enjoy the view." He turns to his soldiers and gestures to the surrounding area of the village. "Fan out," he instructs them, "and kill any survivors you come across."

My heart sinks. The women, the children . . . Chyou, Ming, little Jia.

I choke. *"No—"*

A soldier strikes me across the back of the head with the scabbard of his sword.

My vision blurs, and then all goes black.

37

There are few things as startling as a mother's intuition.

Sensing something gravely amiss, Her Majesty beseeches her husband with an inexplicable sorrow that has been tearing at her heart.

"Our son is in danger. I can feel it, clear as daylight. Please, my love, we must make haste and set out to find him."

The red dragon, despite his reservations, agrees. There is precious little he will not do to protect his only child.

They leave the safety of their eastern paradise and venture west through the lands where mankind roams. Humans are truly curious creatures, capable of carving out the earth, controlling the flow of the rivers, and molding structures of clay and stone. It is unnatural. They have built temples and statues and carved their likenesses into buildings, bestowing upon themselves a reverence befitting the Gods.

Her Majesty notices something strange as they pass through the lands. Villagers boast necklaces made of sharp teeth to ward off evil spirits. Soldiers are wielding weapons of sharpened bone. Merchants peddle bottled medicines of sparkling blue scales.

As a growing dread builds, the green dragon realizes what has come to pass. The cry that erupts from her chest is so powerful that the fields and forests wither and die. She knows they are too late to save her child. All must suffer as she suffers.

But even then, she knows of only one way to sate her need for revenge.

"Bring me the emperor," she says. "I crave a heart for a heart."

38

S *now.*

    The first thing I notice when I finally wake is that we are surrounded on all sides by a blanket of soft, frigid white. The wind is unforgiving, freezing everything it touches. The metal cuffs biting into my wrists serve only to amplify the harsh temperature, scraping away at my tender flesh, which has turned a jarring blue.

    My vision is blurry, coming back into focus at a snail's pace. Whether it's due to hunger or the ice frosting over my lids, I can't tell. They have broken both my legs, my bones shattered and muscles torn. The only reason I don't cry out in pain is because I'm far too numb to feel anything.

    It takes me a long while to make sense of my surroundings. I'm in some sort of open-air atrium carved into the top of a high mountain. The Winter Palace is a magnificent structure, chiseled into the grand rock face. Smooth columns hold up pointed roofs covered in red clay tiles, and a large red moon door with two gold dragon-head knockers is bolted to the front. I would marvel at the sight, were I not teetering on the brink of death.

When my vision finally clears, I realize why I can no longer feel my hands or feet. I'm bound in a kneeling position to an iron post, chains pulling my arms back behind me while my ankles are strapped down to the cobblestones beneath.

There's not enough slack in the chain for me to lie down, but just enough to keep me in this stress hold. There's a chain around my throat, too, secured to the post so that I have no room to move my head. I can't lean back without putting stress on my knees, but I can't lean forward without choking myself.

There's no telling how long it's been, though the sticky haze over my thoughts leads me to believe the emperor's men might have slipped me something to dull my mind. Poppy sap, perhaps? Whatever it was, it's wearing off—much to the chagrin of my screaming nerve endings.

It takes me far too long to realize that there's another figure bound on the other side of the atrium. Her hair spills over her face and shoulders; her robes are tattered and stained. While she has thrice the number of restraints on her, I have triple the number of armed guards. The ends of their spears are all pointed toward me, hovering dangerously close to my face, my chest, my stomach— ready to kill.

"Jyn!"

She doesn't move.

A low chuckle reaches my ear, the sound of the emperor's voice igniting my simmering rage. I strain my neck in order to see him. Seated beneath the cover of a large tent, the emperor gorges himself on a succulent buffet of roasted meats, steamed pork buns, and hearty stews. My mouth waters while a painful cramp runs through my empty stomach. How many days has it been since I last ate? Or has it been weeks?

"Glad to see you're finally awake," the emperor says, chewing with his mouth open. "I was beginning to worry I had killed the red dragon's newest reincarnation."

My brow furrows. "But . . . how do you—"

"How do I know?" the emperor scoffs. One of his concubines climbs onto his lap to wipe at his lips with a silk napkin. "You weren't exactly discreet, my boy. The famous Thread-Seeker . . . Not just anyone has the magic to see red threads of fate. Only those descended from an ancient line of power can do so. Stories of the matches you made spread much farther than you thought. It was an easy enough task to discover you. The mighty red dragon, returned once more."

I seethe. "So you sent me to find her on purpose?"

"I figured, why not let you do the work for me? If you did manage to find your own Fated One, all I had to do was keep an eye on you from afar and follow."

I spit at the ground, my opinion of him clear. "Wipe that smug look off your face, you rat."

The emperor leans back on his low chair, carved of varnished mahogany. He pops a soured plum into his mouth and chews on it gracelessly. "I suggest you choose your words carefully. You are in no position to speak to me in such a manner."

I struggle against my chains to no avail. "Let her go. I will do whatever you command, but please, let her go."

The emperor rises to his feet and wraps the long sleeves of his robes about his forearms. Then he approaches me slowly, without the slightest hint of urgency, as if he were out on a leisurely stroll. He stops just in front of me and peers down with a cruel satisfaction.

"Plead all you wish," he says, dragging the tip of his pointed finger guard my cheek. "Neither of you will ever know the taste of freedom again, now that I have you within my grasp."

His words sink in, and I understand their ominous implications. He has no plans to release us, nor will he let us die, for at least in death, we might have escaped him. We could have come back, reborn. But now he has us captured and restrained; we are truly trapped, his prisoners to do with as he sees fit for all eternity.

I consider strangling myself on my restraints, biting off my own tongue to drown in my blood, refusing all food in captivity. I will come back as many times as it takes. But what about Jyn? She might never recover from losing me after we've finally come this far; would she give up when offered another life? It is a horrifying realization that even death can't save us.

On the other side of the atrium, Jyn groans as she blinks herself awake. Focus alights in her eyes the moment she spots the emperor; they flash a dangerously dark shade of green.

"Get away from him!" she screams, so loudly and viciously that her guards jolt back in surprise.

The emperor laughs. "About time. Now the fun can finally begin."

My eyes widen. "What do you mean?"

"Seven thousand years I've spent hunting you, and *finally*, you have been reborn with your dragon magic. I shall have not one, but two mighty beasts at my disposal."

I'm adrift, my body so numb from the cold that I can't distinguish where I end and the rest of the world begins. He means to strip us for parts; little by little, or perhaps all at once. If he was willing to kill his own Fated One for such selfish gains, there's no telling what else he's capable of.

He frightens me more than any fei or yayu. More than illness, than war, than death. The longer I stare at him in helpless disbelief, the more I understand that there's truly no creature in all the realms with a blacker heart. He's a demon, destined for Hell if I ever find a way out of these restraints.

"Go on, then," the emperor says, nudging my thigh with the tip of his foot. "Transform, boy. Show me the red dragon in all his glorious splendor."

I only glare at him. "Mark my words: when I kill you, I will savor every one of your screams."

For only a moment, I catch a glimpse of something behind his stony expression, the faintest trace of fear. He's a cruel man, yes, but he's by no means a fool. He remains breakable, which I will certainly not forget.

"You will transform," he repeats, a hard edge to his tone. "Or I will bring down every manner of hurt unto your Fated One."

I lurch against my chains. "Don't you touch her!"

The emperor bends at the hip, his face a mere inch from mine. "Would you like to test me, boy? Even if I kill her, she will come back. I will dispatch her again and again until she returns as a dragon. As many times as it takes, just as I did with you. I'll make you watch every single time until you do as I ask."

A chill tears at my tender flesh. I close my eyes, and my mind finally sees through the haze and pain.

The first time I came back, I was a boy. My village was punished by an unforgiving plague. When I focus hard enough, I can see him; the mysterious stranger with vials full of blue gems. No, not gems—*scales*. I suddenly remember my mother and father from many lifetimes ago, pleading with the stranger to let them have the medicine that had worked wonders for their neighbors, only for him to deny them outright because they couldn't pay.

When I came back as a bird of paradise, it was the emperor's cage in which I sat, alone and helpless until the day I died. And who led the charge when the hunters attacked me when I was re-born a fei? None other than the emperor himself, all so he could keep an eye on me to see if my magic had returned.

In every life, in every possible capacity, this monster has haunted me. There's only one way to escape his clutches. I must free his soul from his body to break this cursed cycle—and in doing so, free A-Qian's own soul as well. Only then will my son have a choice to return once more.

"Enough!" Jyn screams. "You have it wrong. He's no dragon."

The emperor arches his brow, casting her a sharp look. He abandons my side and starts toward her. "Come again?"

"Sai is mortal. He has no powers."

"You're lying. The huntress informed me of his red eyes. Of his inhuman strength."

Jyn nods at me. "Look at him," she says, completely serious. "If it were true, would he not have shifted by now and freed us? The red dragon was thrice as strong as I."

The emperor scoffs, nothing but doubt in his tone. "Do you think me daft?"

"It's the truth."

"I'm sure I can help tease it out of him."

"You'll only end up killing him," Jyn says.

"That's a risk I'm willing to take. Until then, the burden will lie upon you. Go on. Unleash your power so that I may finally take what is mine."

"Stop!" I scream, choking helplessly against my restraints. "If you lay a hand on her—"

"What? Like this?" He snatches Jyn by the hair and yanks her head back. She yelps, the tears welling in her eyes immediately frosting over from the cold. "I could slit her throat here and now. Perhaps I will drain her of her blood if I cannot have her scales. At least then she will be worth something."

I can feel my anger rising to the surface, an overwhelming force that makes my skull vibrate and my chest burn. I'm held together by a loose thread, ready to unravel and pull apart at the seams. All I would have to do is give in to the urge, to pull at the end of my resolve and allow the magic flowing through my veins to tear the emperor asunder.

Sensing my thoughts, Jyn shoots me a warning glance. I can feel her pleading with me over our bond, cold water desperately thrown onto a roaring flame. I'm barely—just barely—able to tamp down my emotions.

We can't give the emperor what he wants, two dragons in hand. Even if I have no clue yet whether I have the ability to transform in full, I would rather he not be sure of our collective power.

After a few moments of contemplation, the emperor circles back slowly, glaring at me down the length of his nose. He looms, a silent sentry in his watchtower, so impossibly still that I can't tell whether he's even breathing. With a sharp click of his tongue, he turns swiftly on his heel to return to his seat beneath the cover of his tent. He snaps his fingers at a different one of his many waiting concubines, prompting her to pour rice wine from a hefty jar into a much smaller cup.

"You will transform," he tells Jyn flatly, "either of your own volition or by force."

I tilt my head back and stare at the growing snowstorm above. Ice shards pelt my skin, so cold they burn on my cheeks. I hate it here. "We will give you nothing," I rasp.

"Oh, but you will, boy." He sits back and sips his wine. "I always get what I want, no matter what I must break." He turns to one of his guards and snaps his fingers. "Bring out the table."

Before I can even blink, the guards standing behind me release me from my bindings and drag me over to a wooden table that is deliberately set out in clear view of Jyn. Save for the iron cuffs bolted to its surface, it looks much like any other table. The guards carry me toward it, practically tossing me onto my back before pinning me down and securing me to my new confinement.

"What are you planning to do?" I growl. "Brand me? Break my bones? Shred my skin?"

The emperor replies with a wicked smile before gesturing with his hand. "Bring out the water."

39

I scoff. *"You mean to drench me into submission?"*

My question goes ignored as the emperor returns his attention to his feast. I am evidently not worthy enough to warrant a reply. While he eats to his heart's content, the guards busy themselves above me, securing a large bucket of water to a hook suspended several feet above my head.

They force me to lie flat upon the uncomfortable wooden table, hard ridges designed onto its surface to bite into the meat of my back. My wrists and ankles are secured on either side of me, an iron bar clasped over my throat to keep my neck rigid. I can hear the foreboding clink of ice against the wood as the guard scrapes free some hardened wax that was covering a minuscule hole in the bottom of the bucket.

Water drips sporadically, hitting me square on the forehead. I flinch. It is cold enough as it is here on the mountaintop, but I refuse to be bested by a few drops of moisture. Has the emperor lost his mind? Is this truly how he wishes to break me? It's uncomfortable, to be sure, but a genuine surprise, considering all the other methods he could have chosen to torture me.

Drip. Drip, drip, drip.

The droplets hit me, their timing impossible to calculate. Some fall hard, while others are a light tap on the forehead. The skin there begins to swell from the cold. After a couple of hours, my head aches. A terrible pressure builds behind my eyes as water trickles down my temples, slithers past the backs of my ears, and kisses the nape of my neck before soaking into the collar of my robe, where it then begins to freeze from the frigid mountain air.

I am so tightly restrained that I can only stare at the sky. My discomfort grows, slowly but palpably, with every passing second. Because there is no rhythm to the water drops, long stretches of nothing are followed by an onslaught of fast drips. I try not to dwell on it, but before long, it's impossible not to anticipate each drop. It's maddening.

Drip, drip, drip . . .

My neck strains. Any attempt to blink away the moisture gathering on my eyelids is futile. The water either gets stuck in the wells of my eyes or freezes to my lashes. I squirm against the table, try to move my head to avoid the next droplet, but the clamp on my neck prevents me from doing so.

Drip.

The more I struggle, the more I feel as though I am drowning. Whatever confidence I had before fizzles out with the water. Panic strangles the breath from my lungs. By the end of the day, I'm a blubbering mess. I want it to stop. When will this blasted bucket finally drain?

"Sai!" Jyn calls to me, her voice barely reaching my ears. "You have to focus!"

"I . . . I'm trying—"

Drip, drip.

The emperor chuckles and smacks his lips as he tears into the endless assortment of food presented for his enjoyment. "Effective, is it not? A little technique my war generals came up with to interrogate their prisoners. Bones mend and skin heals, but it is different to break one's mind."

I hear some shuffling. The emperor is suddenly at my side, bending to hiss in my ear, "I wonder how you will fare overnight. Have a good sleep, boy, if you can manage it."

"Go fuck yourself," I spit.

He leaves as quickly as he came. I'm suddenly alone again, still hopelessly trapped and at the mercy of the water. The pain comes in cycles. My body goes numb, only for parts of it to scream seconds later. My muscles cramp, my joints ache, my throat chafes against its restraint. I try to concentrate on my breathing, in and out and in again, but the nature of the drops makes it impossible to focus for long.

So simple, and yet so torturous.

"Sai," Jyn says, starting to cry. "Sai, I'm so sorry. I'll get us out of this."

Drip.

My teeth chatter with every new drop that assaults my forehead. A sob escapes my throat, too, choked and desperate. It's so cold and sharp that it feels like someone is stabbing me with the tip of a dagger. "I . . . I can't breathe—"

"Sai—"

"I want to go *home*."

The confession rips itself from my hollow chest. It's a plea from my battered soul. I long to return to the teahouse, where safety and comfort come easily. I wish to see my poor mother again; I'm worried about her health and miss her kind hugs. I have been away for so long. . . . Is she all right? Does she wonder what became of me?

I was a fool to underestimate the emperor. No matter how hard I try to clear my mind, every new drop yanks me back to reality. My fear is insidious; a long, dark hand piercing through the front of my skull and latching onto my brain. It claws and it seeps into the deepest crevices of my mind, reminding me that there's no escape. There's no escape until Jyn gives the emperor what he wants.

Harvested like a common crop: her scales peeled away for medicine, her teeth pulled out to be forged into weapons, her eyes gouged from their sockets for sheer sport.

I reach out to her over our connection, seeking out her warmth like a moth to her dwindling flame. She's in no better state than I, her sorrow cold and heavy. Watching me suffer is just as torturous for her as being strapped to this table.

"Tell the emperor I'll give him what he wants," Jyn says to the guards nearest her, her voice breaking.

"No!" I yell.

"Sai—"

"I will not lose you," I snap. "Never again."

"He will destroy your mind."

"My Fated One, the love of my many lifetimes, for you, I will endure." Even as I speak, my body shakes uncontrollably. The ugly, heavy coil of anxiety boils in the pit of my stomach, causing me to retch. "You must find a way to escape. Give that monster nothing."

"Sai . . ."

I can no longer hear her words. The air, the table, my body . . . It's as though I stop existing altogether. I can only feel each drop, worse than an arrow through the skull. The more I try to ignore the water, the more sensitive I become to it.

On and on it goes, until the sun sets and the moon rises to take its place.

At some point, the guards come to change the bucket of water, replacing it with a full one that is somehow colder than the first. I find no reprieve in the few minutes it takes them to refill their torture device, because I know what is sure to come.

40

The emperor is ready and waiting, his legions of soldiers prepared to lay down their lives for the man they believe to be a god. How else can they explain the thousands he has saved from grueling plagues and disastrous famines? They are happy and willing to fight for the emperor against these great beasts. They shall slay the monsters at all costs.

They prepare their bows, swords, and spears. When the red and green dragons swoop down, their furious roars tearing through the air, the army rises to meet them.

Carnage, pointlessly bloody and horrifyingly vicious.

Many good men lose their lives, their dying thoughts spent struggling to understand what could have outraged these dragons so. But they fight on, sporting the emperor's colors with pride, slowly but surely beating the red and green dragons back toward the mountain pass.

It is there that the dragons are lured into a trap. The soldiers have hidden cannons beneath the underbrush, set to fire at a moment's notice. Fire rains down upon the dragons, burning them alive. They fall to the ground, and an entire army rushes them with swords drawn and spears tipped in poison.

Like an army of ants, they swarm—slicing, piercing, hacking.
One of their tails is torn off, their tongue sliced clean through.
It is not long before the land turns crimson, soaked with the blood
of dragons.

41

The emperor doesn't visit the next morning, nor the morning thereafter. I lose track of how many days pass. Weeks, maybe. Or perhaps a whole moon? It doesn't matter anymore. They blend together into one inescapable nightmare.

I'm parched despite all the water, and starved within an inch of my life. I no longer have the strength to lift a single finger. The guards come to feed me, but only enough to keep me alive. Sometimes, when they're feeling particularly cruel, they'll eat their own meals right beside me, or worse—spill what little there is of my food on the floor.

I want to bite their damn heads off.

Dreams and waking thoughts have become indistinguishable from one another. I see things as plain as day up in the sky, though I can't tell if they're real or machinations of my fracturing mind.

Sometimes I see him, my little prince. Bluer and more brilliant than all the glistening seas. He flies overhead in loops, chasing his own tail with a gleeful heart. The snow doesn't even faze him as he glides through the clouds. Every now and then, my son looks at me, something familiar in his sapphire eyes. A hint of pity, I think, for his withering A-Ba.

Where is your fight, dear Father? he asks. *You must not give up now. You must save yourself and Mother.*

Memories from past, present, and even future lives play out in real time. In every single one, I'm without my Fated One. I'm incomplete without her: totally, irredeemably alone.

Is there really no hope for us? Are we truly doomed to tragedy in every new life?

I know that I'm not the only one suffering, not the only one who has questioned whether this is worth the torment of losing each other a thousand different ways in a thousand different lifetimes.

Jyn deserves better. She deserves to be free.

Maybe this time when I find myself at the Steps of Heaven, I will choose not to return. Maybe I will choose to let my weary soul rest, and in doing so give Jyn the chance to live without the burden of me. At this point, it would be a mercy for us both. I can choose not to subject her to another missed lifetime.

Something cold licks at my little finger. I don't notice it at first, too numb and too broken. But then the cold begins to eat away at my flesh, starts to singe my muscles. I strain my eyes down to look at my thread of fate and am alarmed at what I find there.

The end of my fraying gray thread is starting to turn black.

I think I hear Jyn screaming for me, but I can't make sense of sound nor sight. I'm an empty husk, my mind breaking into tinier and tinier pieces. My hunger pangs reverberate through my thin bones, every part of me aching. This is by far the cruelest way I have ever died, but at least the pain will be over soon. At least this time, my soul will finally know peace.

For her sake, as well as mine . . . I don't think I'll come back. I will release her from this torturous cycle.

"Sai!"

The sound of my name snaps me back to reality. What was I

thinking just now? I really must be losing my mind. My hope was nearly snuffed out. So long as I yet breathe, have the chance to make my way to her, I could never willingly leave her. There must be a way out of this, but *how*?

A fearsome roar shakes the air, the mountains, the seas. I detect movement, though I'm unsure whether it's real or merely a strong breeze whipping over my body. My eyes can't focus, though I'm able to make out the blurry movements of the guards, the flick of a winding green tail. There's yelling, and though I don't know what they're saying, their tone suggests rising alarm.

Drip, drip, drip.

Soldiers scream as they charge her with swords and spears and arrows. It's not until I smell the heavy scent of iron that I realize it's not water tapping me on the forehead. It's far too warm, too thick, too *red*.

I catch the whiff of jasmine before I see her, Jyn's shaking hands desperately trying to unlock my restraints. Her own wrists are badly bruised, and several deep cuts to her arms and her side are soaking her silk robes with blood. She must have wrenched herself from her restraints with what little strength she still had, but in doing so, has grievously injured herself.

"Stay with me," she wheezes. "Stay with me, Sai!"

She frees me of my iron collar, my head and neck so heavy that I wince at the sudden ability to move. My wrists and my ankles are next, but my limbs are too weak. There's a scuffle, soldiers bearing down on us. With a vicious snarl, Jyn transforms back before my very eyes, the normally vibrant green of her scales muted and fading. With a whip of her tail, she knocks the bucket of water and its stand aside, spilling it onto the cold stone floor of the atrium.

I attempt to move, but my body is too broken to cooperate.

Jyn fights. She fights like her life depends on it, and it *does*.

I can only watch in stunned shock as my thread turns a deeper black, trailing farther down our connection. This is what it must feel like to *die*.

Facing wave after wave of soldiers, my dragon shows no signs of slowing. With one swipe of her claws, she slices a man in twain. With the gnash of her teeth, she rips heads from shoulders. With a flick of her tail, she sends a man flying into the mountain's jagged rock face. She endures spears through her legs, arrows to her chest, swords to her face—and yet she fights on.

Her desperation awakens something inside of me. I can't let this pass. She needs me.

If we are going to die, then let it be with a fight.

One foot before the other. It takes every ounce of my concentration to even take a step. My legs are indeed broken, the shattered pieces of my bones slicing from within. In a way, I'm grateful that the emperor's torture has left me too numb to feel.

I stumble and fall, only to get back up again. I clamber over corpses and pick up someone's bloodied sword. My vision is far too blurry to make sense of my surroundings. All I do is hack and slash at anything that comes barreling toward me.

I take my share of injuries—they slice the backs of my knees, run my shoulder through with the tip of a spear—but I keep fighting. Pain no longer frightens me. I need to get to my Fated One.

Now that I have accepted certain death, I am unstoppable.

The Imperial soldiers circle us. We're outnumbered and trapped. Archers position themselves on the roof of the atrium, pelting us with arrows with their tips set ablaze. Between the slash of swords, the unforgiving snow, and the hail of fire, it's frankly a miracle that Jyn and I have lasted this long.

"No, you fools!" the emperor bellows from the safety of the Winter Palace. He watches in fury from one of the many windows carved into the mountainside. He must have been asleep and rushed from his bedchamber at the first news of the fight. "You musn't kill the dragon!"

Jyn and I fight on, determined to thin out the crowd. The air reeks of death. Some of the soldiers heed their emperor's orders and retreat, but the unlucky few who remain in our path are slaughtered without remorse. Before long, the chaos subsides. A horde of armed men is back in formation at a distance, still ready to tear us asunder if given the command.

The emperor leaves the safety of his palace and steps through its large moon door. He remains behind his sea of soldiers, sporting a slight grin. "Well," the emperor says, clapping his hands slowly. "I'm impressed. And here I thought I'd broken you. Thank you for helping me draw out my dragon."

I place myself between him and Jyn, snarling through bloodied teeth.

"She is *not* yours," I seethe. "You've already stolen our son's immortality. Is it not enough for you to have murdered him?"

The emperor goes rigid, and he stares at us in silence for a few long seconds. He takes a deep breath before he says, "I have spent the last millennia regretting it. But my shamans believe that we may be able to bring him back."

I frown. "Bring him back?"

"It would require sacrificing one dragon in exchange for another. But you know as well as I do that there's nothing we would not do for our Fated Ones."

A growl rises from my throat. "You *killed* yours. Our son. After taking him from under our protection for your own gain!"

For the first time, I see shame wash over his expression. "I will make amends by giving him life again. But I need enough dragon's blood to summon his soul."

I shake my head. "You're a misguided fool."

"What?"

"You devoured his heart and his soul along with it. So long as his spirit remains within you, there's no bringing him back."

"No . . . you're lying." The emperor shakes his head, confusion swirling on his face. He's utterly unwilling to listen. "My shamans have assured me—"

"You can't bring him back without sacrificing yourself. He remains trapped within you, and even then, he cannot come back to life. Once his soul is free, he can be reborn, but the man you knew is no more."

His expression darkens. "There's little dragon's blood cannot accomplish. And I'm willing to test your limits."

"You're mad," I say. "Absolutely mad."

"Guards! *Seize them!*"

The soldiers advance, but not before Jyn throws her massive body in front of me. She takes every spear, every arrow, every sword, shielding me from those who wish us harm. Her roar is reduced to a whimper, the damage sustained too great for her to bear.

"Jyn, we have to get out of here!"

She stands firm, but I can feel her resolve shattering. She knows as well as I that there's no escape from this hell. Too weak for escape, too tired to fight on. We're done for.

An arrow slices through the air and hits Jyn square in the chest. It pierces through her bloodied scales and sinks deep. With one final wail, she shifts, her body shrinking as her magic begins to fade. I catch her in time, but we fall nonetheless.

I cradle her body close, tenderly brushing strands of her hair away from her face. She's distressingly pale and growing colder by the second.

"It will be all right, my love," I whisper against her cheek. The throbbing ache in my lungs leaves me gasping, sobbing. "It will be all right."

With a trembling hand, Jyn reaches up and caresses my jaw. "I will be back," she rasps.

"No, please—"

"I *will* be back."

"Jyn, I—" I choke on my own tongue. "There's still so much I wish to do with you in this life." I press a kiss to her forehead. "I wish to braid your hair." A kiss to her temple. "To watch the morning sunrise with you." A kiss to her lips. "To annoy you with my stories."

Jyn coughs. Her weak smile breaks me. "I don't mind your stories."

I want to scream.

Gods above, please—*not now*. Not when we've finally found each other.

"Let me rest," she whispers, impossibly quiet. I hear my own heart shatter around her words. "I'm so very tired."

My eyes sting with tears, and my chest threatens to cave in. I can already feel her slipping away.

"How am I to live without you?"

"Promise me," she mumbles. "You must return so that we might find each other again."

Her light is quickly fading, drifting out where I have no hope of following. My mouth is dry. "I promise."

"I love you, Sai," she says on a weak exhale. "I have loved you in every life, and I will love you in every one hereafter."

"I love you, too," I mumble back. "Always."

It happens quietly. One final breath, and then she's gone. She's gone, and I suddenly know a fraction of the pain she has endured all these years. When she dies, I die along with her; yet I am cursed to remain on this wretched earth.

The thread between us—our sacred connection—turns an inky black. And then it crumbles away, mere dust on the wind.

I am hollow.

Broken.

He has taken her from me.

I look up at the emperor, who raises an amused brow. "What a shame," he says. "It appears I have finally vanquished the last dragon of the east. But I'm sure we can do something with the meager amount of dragon's blood she has left us."

I lay Jyn's body down onto the tile floor, silently promising her a resting place more befitting of her station, that of a forgotten queen. I rise slowly, my knees cracking as I do. As I stare up at the emperor, the grief I feel quickly becomes something darker. It threatens to tear me in two.

"You're wrong," I hiss. I tap into the unbridled rage, so intense it threatens to consume me. I have felt it before. But it's far stronger now than I remember it being in any of my other lifetimes.

The rage of a beast.

"Oh?" the emperor asks. "How so, boy?"

The magic that has been sealed away within my blood finally ignites, a million sparks arcing at once as my skin transforms, rigid red scales the color of an inferno taking its place.

"She wasn't the last dragon," I say with a low, vicious snarl through sharpened teeth. "*I* am."

Part 5

The
Red
Dragon

42

I *crave destruction. With this overwhelming* rage, the magic sealed away in my veins unleashes itself, erupting with such intense heat that it threatens to swallow not just me, but the whole world.

Jyn in her glorious dragon form stood taller than the most opulent buildings of the Pearl District back home. She was longer than eight carriages lined up back to front, muscles thick and posture poised. But if she was huge, then I'm massive.

I tower over the emperor and his men, nearly half the size of the adjacent mountain. My body wraps around the atrium three times, my tapered tail whipping and crushing anyone in its path. I suck in a sharp breath, a wealth of power coursing through me.

My sharp claws dig into the ground, scraping up stone and dirt and roots. My jagged rows of pointed teeth are fiercer than any blade. It's my own scales that bewitch me the most, a deep and vibrant ruby that stands in stark contrast to the snowstorm flurrying around us. The emperor has an army of no fewer than a thousand men, but they know as well as I do that they stand no chance against the red dragon of old.

I am His Majesty, King of the Skies. My rage knows no bounds, and there will be no salvation for those who've crossed me.

This is who I was always meant to be. Feeling the stretch of my skin into diamond-hard scales, the shift of my fingers into deadly claws, and the whip of the wind through my crimson mane is as natural to me as breathing. An old glove, a familiar outer robe I once thought lost, a warm bed at home after years away.

I lash the end of my tail against the mountain wall, the force so mighty that it crumbles and gives way. An opening—and the only mercy I will show to those with enough sense to abandon arms and escape with their lives. It's not long before more than half of the emperor's men drop their weapons, tripping over one another as they flee.

"Where are you going?" the emperor howls behind a wall of his most loyal guards. "Traitors! Return at once or I will have your heads!"

I stare him down, relishing the full-fledged fear in his eyes. This is the face of a man who realizes too late that everyone must get their comeuppance. No amount of status or gold or influence can protect him now.

"Don't just stand there!" he screams. "Kill him! *Now!*"

Their attempts on my life are pitiful. I'm too great, too mighty for their pathetic weapons. With one bat of a colossal claw, I crush his men instantly. Their screams are wasted on me, drowned out by the sound of their bones being ground to dust underfoot. I pick them off by the mouthful. The lucky ones die quickly, torn to shreds between my unyielding jaws. The unlucky ones are swallowed whole, awake for their every dying second.

These fools were born and raised in a time where dragons were long thought lost. They know not the enemy they've made of me. Whatever luck these pitiful creatures had that saw to our initial demise is gone. Now, I will be their reckoning.

A few of them manage to nick me, stabbing at a point between my thick red scales. It's their mistake, however, for they can't retrieve their swords from my hide. A quick twist of my body sends them flying, their skulls crushed and their limbs twisted the wrong way. Most are dead before they even hit the ground.

Before long, I have the emperor cornered. I purposely saved him for last. The emperor has his back pressed against the mountain wall, his knees trembling. I can hear his heart railing inside his rib cage; his breathing is fast and shallow. A mighty ruler, now reduced to a quivering rabbit facing his doom. It's his turn to know endless fear and pain. To feel hopeless.

And I will savor every moment of it. I will not rest until I have wrought on him the same pain he has caused me.

Terror has an awful stench, equal parts sour and bitter. It's worse than curdled cow's milk mixed with soggy day-old market meat and horse piss. And now it radiates off him in endless waves.

"H-have mercy," Róng begs.

I fight the urge to rip his head off on hearing the word. Mercy? After everything he has done to my family? The gall of this man.

It's time to put him in his place.

I snatch him up in my jaws, my teeth shredding through his golden silks. But I'm careful not to give him any fatal wounds—he doesn't deserve a swift death. He screams, beating my face with his closed fists and kicking his legs out helplessly, his crown falling away.

"Please! Release me, and I will never pursue you again!"

I turn instead and carefully move toward Jyn's body. My heart hurts as I pick her up as gently as I'm able in my claws, careful not to scratch her. I take a deep breath before looking to the sky. A new sensation—hope—brews deep within my core.

Flight comes to me as easily as breathing or walking. I launch into the air, the rest of my long body trailing behind me like a vibrant red cord. It feels good to be one with the clouds once more, surveying the lands from up above. Thousands of years ago, I blessed every one of these mountains, streams, and rolling hills. It's a bittersweet return without Jyn.

If only my heart were not broken, I might truly enjoy it all.

Róng screams himself hoarse from my mouth, giving up only when we make it out to sea. I'm unsure where we're headed. All I know is that something is pulling me in this direction, an internal compass. I can feel it tugging at me, leading me east—leading me home.

The coastline is now a distant dot on the horizon, long stretches of endless blue sky reflected in the salty waters below. I soar through the clouds faster and faster, chasing after some unknown target. When the island finally comes into view, I instinctively begin my descent, the warm earth welcoming me like an old friend.

It's paradise, hidden away from the rest of the world by thick fog and rough seas. The rich bamboo forests provide the perfect amount of cover. I land near a large lake, all manner of beasts gathered around. There are fei and yayu and a number of other species drinking peacefully from the water's edge. They move aside as I approach, but I detect no threat of danger from them.

I open my mouth and let Róng fall into the lake. He breaches the surface with a wheeze and a cough, flailing about chaotically. He thrashes like a drowning pig, weighed down by his ostentatious robes, which are now soaked through and heavy.

"What do you plan to do to me?" he rasps. "Drown me? Eat me? Whatever it is, just get it over with."

Ignoring him, I carefully lay Jyn's body down on a bed of soft grass before transforming back into my human form. With careful fingers, I brush her hair away from her face, now at peace in eternal sleep. Bending down, I press a tender kiss to her forehead—a farewell, as much as it is a promise.

I rise once more and turn to the emperor, wholly unimpressed when he attempts to charge me. All it takes is a step to the side and a hard strike across his cheek to send him tumbling to the ground.

Dazed, he sits up and looks around; then Róng swallows hard. Behind us, the beasts of the forest gather, watching with hungry curiosity. How many years has it been since a human wandered into their home? What a rare, lovely treat he might make.

I step forward and snatch him up by the chin, digging my nails into his pale cheeks. He whimpers when I pierce his skin, angry red beads forming at my fingertips. I allow his blood to coat my palm, and drip down my wrist.

"You will not receive the mercy of a quick death," I say. "You killed my wife. My son. My parting gift to you is one final hunt, to commemorate the millennia you have hunted us."

He looks over at the hungry beasts, eyes widening at the sight of their bared teeth and pronounced rib cages. "You—you would set them on me?"

"A rather fitting end, wouldn't you agree?"

"Wait, I beg of you—"

"Go on, then," I say, glaring at him down the length of my nose. "On your knees, *boy*."

A shaky breath escapes the man as he struggles onto his hands and knees, his eyes keeping a wary watch on the forest beasts. Humiliation scorches his face, a bright crimson. Slowly, he lowers his head to the ground in a full kowtow, his entire body trembling with fear and perhaps fury. I wish I could say it's satisfying, but I find no pleasure in the cowering of a useless rat.

"Run, then," I tell him. "I'll give you the courtesy of a head start."

Róng rises onto shaky legs and stumbles back one step at a time. The beasts of the forest growl and hiss, prompting him to spin on his heel and break into a sprint. He runs deeper into the bamboo forest with a pathetic whimper.

I let out an exhausted, heavy breath. I silently count backward from ten before flinging the blood upon my hand to the forest floor. The beasts sniff at it, drool dripping from their lips. I've marked Róng for death.

I step out of the way, cautious of their snarling fangs, and whisper, *"Eat."*

The beasts lurch forward in one giant horde, growling and barking and snarling as they track Róng's scent. It's not long before the sounds of the hunt fade in the distance. They will find him sooner or later, I'm sure. I won't give him the honor of a dignified death by my own hand.

He once hunted me and Jyn like dogs, and now he will die knowing the same terror.

I set to work instead, carrying Jyn to a neighboring hillside near a large field of soft grass. Blanking my mind, I begin to dig into the soft earth with my bare hands. Sweat drips from my brow, and my knees are stained brown from the damp soil. It's pleasantly warm, a nice reprieve from the bitter winters back home. This place has a clear view of the sunset over the ocean, surrounded by fields of blue wildflowers.

She would like it, I think, if she were here.

I bury Jyn with great care, resigned as I return her to the earth. I carefully remove her hairpin and smooth out her locks so that she may rest in comfort. Grief bears down on my shoulders, sorrow squeezes my throat tight. As I lay flowers over her resting place, I can't stop rubbing the closed black loop around my little finger. It's terrifying, not being able to sense her on the other end of the line. I'm missing a part of myself now that she's gone.

I sit beside her for what feels like hours until the sun sets and the moon rises. A part of me feels guilty for the lack of tears, but despite my overwhelming sadness, they do not flow. She promised she would be back, and I have no choice now but to take her word for it.

Somewhere in the distance, perhaps on the other side of our island paradise, I hear Róng's scream. It's a bloodcurdling sound, desperate and raw and pitiful. It cuts short.

The deed is done. Róng and his insatiable greed are no more.

And with it, I swear I feel the ocean sigh. The wind whispers past me. My son's soul has finally been released, free to slip back into the natural cycle of reincarnation. I pray he'll come back to us one day, too.

"Rest, my heart," I whisper, one hand on the gravestone I placed here for Jyn. "I'll wait for your return."

43

It's strange coming home again after a whole moon away. Every-thing's the same, and yet it's all so different. The run-down shan-ties, the dirt roads, the bustling marketplace. People go about their business, some haggling with vendors while others gather in groups to share idle gossip and news from the war front. Maybe *I* am the one who's changed.

A-Ba's teahouse is exactly how I left it, though it feels like de-cades ago. I was a different man then, so full of hope and quips and energy. Now I can barely find the will to breathe. When I slide the front door open and step inside, I find a few customers enjoying pots of tea. Our cheapest blend, judging by the mild scent. It's a relief to see the place is still afloat, although I'm concerned at my mother's absence.

She's nowhere in sight.

"Sai?"

A woman approaches from out of the corner of my eye. She's familiar to me, sharing A-Ba's long black hair, pinched nose, and rounded cheeks. Auntie Ying wipes her hands on a cloth, looking me over with clear surprise.

"My goodness, it really is you!" she says with wide eyes. "Where have you been? We've been so terribly worried about you. Nine suns, you look as though you've been dragged beneath a horse!"

"Where's A-Ma?"

"In the kitchen, dear. She'll be so happy to see you."

I make my way through the teahouse and round the corner in a hurry. I find A-Ma seated on a wooden stool next to the burners, tending to their flames as clay pots full of water come to a boil. She has thinned out again, but she's nowhere near as sickly as she was before I left. It appears that the green dragon's scale has managed to tide her over in the time I have been away.

"Sai!" A-Ma gasps when she sees me, and springs up from her seat. She cups my face in her hands and kisses my cheeks. "Oh, my boy, my sweet boy, you've come back!"

I've missed her warmth and the smell of tea leaves lingering on her robes. After the hellish weeks I've endured, seeing her again feels like a dream. It's no small relief to discover that Róng's threats to harm her turned out to be empty.

"I'm so glad to see you," I say in a rush. My words come as a raspy croak, exhaustion weighing them down. It's good to finally be home.

My mother takes a step back to inspect me, her smile slipping as she does. "Good Heavens. What happened?"

I reach into one of my pockets and pull out a single red scale. It shimmers in the light, dazzling wildfire in my palm. I move about the kitchen and retrieve the stone mortar and pestle from one of the lower cupboards. I'm quick to grind my scale into dust, then move to mix it into a nearby pot of tea. Finally, I pour a cup and hold it out to A-Ma.

"Please, drink this," I instruct her.

She arches a brow. "This is the first thing you have to say to your mother? I was worried sick after those soldiers showed up and took you away. And what was it that you just put in my drink?"

"Please, A-Ma. I'll explain everything while you drink. Trust me."

My mother eyes me suspiciously, but takes the cup all the same. She takes a seat on a nearby kitchen stool and takes a few sips. The effects of my scale are far more potent than that of the green dragon's. Within moments, I see her cheeks fill with color and her hair become glossy. A-Ma glows with a youthful vibrance, her health further restored with every sip of tea.

"There," she says, dabbing her lips with a nearby napkin once she's downed the entire cup. "Now, tell me where you have been all this time. Your complexion has gotten darker—have you traveled far? Could you not have written your poor A-Ma just one letter assuring me you were well?"

She rattles off question after question, boisterous and full of life. I'm relieved that she's not so much angry as she is anxious for answers, though I'm not ready to give them. It's a slice of normalcy I believed long gone for me. Gratitude sits high in my chest, mixing with the grief I have been carrying, both newly and for centuries.

My bottom lip trembles.

And then I fall apart.

I drop to my knees, wrap my arms around A-Ma and hug her tight, sobbing against her shoulder. Startled, she embraces me, patting me gently on the back.

"My son, what has happened to you?"

"It's a long story," I say wearily. The tears I couldn't shed during Jyn's burial suddenly pour forth, streaking my cheeks and burning my skin. "I met my Fated One. She was . . ."

My chest caves in. I can't get out another word.

My mother stands and has me take a seat on the kitchen stool, clasping my hands tight. "Tell me, Sai. I'll listen."

I take a deep, labored breath and start from the beginning—the *very* beginning.

"According to legend, they were a family of three."

44

The first thing I do when I wake each morning is check my hand.

Still a closed black loop.

I do my best not to sit in my disappointment. It has been almost a year and three moons, but I haven't given up hope. Jyn promised she would come back, so it's only a matter of when. She waited seven thousand years for me; surely I can do the same for her.

Tending to the teahouse is as good a distraction as any. There's a lot of work to do now that the war has ended and the traders from the South have been permitted entry once more. Business booms with the start of the new year, the springtime months bringing with them warmer weather and the promise of new beginnings.

"Ridiculous!" one of the teahouse patrons at the far end of the room says to the man sitting across from him. "Surely these are the ramblings of a madman."

"It's true, I swear it! There were soldiers there who escaped the carnage. They say that the emperor was holding captive the red and green dragons of old!"

"That's preposterous." The patron turns to me with a friendly chortle. "What do you think, Sai? Surely it's impossible."

"Dragons?" I ask, setting a fresh pot of tea on the low table. "Unbelievable, if you ask me. There are no such things as dragons."

"Then how do you explain the emperor's sudden disappearance?" the second customer asks with a huff. "His Imperial Majesty went missing without a trace. And there were hundreds of witnesses to the event!"

"You know what I think it is?" the first customer says, lowering his voice. "Probably just a tale by one of his advisors to help them claim the throne. You know those shamans are always scheming."

"You shouldn't say such things," the second patron warns. "The newly crowned emperor could have your head for such slander. Right, Sai?"

"I'm just a teahouse owner," I say easily, gathering up a tray of empty cups. "I couldn't care less about the goings-on behind palace walls."

"Ah, to be young and carefree! How I envy you."

"Our new emperor is already doing a lot of good," the other man at the table says. "They say he was a most respected advisor. He put an end to this stupid war, and I hear he's lowering taxes come summertime."

"You don't say? That's a welcome change, indeed," his friend replies.

"Another refill, gentlemen?" I ask. "My mother has just made a fresh batch of steamed buns."

"That sounds wonderful. Bring us a plate of pork dumplings, too."

"As you wish, good sir," I say, heading toward the kitchen.

A-Ma keeps herself busy with all manner of fried doughnut sticks, flaky scallion pancakes, and soup dumplings made lovingly by hand. Her hair is pulled back into a bun, her sleeves are rolled up and tied out of the way with long white ribbons, and the heat of the fire brings color to her cheeks.

"Wonderfully busy today," she comments. "How are things looking up front?"

"All of our tables are full," I inform her with pride. "We'll likely be open well after sundown."

"Perhaps we should consider hiring some help. We could use an extra pair of hands."

"That would be wise. I worry the customers will race me off my feet at this rate."

"Speak to Auntie Ying tomorrow on your way to the market. I heard that her son-in-law's cousin is looking for work."

"Very well, I'll—"

I freeze midsentence, an odd sensation suddenly washing over me. It's a spark, light and pure and good. The birth of something new. I nearly drop the kettle of hot water I'm holding, so stunned that my mind momentarily goes blank. This feeling is new to me, and yet . . .

It's strangely familiar, too.

"Sai?" A-Ma calls to me. "What's the matter? Is something wrong?"

An invisible force tugs at my hand. I look down, curious and excited. Wrapped around my little finger is a brand-new thread—a brilliant red.

Hope leaves me lightheaded.

"Nothing's wrong," I say, a smile forming on my lips. "Nothing at all."

45

Y*ou've packed enough water, yes?"* my mother asks, fussing over me as she crams red-bean buns into every available pocket of my robes.

"Yes, I have."

"And your compass? You know as well as I do how easily you get lost."

"I know, A-Ma."

"A change of under robes?"

"A-Ma."

She wrings her fingers together nervously, buzzing with so much excitement I fear she might vibrate right out of her skin. "I just want you to be prepared, that's all. Who knows how long this trek could take?"

"I found her once," I say with a grin. "I'm sure I can do it again."

"Please remember to write. You know how I worry otherwise. I expect to hear all about your grand adventures."

"I promise."

She gives me a tight hug. "Please be safe, Sai. And good luck."

"Thank you, A-Ma."

With a nod and a reassuring smile, I set off with my hand out-stretched before me. There's a great deal of slack as it trails off—according to my compass—due north. There are very few large cities in the northern regions; the land is too cold and hard for the growth of enough crops to sustain a large population. It will take at least two weeks on foot.

But not so long by flight.

Once I'm well and clear of the city, I duck behind the shade of a tall row of trees, shifting quickly before launching into the sky. I ascend at a sharp angle, determined to keep out of view. Ever since the attack at the Winter Palace, rumors about dragons have been impossible to avoid. Most people—thankfully—have the good sense to ignore them, writing them off as tall tales, but I would much rather avoid detection where possible.

I follow my red thread, allowing it to guide me as I sail through the clouds. I have no idea what to expect. What form has Jyn taken? Will the memories of her previous life return to her as they did for me? I hope that I'll reach her before anything befalls her. Róng may be dead and gone, but the world remains full of unseen dangers.

Plant life in the northern regions is sparse. The terrain here is rocky, covered in frost, and largely clear of trees, making it easy for me to spot the small village of tents on the northern coast.

My thread slowly edges downward. My Fated One is some-where near.

I descend a good distance from the village, shifting into my human form before anyone can spot me. I walk the rest of the way, entering the main road that leads straight through to the village center. The place bustles with life. People go about their usual business, while most eagerly catch up with the traveling merchants who have made it all the way up with their goods. I blend in with the lot of them, a stranger to this area, yet still wholly welcomed by the locals. They pay me no mind as I wander through the village in search of my Fated One.

My thread is now drawn taut and vibrating, a glorious warmth emanating from our connection with our nearing proximity. I will my heart to settle, but there's no denying the brewing excitement in the pit of my stomach. I'm close.

I come across a humble shack at the far edge of the village. Its thatched roof is made of woven water reeds, its walls of baked white clay. There's a meager fence of thin sticks around the perimeter of the property. A strong breeze could easily knock it over, but it seems to work just fine to keep the family's chickens from wandering off.

Strings of thyme, garlic bulbs, and red peppers hang above the wooden doorframe to dry. There's an outdoor kitchen just beside the shack, boasting two woodstoves and a large, tightly woven basket for uncooked rice. All in all, this is a humble abode, though I can't tell if anyone is currently home.

The sharp cry of a child answers my question.

I wander around the front of the shack and find a young woman seated on a log amid a thriving vegetable garden. She looks to be in her mid-thirties, her long black hair in tangles. Though my thread of fate points in her direction, she and I are not connected. Hers is connected to another, leading off to the left, back toward the village center.

The woman hums a gentle tune, gently shushing the crying bundle in her arms. The newborn is only a few days old, with chubby cheeks a cute shade of pink. The child cries and cries and cries, wriggling uncomfortably beneath thick blankets.

"Please, my darling," her mother says. "Please, stop crying. Why won't you sleep?"

I clear my throat gently. "Excuse me, madam?"

The woman rises, startled. "Yes?"

"Apologies for the interruption. I was traveling through and couldn't help but overhear the child's distress. Is everything well?"

The woman gives me an exhausted nod. "Oh, I do beg your pardon. My daughter . . . She has not taken to my milk. No matter what I do, I can't get her to latch on. My husband will be back shortly with the doctor, but I fear . . ." She sighs, the dark circles beneath her eyes deep and weary. The new mother's bottom lip trembles. "I fear I may lose my little one if she doesn't eat soon. It's been a hard winter. I'm not sure we can afford the medicine."

My heart aches for her. She's clearly doing her best.

"I happen to be a healer of sorts," I say. "With your permission, might I hold her for a moment?"

The woman frowns slightly, her hesitation not unwarranted. She gestures with a hand to the free space on the log, inviting me over. We sit together as she carefully hands the child to me.

The crying stops at once.

The little girl peers up at me with big brown eyes. There are dazzling specks of green around the edges, as beautiful and brilliant as emeralds. She manages to wriggle one of her arms free of the blankets, exposing her thread-bearing hand.

We are connected.

I cannot help but laugh as she laughs, joy radiating over our bond.

"Amazing," her mother breathes, her eyes wide with pleasant surprise. "Goodness, how is this possible? She hasn't stopped crying since her first breath!"

I shrug a shoulder, keeping my hold on the child as tender and careful as possible. "Have you any goat's milk?" I ask.

"That I do."

"Mix in a small amount of honey and soak a clean cloth in the mixture. It will tide her over until she learns to suckle."

The woman hurries inside, keeping an eye on me through the small window of her home as she diligently gathers the ingredients.

She returns with the soaked cloth and hands it to me, then takes her seat at my side to watch everything unfold. I bring the cloth to the child's lips. She whines softly before finally opening her mouth and hungrily sucking up the milk and honey.

Her mother gasps. Tears of happiness well in her eyes. "You're a miracle worker. Pray tell, what's your name, good sir?"

"Sai," I answer.

"It's a pleasure to meet you, Sai. I'm Luobing."

"And the little one? What's her name?"

"In all honesty, my husband and I are still struggling to come to an agreement on what we should call her." The woman shifts in her seat. "Tell me, dear sir. What would your suggestion be?"

"You would have me pick her name?"

"I was in dire straits before you happened along. It seems that you have the right instinct."

The little girl in my arms coos, staring up at me with wide eyes. She mirrors my smile, her free hand reaching out toward me with a flex of her little fingers.

"As luck would have it," I say, "I have the perfect name in mind."

46

Twenty years come and go.

I have settled on a small plot of land in the rolling hills north of Jiaoshan. It's surrounded by towering trees and bisected by a winding river full of enough fish to keep me fed year-round. I built my home by hand, digging the foundation into the earth and diligently setting each one of the roof's glazed tiles. My humble shack stands alone against the backdrop of trees, solitary and proud atop a steep hill.

I visit the markets every now and then to restock on supplies and to check up on the teahouse. Business has flourished. People come far and wide to taste A-Ma's baked goods. They say she makes the best red-bean buns in all the land. The teahouse is self-sufficient at this point, a whole team of servers and cooks working throughout the day to fill the bellies of paying customers. As much as I enjoy visiting my mother, who is completely healthy thanks to a good dose of dragon scales all those years back, I find quiet pleasure in my solitude, too.

It's just as well. I'd overheard the curious whispers and suspicious rumblings as I passed through town over the years. Comments about my miraculous lack of aging grew more and more frequent. I chalked it up to a healthy diet and the medicinal prop-erties of tea, but my crafty lies and easy charm were eventually not enough to explain my lack of wrinkles, sunspots, or even graying strands of hair.

It seems that I am forever stuck at five and twenty—amortal.

I suppose dragons age slowly once we've reached maturity, Jyn once told me. *To the human eye, it looks as though time has stopped altogether.*

There's peace to be found out here. I spend my days tending to my vegetable garden or feeding the gentle critters of the forest. Every now and then, a traveler will show up at my front door re-questing an audience with the Thread-Seeker. I help them if I'm able, though my heart rarely has the will for such a journey. Where the coupling of a fated pair once brought me endless joy, it now serves as a reminder of what I have lost.

Though hopefully, soon, my darling one will return to me once again.

My mornings begin at the crack of dawn with the call of the rooster I keep in an outdoor pen. I feed the chickens before cutting up the next day's firewood, and then promptly get to cooking a hearty, filling meal of steamed eggs, green onions, and fluffy white rice.

I spend the afternoons writing, not just to record the stories of my childhood, but also my grand adventures across the Five King-doms. I write letters, too, keeping in touch with Luobing every few moons or so, though I choose to keep my distance.

Jyn was far too young when I first found her. After the millen-nia of turmoil she endured, I wanted to give her the chance to live a normal life—to enjoy childhood, adolescence—before we find each other again. Was it selfish of me? I'd argue not. I'm sure she will come and find me once she's ready. Until then, I will wait. As long as I know she's happy, I can make peace with the distance I've placed between us.

One sweltering afternoon, I find myself in my garden watering the vegetables. I'm particularly proud of the succulent wolfberries that I've managed to cultivate this year. Once dried, they will make a nice addition to wintertime soups. I'm so engrossed in my garden work that the sudden tug I feel on my little finger takes me by surprise, along with the faint scent of jasmine sweeping in with the breeze.

"Excuse me?" comes a woman's soft, sweet voice.

I turn to regard the stranger, except she's no stranger at all. Before me stands a woman so radiant, so beautiful that I'm left without breath. The light green of her robes complements the soft porcelain of her skin, and her long black hair is tied back in a simple, clean braid that trails down the length of her back.

There are enough similarities to know exactly who she is, but there are also many differences that I take great pleasure in studying. From the new shape of her rosebud lips, to the gentle slope of her nose, to the curve of her chin and the height of her sharp cheekbones. She has freckles in this lifetime, a delicate splash of faded color across her forehead and the bridge of her nose.

"I apologize for disturbing you, good sir, but . . ." Jyn sucks in a sharp breath, picking at her fingernails. "Well, this might sound a bit ridiculous."

I tilt my head to the side, basking in the light of her bashful smile. It's a thrill when she finally musters up the courage to look me in the eye.

I can't help but tease. "Is something wrong? Is there something on my face?"

"What? Oh, um, no." She swallows hard, anxiously opening and closing her fists. "You're my mother's benefactor, are you not?"

"Benefactor?"

"Yes. For as long as I can remember, my family has received a generous sum of coin every moon without fail." She reaches into the silk purse she has tied around her dainty wrist, pulling out a few pieces of neatly folded parchment. "I have your letters, though you never signed your name."

"What makes you believe it's me?"

"Because you have yet to deny it."

I chuckle. "Is it coin you seek?"

"I'm no beggar, sir."

"Then, pray tell, what brings you to my humble abode?"

She shifts her weight from foot to foot, clearly flustered. As elated as I am that she has arrived, I don't wish to see her upset.

"You said it might sound ridiculous?" I prompt gently.

Jyn takes a deep breath. "Ever since I can remember, I have . . . I don't know how to explain it, but I'm able to see red threads of fate."

"Oh. Is that so?"

"You're laughing at me."

"No, my mooncake, I would never."

"Don't call me—" Jyn pauses, her expression melting into confusion. "Wait . . . Do I know you?"

"Can I interest you in a pot of tea?" I ask, gesturing to my outdoor kitchen. "I make an excellent brew of Longjing."

She shakes her head. "No. I mean, yes, thank you, but . . . Please, what is your name?"

I take a step forward and search her eyes. I wonder how close to the surface the memories of her past life sit. "You know my name, Jyn. Think back. The answer is there."

She watches me in thinly veiled suspicion but accepts my offer of tea regardless. I'm filled with a giddy excitement as she follows me through my humble garden, taking in the little knickknacks that I've collected over the years—everything with her in mind. Scrolls of poetry set out on the porch table, collected in the hopes of sharing them all with Jyn one day. Rare tea leaves that I bartered for so that we may taste them together. My garden is full of delicate blue wildflowers, the very same from our homeland, planted in thick, flourishing bundles so that she might feel more at ease.

I get to work in my small kitchen, bringing water to a boil so that the tea can steep, all the while observing Jyn out of the corner of my eye. She takes a seat at the low porch table and looks around in quiet awe. I can tell she has questions, and I'd be more than happy to indulge her were I not so worried about overwhelming her. Recalling all my past lives in one fell swoop shook me to the core. I'd much rather let Jyn in slowly. There's no rush now, no threats lurking around the corner. We can finally take our time.

"I'm surprised you're willing to listen," she admits. "There are only a few people that I've told about the red threads, but they've all laughed at me."

"That's not very nice of them," I reply, pouring hot water into a clay pot full of dried tea leaves. The satisfying glug of the steaming stream fills my ears, harmonizing with the gentle crackle and snap of the stove fire before me. "In my experience, people often laugh at things they don't understand."

Jyn arches a brow. "But *you* understand?"

"Oh, yes. I'm a bit of a know-it-all, in fact." I sit down across from her and pour her a cup, delighted when she brings it to her lips and takes a thoughtful sip.

"I've come seeking answers," she says after a moment.

"And I'm happy to oblige."

"I don't even know where to begin. You'll think me mad. *I* think I'm mad."

I pour myself a cup of tea, breathing in the herbal steam. "You'll find no judgment from me. Tell me what's on your mind."

Jyn chews on the inside of her cheek, an adorable little quirk she's picked up in this lifetime, it would seem. And yet the familiar furrow of her brows, as well as the way her shoulders tense with concentration, remain the same. She takes a deep breath and steels herself, her eyes peering deeply into mine.

"I think you're my Fated One," she says.

I grin so wide that my cheeks ache. "I know I am. Now, if you'll drink your tea, I would share with you a story."

It's well into the evening by the time I'm finished. Jyn sits at the table overlooking the flowers, her delicate features painted in the soft orange sunset. Her eyes are closed, her fingers rubbing at her temples. She didn't speak a word during or even after I recounted our tale.

"I don't understand," she says eventually. "I don't remember anything at all."

"Give it time," I reply patiently. "It's a lot to take in."

"Are you sure you're not lying?"

"No, sunshine. This is far too important for me to lie."

Jyn shifts in her seat, frustration bubbling off the surface of her skin. It's fascinating how much clearer her feelings are to me over our connection. Where before they were muffled, like listening to her speak from another room, now all is unobstructed and clear. I can sense her blazing curiosity, can feel the butterflies fluttering in her stomach. I'm even able to partake in the headache pulsing behind her eyes as she racks her mind for memories she can't seem to summon.

"I'm sorry," she says after a long while. "Everything you've said feels so familiar. Almost like a dream . . . but nothing's coming to me."

I was scared of forgetting you.

I push away a great disappointment in favor of hope. Of course I hoped her memories would sit closer to the surface, since her soul hasn't endured the cycle of rebirth as many times as mine has. But even if Jyn never remembers everything, what matters is that she's *here*. Whatever the future may have in store for us, I'm confident that we'll figure it out together. Nothing but possibility stands before us.

"There's no need to fret," I say, rising from my seat at the table. "We have plenty of time to get to know each other again. Are you staying somewhere in the city?"

Jyn nods, the rims of her eyes red and puffy. I so hate to see her upset. "I have a room at the inn."

"It's getting late. Allow me to see you back."

She takes my hand when I offer it, her skin soft against my rough palm. My heart skips a beat when I notice the faint blush of her cheeks. "Thank you, that's very kind."

A thought suddenly pops into my head. "Before we go, I have something for you. A gift."

Jyn gives me a quizzical look. "But how did you know I was coming?"

Holding up my hand to show off our taut red thread, I reply, "I had a feeling."

I momentarily leave her for the entrance of my home, stepping through the doorway to rifle through the cabinets next to my writing desk. After a bit of shuffling, I find a small box stashed away in the very back. The box itself is brown and plain, easily overlooked. It's the contents *within* that are of immeasurable value. I return to Jyn and place the box delicately in the cup of her hands.

"What is it?" she asks, prying the lid open to reveal something wrapped in soft green silk.

"Something that was once yours," I explain. "I wanted to keep it safe for you."

Jyn carefully peels away the layers of silk to reveal a silver hairpin, the one I gifted her all those lifetimes ago. She stares at the intricate piece for so long I fear her mind has wandered too far. She's in a world entirely her own. I silently pray that it will help jog her memories. Maybe a trinket, something to hold, will help spark something.

It doesn't.

"Thank you," she says, quickly moving to secure it in her hair. "It's beautiful."

"I'm glad you like it. Now, give me your hand."

"Why?"

"So that you can climb onto my back."

"*Why?*" she asks suspiciously, arching a brow in true Jyn fashion. "I thought you said you'd see me back to the city."

"I did, but I never said anything about walking."

I step out into the garden and transform, my body curling around the planters, the chicken coop, my shack. I can sense Jyn's fascination, feel her thrill over our thread, without the fear I would've expected from anyone else. Holding my head up high with pride, I crouch so that she can climb up.

"Wow," she breathes, throwing a leg over. She's mindful of my mane, leaning forward to hold on tight. "Are you sure this is safe—"

I launch into the air. At first, her scream is one of pure terror, but it quickly morphs into a delighted burst of laughter. We soar ever higher, up above the forest and the clouds, close enough to touch the silver moon. Her glee is unfettered, her elation unmatched. It brings me endless joy to feel her breathless exhilaration.

Jyn looks down upon the sleepy world below us, and I sense something almost bittersweet thrumming over our connection. A memory stirs. The locks in her mind slowly come undone. I turn my head to look at her. Recognition, just out of reach, flashes across her face as her mouth falls open. All she has to do is concentrate and grasp for it.

"Sai?" she whispers.

Suddenly, I feel her slip off my back. Jyn plummets from the sky, but I sense no panic. She stretches her arms out toward me, green scales forming along her arms. Her eyes turn a brilliant green and then—

She shifts, her magic unlocking from within as she transforms. I chase after her, our bodies entwining as we fly. Tears well in her eyes as she presses her head to mine. We are the red and green dragons of old, reunited at long last. Fated Ones, destined to find each other through countless lifetimes.

Sai.

Hello, my love.

Acknowledgments

I'd like to begin by offering my sincerest thanks to my agent, Jim McCarthy, who believed in Sai and Jyn's adventure from the very start. I'm so grateful to have you in my corner. Thank you for putting up with my silly phone calls and never-ending questions (that I'm sure I probably could have just Googled, but asked anyway). Here's to many more projects together!

I owe a massive thank you to my editor, Amara Hoshijo. Thank you so much for your faith in this story and giving me the opportunity to share it with the world. Your guidance and support throughout this journey has been invaluable, and I can't wait to work with you on the next grand adventure.

I'd also like to thank everyone on the Saga Press team who worked tirelessly behind the scenes to put *The Last Dragon of the East* together: Karintha Parker, Savannah Breckenridge, Alexandre Su, Chloe Gray, Zoe Kaplan, Lauren Gomez, Lewelin Polanco, Meryll Preposi, Matt Monahan, and Caroline Tew! A huge thanks to Kuri Huang, as well, who illustrated the book's gorgeous cover!

Thank you to Kirsten, Camri, Ashley, Beka, and Erin. We may be hundreds of miles apart, but I will forever be grateful for your love and support. Thank you to everyone who read the book, as well!

And finally, thank you to my husband, who believed I could be a published author well before I did. I love you to the moon and back!